PENGUIN BOOKS

When We Were Friends

Tina Seskis grew up in Hampshire, and worked for more than twenty years in marketing and advertising before turning her hand to writing. Her first novel, *One Step Too Far*, was published in 2013, and it became an instant bestseller with over 100,000 copies sold in just four months. The rights have since sold to fifteen publishers worldwide. Tina lives in North London with her husband and son, where she writes full time. *When We Were Friends* is her second novel.

When We Were Friends

Tina Seskis

PENGUIN BOOKS

PENGUIN BOOKS

UK | USA | Canada | Ireland | Australia
India | New Zealand | South Africa

Penguin Books is part of the Penguin Random House group of companies
whose addresses can be found at global.penguinrandomhouse.com.

Set in 12.5/15.5 pt Bembo Book MT Std
Typeset by Jouve (UK), Milton Keynes
Printed in Great Britain by Clays Ltd, St Ives plc

A CIP catalogue record for this book is available from the British Library

B FORMAT ISBN: 978-1-405-91795-7

www.greenpenguin.co.uk

MIX
Paper from
responsible sources
FSC® C018179

Penguin Random House is committed to a
sustainable future for our business, our readers
and our planet. This book is made from Forest
Stewardship Council® certified paper.

For Alex, Annabelle, Brigette,
Jackie, Lisa and Rachel

Part One

Part One

1

The evening was set to be balmy, perfect for a picnic, even one destined to end in disaster. Light was dappling in the sloping back garden, enormous for London, and it had rarely looked so lovely. A glass of white wine stood gleaming on the window-ledge, chasing shadows across its surface. A squirrel hot-footed it across the lawn.

Juliette stood at her state-of-the-art white sink looking out of the window fuming, ignoring the too-loud sounds of children misbehaving. Stephen had just called, and he would be home late again, although he'd *promised* he'd be back by six. He knew she was going out with her friends, and she really didn't want to be late for once. Her children were sat at the table behind her, throwing their food around like hand grenades, and she just didn't have the energy to stop them. She'd been effectively a single mother (apart from the nanny of course) all week, and she was tired of it now. She trusted Stephen, he was way too obsessed with his job to have time for affairs, but she was sick of taking second place to his career. He was only

3

editor of a newspaper, she always used to remind him when they still had that kind of relationship (you know, the one where people talk, really properly talk). No-one died, she'd joke, but then he would remind her that people did, that the stories he told could wreck or make a life, depending on his whim (or perhaps savagery, she'd thought) at the time. She often wondered how she could have married such a man – maybe it was because she'd met him when they were both students at university, before she'd had time to grow into who she wanted to be, instead of who *he* wanted her to be. He'd been behind her at the queue for the pay phones and they'd just got chatting, and she'd thought he was nice enough, but not like *that* at the time, he'd been wearing a rugby shirt for a start. And after that they'd said hello to each other around campus, in that polite way where you don't really know someone, until eventually one night he'd come and chatted to her in the student bar and, despite them both knowing he was doing well for himself, that had been that. And although he was keener than she was, before she knew it they were seeing each other *every* day, until somehow by the final year they were even living together in a shared house, and despite a brief split when he'd gone to America after they gradu-ated, once he came back he'd pursued her until she'd succumbed again. And when they both moved to London, he'd thought they may as well get a place together, they could just about afford a studio if they both pitched in, he'd said, and somehow she found herself agreeing, and then she'd never quite got around to dumping him again. And so here they were now, over two decades later, married with three children and happy, apparently. Juliette couldn't complain from a material point of view – the rented studio was long gone, their house was done up and beautiful, the kids were in private school, they had a place in Italy, and Stephen was making loads from his career, especially now he'd become a quasi-celebrity, appearing on late-night game shows and being asked to present televised awards events. It was odd how other people always found him funnier than she ever had.

Juliette kept her back to her children and thought about the evening ahead. She was meeting up with five of her oldest friends from university – every summer they got together, and although they had all been so close once, that was a long time ago now. Privately she thought that these occasions felt uncomfortably forced these days, there were far too many conversational no-go zones for a start, and she still found it hard to see Renée especially – but she wanted to go, for Sissy mainly, although she wasn't even sure if Sissy would be happy to see her, not after what had happened. This year they were having a picnic in Hyde Park, and it wouldn't be some half-hearted affair, but a traditional picnic, with old-fashioned dishes like coronation chicken and home-made potato salad served in handmade Italian bowls on real china plates with knives and forks, no plastic rubbish. It was all too heavy to carry really, but her friend Camilla was posh and liked to do these things properly, and so everyone indulged her, of course. Even when they'd been students a few bought pork pies and a family bag of Twiglets would never do in Camilla's book. It was all such a lot of work, but Juliette had acquiesced as usual. And it wasn't cold or raining for a change, so hopefully they'd all enjoy it.

Juliette turned wearily from the sink, exhausted suddenly by the thought of seeing everyone, fed up with her husband for letting her down again, and as she looked across to the table she felt her back stiffen.

'Noah, put that bowl down, darling.' Her tone was pleasant, cajoling. Her middle son pretended not to hear her.

'Noah, I said put it down, please.' He lifted the bowl further off the table and, ignoring her still, raised it to shoulder height.

'Put it down, Noah.' Her tone was becoming strained. Noah smirked at her, took aim.

'NOAH! Will you put that bowl down NOW,' she yelled, as he was about to fling the yoghurt at his little brother, who was racing, screaming, out of the kitchen to avoid it.

Noah looked at Juliette and his expression was one of reciprocal hostility, a look she was becoming used to. He hesitated, went to put it down as requested, and then just as it touched the solid oak table, he changed his mind and flung it anyway.

Juliette stared into her wine glass as she counted to ten. Then she walked without speaking over to the spattered yoghurt, its garish patterns perversely making her think of the markings on some type of cow (*Friesian, she thought, or was it piebald?*), and she picked the melamine bowl out of the pink bovine-shaped mess as if it were contaminated, and took it to the sink and put it down, too calmly now. The two children still in the kitchen (Jack had escaped unmarked and hadn't reappeared) sat at the table motionless, watching their mother – the magenta violence of the incident had shocked them all, and none of them was sure which way this would go. Finally she turned to Noah and said wearily, 'Go to your room,' before she pushed her tumble of hair behind her delicate ears, went down on her delightful knees and got busy with the dishcloth – they'd run out of kitchen roll, and Mrs Redfern had left for the day.

2

Chelsea, West London

On a street tucked away off the King's Road, where long-dead artists and poets used to scrape a living, and a movie star had once fallen out of a window of the house diagonally opposite, and where the handsome flat-fronted terraced house had been bought for her for a tenth of its current value, Camilla was standing with her phone propped between her shoulder and chin, amidst a maelstrom of cooking. With the back of her free arm she pushed a stray strand of her Alice-banded hair out of her face as she ended the call with a forced, 'OK then, see you later, bye-bye,' and, bending over to drop her phone onto a cleanish part of the kitchen counter, frowned at it. Really, there was no need for Juliette to be so stroppy, she hardly recognised her friend these days. She used to have the sweetest nature, but over the years seemed to have transformed into the archetypal fiery red-head. Perhaps she'd just been married to Stephen for too long, or maybe she'd still not got over all that business with her mother – she seemed to get more bitter about her as the years passed somehow, instead of letting it go like she should do. We all have our crosses to bear, thought Camilla as she finished skinning the salmon fillets, and although she wasn't prone to self-pity she thought that hers was probably greater than most, yet *she* didn't go round taking it out on everyone else.

Camilla tried so hard to keep the six friends together, but sometimes she wondered whether she was wasting her time, whether she should finally let them all drift their separate ways – just because they'd, in effect, saved her life once, that was over twenty-five years ago now. Maybe the bonds simply weren't there any more, perhaps she was kidding herself that she could recreate what they'd had before.

Camilla had another private concern about the evening ahead, aware that, what with the children's activities and all her charity work, James seemed a little put out at how much she was going out lately, and she hated upsetting him. Although he tried so hard to control it, it seemed he had an innate jealous streak that occasionally reared itself, and that over twenty years of happy marriage still hadn't quite fixed. She even wondered briefly whether she should call the evening off, it might be easier all round, and she could always freeze the torte. But then she remembered the hell that Sissy was going through, and she was still worried about Juliette, despite her occasional obnoxiousness, and poor Siobhan's life seemed to be as disastrous as ever; and she thought, no, they did all still need each other, and besides, it would be lovely to see everyone. She always had been an optimist.

Camilla washed her hands in the enormous butler sink, checked the timer and went over to the oven – she pulled out the wire rack and admired the way the frangipane had risen around each individual raspberry, cushioning each one like a precious jewel. She pushed her finger gently into the torte, and the sponge sank under the pressure. Never mind, she thought – five more minutes, and it should rise again, the dent would hardly notice. She closed the oven door and picked up her phone once more, tried to call Natasha to confirm that she was definitely making tabbouleh as well as a potato salad, but Natasha didn't pick up, so instead she sent a group text to everyone, saying how much she was looking forward to the evening and reminding them all to bring chairs.

3

Siobhan stared at the long brown smear down the left thigh of her coral-pink skinny jeans, the broken cake stand, the torn carrier bag on the ground, and felt like wailing. At least the wine bottle hadn't broken, instead it was rolling drunkenly towards the gutter, and she managed to catch it just before it dropped off the pavement into Marshall Street. A young man in indigo jeans and a dark shirt, thin white tie arranged just so, black glossy hair swept asymmetrically across one eye, sidestepped the Tupperware as he walked by, his gait almost as graceful as the sweep of the eight Georgian arches that rather improbably made up the facade of the leisure centre she was outside. He studiously ignored the catastrophe that had befallen her, focused instead on the trendy boutiques on the opposite side of the narrow street, as if stopping to help or interact with this dishevelled, slightly deranged-looking woman would be bad for his image.

Shit! Why was it always when she was meeting her

university friends that disaster befell her? She was a successful career woman these days: a million miles from the girl at college they'd known, the one who was always losing her keys, scoffing her flatmates' food, forgetting her library card, going to the wrong lectures, mangling her washing. She'd wanted to turn up in Hyde Park looking cool, happy, confident, successful – a shining example of how you don't need marriage and kids to be a complete, fulfilled person. She'd made a special effort with her hair this morning, had blow-dried it into languid honey-coloured waves (the hideous perm she'd sported at college long gone), and she'd thought her outfit made her look willowy, California-glamorous. She'd even been fine with Camilla's somewhat long-winded picnic instructions, pleased with her profiteroles, which had risen really well for a change – but now they were strewn halfway across the pavement as well as all down her trousers. She wished Matt were here to help her, but he was miles away, and anyway when she'd tried to ring him earlier his phone had gone straight to voicemail. Again. She remembered the last time she'd spoken to him, four days before, how although she'd tried not to be, she'd been silent and sulky, and she wondered with a pang whether he'd deliberately turned his phone off, was maybe even about to dump her. She wouldn't blame him if he did – she'd been such a nightmare lately, her fixation on their future, or otherwise, utterly joy-sapping. What was wrong with her? Why did she always manage to push men away, especially the nicest ones, the ones she liked the most?

Siobhan felt even more miserable now, and wondered whether she should just ring Sissy and cancel – Sissy wouldn't give her a hard time, out of all of her friends she'd be the one to understand. She felt so inadequate turning up like this, plus she didn't really know where she was going, and it would take ages to get there on the Tube. She wanted to go home, get into her pyjamas and watch something slushy on the telly that she could have a good cry to, that always helped. Work had been so stressful today – although she was pleased she'd been promoted again she wondered whether she could cope with her new job, and she found the high-octane aggressiveness of her boss exhausting sometimes. Advertising sales was a tough business, no matter that everyone else said it was just talking.

In the end Siobhan bent down and rescued what profiteroles she could, relieved she'd made so many. The rest she kicked into the gutter. She picked up the broken pieces of the cake stand and grimaced as she threw them in the bin. She put the lid back onto the Tupperware, retrieved the wine and rammed it into the depths of her handbag, placed the box of profiteroles back in the carrier bag, and slung the fold-up stool over her shoulder. It was such lovely weather, and it *would* be great to see everyone – hopefully they'd not tease her too much for a change, she wasn't in the mood for it today. She was also a little worried about how Juliette and Renée would be with each other – normally one or other of them managed to make some last-minute excuse, but according to Camilla they were both definitely coming this year. Siobhan checked her phone one last time – just in case Matt had called after all – and then she tottered in her cream-smeared heels in the direction of the Tube station, positioning the carrier bag carefully in front of the stain on her jeans, hoping no-one would notice.

4

Sissy was the first to arrive, as usual. She had never succeeded in quite shaking off her need to be not a minute
late, although she knew all the others would be at least
another fifteen minutes: seven meant sevenish to most of
them. Camilla was the only other one of the group who
was normally punctual, and she had texted to say the traffic on the King's Road was even more terrible than usual.

Sissy felt anxious on her own, unsure where she should
lay out the rug, which was the nicest spot, which way
the sun was moving. It was odd how much she worried
about it, as if it really mattered, but she didn't want to
upset anyone, particularly Siobhan – she was the one who
got het up about these things, none of the others were
that bothered, not even Camilla (as long as there was a
proper tablecloth), and Sissy *hated* it when Siobhan had a
strop. Siobhan was one of those people who could turn
the whole tone of a social situation, depending on her
mood, on whether she'd had a bad day at work or had just
split up with someone. Sissy knew some of the others

found Siobhan more than a little tiresome these days, and even Sissy had to admit she seemed to be getting worse as she got older, but she had a heart of gold, Sissy was certain of that. It was just a shame the others couldn't see it – a couple of them seemed to treat Siobhan almost with contempt now, which she most definitely did not deserve. After all, it was Siobhan out of all of them who'd been there for her when Nigel had died, unlike some of the others Sissy could mention, and she had stepped in to help Sissy cope, a widow at not much past forty, with a clapped-out house to renovate and two little children still in primary school. Siobhan had been amazing, looking back, and to this day Sissy's children adored her, but then Siobhan always had been good with kids (she was like one herself, she'd used to laugh, before she'd got upset at everyone else saying it too).

Sissy looked at the grey granite circuit that had been designed to be smooth, water-worn, but if you looked closely had had little crinkle-cut gouges added as a safety afterthought, and as she watched the gushing water she felt sure that Diana would have preferred it all to be a bit prettier, more playful somehow. Sissy admired the sentiment of the memorial, thought it was *nearly* right, but it lacked something visually, maybe some flower borders to soften the stark of the grey next to the plain green grass. It all seemed a bit industrial to Sissy – she could see why the early comments had been that it looked like some kind of drainage system. Sissy wondered how the artist must have felt, to take that much criticism over something so personal, something she had created; particularly when that child had fallen and banged her head, and everyone had been up in arms about the fountain's suitability as a children's playground, and they had even closed it for a while. And then when they did finally reopen it they'd installed No Fun patrols to stop children walking in the water, it was quite ridiculous really. *Let the parents take responsibility for their children*, thought Sissy, *that's their job, life is full of risk after all*. And then that made Sissy think about Nigel again and she almost felt like crying here on her own with her stupid picnic that she'd humped all the way from Balham, and she thought maybe she should just get up and leave right now – she wasn't sure she could cope with any drama tonight, the unspoken rivalries and resentments that had built up over the years. Why didn't people say what they meant any more? Sissy often wondered why she got so upset about things; she should try to think less, be like other people who didn't seem to notice if there was tension in the air, or care how anyone else was, not how they really were anyway.

In the end, Sissy made her decision on where to sit, she couldn't stand there dithering for ever, and she plumped for an area on the south-east side of the fountain, where the water ran belligerently, with no thought for tiny unstable children, fast and relentless and cold. She could always move again if the others weren't happy, and here she could keep a watch on whether they were coming. She spread out her picnic rug, a wedding present from her Auntie Shirley, made of tartan Scottish wool with a waterproof backing, which despite being over a decade old was still good as new. You couldn't beat quality, it was always worth paying the extra, she thought absently as she shook it out and the year-old creases smoothed away as if the evening sunshine had ironed it. And that thought made her sad again, made her think of her poor dead husband, and she really definitely wanted to go home now. There was a group of young tourists – students probably – looking at her, she was sure they were, alone with her blue and green rug and pathetic pasta salad, and she felt conscious of her short sensible haircut and her floral summer dress that really wasn't her, made her look mumsy, out of place somehow. Her pale-blue eyes pricked and swam amidst her sea of freckles. Why was it *still* happening, when would she ever get better?

As she was fishing in her handbag for a tissue (amongst half-open make-up, old receipts, a hairy brush, her purse full of nothing but small change, a battered writing journal, her mobile phone, a hair pin that went up her nail and shot a pain straight to her heart), she heard somebody call her name and she started, wiped quickly at her eyes. It was Renée, approaching from the northern gate, looking tanned and gorgeous, her huge brown eyes as alluring as ever (like a cow's, she always used to drawl when people praised them), and Sissy felt that familiar pang of envy that had never quite gone away, not since they'd been twenty-one and had travelled around Crete together, and Sissy may as well have been invisible on that holiday. She couldn't help having a tiny, buried feeling of delight when, in their final year, Nigel had asked her, *Sissy*, out although Renée was convinced that he was always calling around and staying for *ages* because he fancied her. Renée would never have been interested in someone like Nigel of course, but she seemed to adore the power she wielded over men, and Sissy hadn't had the heart to disavow her, tell her it hadn't worked on this one.

'Hi, darling, knew you'd be here first,' said Renée, dropping down beside her and crossing her legs, the skirt of her khaki shirt-dress bunched between her thighs, just the right side of decent. A tiny skull tattoo was inked inside her ankle. 'Where are the others?'

'Late as usual.' Sissy smiled, the threat of tears receding now. It was always good to see Renée.

'Love the rug,' said Renée. 'Very *Five Go Mad in Dorset*.'

'It was a wedding present,' replied Sissy.

'Oh. Sorry, Siss.' Renée changed the subject as she opened a bottle of Prosecco. 'Is Natasha coming? Has she managed to organise her incredibly busy schedule to fit us plebeians in?'

'Apparently so,' said Sissy with a half-smile. 'But please *promise* not to take the mickey out of her about it – you know how touchy she gets.' She stopped, suddenly guilty at what she'd said.

'Yeah, and doesn't she?' said Renée, blithely. 'And then she just goes back to telling everyone how important she is. Silly bitch.'

'Ssshh,' said Sissy, looking around nervously, as though the students ten feet from them actually knew Natasha, were perhaps even related to her, and would be offended.

'Don't worry, Sissy, no-one's listening. And anyway, it'll be nice to see her, I haven't had an update on her ghastly children for ages.'

'Don't be mean,' said Sissy. 'They're lovely kids,' although they weren't, of course, but despite everything Sissy still tried to see the good in people.

'I'm only joking,' said Renée. 'You really need to lighten up sometimes.' She grinned and shoved a glass of sparkling wine at Sissy, and when Sissy took it her hand was flecked with tiny spots of blandly neutral paint, Mascarpone perhaps. 'Cheers, darling.'

Sissy put down the glass carefully, untouched, and as she looked up she saw Juliette walking – no, not walking, *staggering* – along the path, lugging a colossal picnic basket, and although Juliette also had one of those fold-up chairs slung across her back, her posture managed to be graceful, like a dancer's. She's still so beautiful, thought Sissy, a little wistfully, is she ever going to look older?

'Hi,' called Juliette across the fountain, plonking the basket down with a dangerous-sounding clank and re-adjusting the chair, which had slipped off her shoulder.

Sissy went to help, trying her best to be normal with Juliette, to not recoil as she was embraced somewhat reticently by her friend – after all *Juliette* wasn't to blame for what had happened. By the time they'd carted everything over to Sissy's chosen spot Renée had lain down on her own rug (which was blood-red and satiny, more porn film than picnic), long dark hair fanning out like a dried-up stain, legs bent into perfect flesh triangles, scarlet silky knickers shamelessly on show – and instead of sitting up she simply smiled and vaguely waved hello, which Sissy wasn't sure was deliberate rudeness, or just Renée being louche, you could never tell with Renée.

Juliette seemed equally awkward, and Sissy wondered if something new had happened for them to fall out over – they usually made a bit more of an effort to at least pretend to get along – or whether it was just the same old feud that had been rumbling on for years. Sissy put down the chair and sat back down on her rug, twisting her wedding ring, wishing she could go home, to Nigel – and then she remembered all over again that he was dead.

'Thanks, Sissy. My God, getting here was a nightmare,' said Juliette. 'First Stephen was late home, and then my taxi didn't turn up, so I had to call some dodgy minicab and it *stank* of car freshener. Thought it was going to contaminate the picnic, ha ha.' Juliette kicked off her silver sequinned flip-flops and sank onto Sissy's rug, her back to Renée, her extraordinary hair glowing in the amber sunshine. 'Is that Prosecco? Pour me a glass will you, Sissy, I'm gasping.'

There were only a few people left at the fountain now, it was getting late: one other picnicking group who were drinking wine from white plastic cups and eating out of carrier bags; a couple with backpacks and zip-off shorts and matching sensible sandals, those Velcro ones, who were sat on the wall eating supermarket sandwiches whilst studying a map of London; a family of noisy, very wet children (the mother had wrung out her little boy's shorts and was attempting to put them back on him again); and lastly a lone man in a business suit who was dangling his bare feet in the fountain whilst reading a book – which, Sissy noticed, was her most favourite war novel ever. He had a nice face, unremarkable yet familiar somehow, but he looked melancholy to Sissy, and she wondered why he wasn't on his way home – he didn't look the type to take off his socks in public, or read Zola's *La Débâcle* for that matter.

Sissy and Juliette sat down and chatted about their children as Renée continued to lie insouciantly on her back, catching the last of the summer sun. It was only when there was a screeching noise that even Renée sat up to see what the fuss was. It was Siobhan, of course, stumbling through the gate, with what appeared to be a folding chair over her shoulder and a wrecked-looking carrier bag in her hand. The bag's handle had broken, and she seemed to have made another hole in the plastic, cutting off the blood supply and making her wrist look angry. Sissy noticed she was wearing heels that were far too high for her, as usual, making her look taller and slimmer than ever, and her skinny jeans had a dark stain down the left thigh.

'Oh, there you are!' she squealed, loudly, so everyone in the fountain's enclosure turned to look at her, everyone except the businessman who carried on reading his book determinedly. 'I couldn't bloody find this place, I thought you said it was by The Serpentine Gallery, Sissy!' Her tone sounded accusing, but Sissy didn't rise to it.

'Sorry, Siobhan, I'm sure I said it was by The Serpentine cafe, near the lido, but maybe I got it wrong. How are you?'

'Hot. Fed up. Dropped my profiteroles, had a row with my boss, he's such an arsehole sometimes. Anyway, whose idea was it to meet here? It's a bloody nightmare to get to on public transport.'

The others sighed inwardly. *Here we go*, thought Sissy with dread, as she continued helping Juliette sort out the food. No-one bothered correcting Siobhan, that in fact it had been her suggestion to have the picnic here – Siobhan was one of those people who managed to fit history to suit her version of the truth.

Siobhan dumped her things down and looked around. 'Don't you think over there's better?' she grumbled. 'It's a bit higher up, so it's got a nicer view of the river.'

Renée gave Sissy a distinctly unsubtle *told you so* look, and Sissy looked down, embarrassed, but she needn't have worried, Siobhan seemed oblivious. Sissy was about to start packing up, to move to where Siobhan suggested, when Juliette spoke.

'Sorry, but I think we're all right here, Siobhan. It's too much palaver to move everything now.'

Siobhan stared at Juliette, unsure whether to argue. 'But it's better over there,' she said eventually, and she sounded forlorn, like a little child.

'Oh, OK, maybe we could –' began Juliette.

'Yeah, well, you shouldn't have been late, Siobhan,' interrupted Renée, as she lay down again, and hitched up her dress even higher. 'The others will be here soon, let's just get on with it instead of fussing about nothing.'

'Oh!' said Siobhan. 'That's a bit rude.'

'Sorry,' breezed Renée, and closed her eyes.

Before Siobhan had time to say anything further, there was a loud, horsey 'Helloooo', and as they turned they saw the final two women approaching along the path from the other direction. Natasha was thread-thin and stressed-looking, aggressively blonde, in a scarlet dress suit that was too hot for the day, too dated for the year, and she walked in her heels like she wished they were running shoes. Camilla was short, immaculately pastel, in white jeans that made her legs look stumpy like iced buns, and a pink stripy shirt with the collar turned up under a string of pearls. A pale-blue jumper was slung nonchalantly over her shoulders. Sissy caught Renée looking at them as she sat up to top up her glass (*already?*) and hoped she wouldn't say anything. Renée was always threatening to take them both clothes shopping, but Sissy could tell that Natasha wasn't in the mood for any dress sense jokes today. Sissy wondered what was wrong; it was unlike Natasha to be miserable, or to show it anyway.

Sissy observed Renée not even bother to sit up to say hello (instead she just murmured hi from her horizontal position), and Juliette hunch into the apparent effort of unfolding the chairs (were they *still* not up?) rather than turning and greeting people properly, which seemed strange to Sissy; and of course Siobhan was looking moody still for a whole host of unknown reasons. In fact the atmosphere felt so odd, off-kilter, it seemed almost impossible to believe they'd all once been best friends – and as she watched them, Sissy knew with the certainty of someone primed to spot trouble these days that she'd been right all along. She shouldn't have come.

5

Bristol

Nearly thirty years earlier

The room was high-ceilinged and elegant, despite the cheap student furniture, the two unmade single beds tucked away under the sash windows, the clothes horse full of damp faded washing in the corner, the Morrissey poster pinned up over the mantelpiece. It was as if the size of the room made up for the student chaos it contained, enabled it to rise above it somehow. Sissy had been glad she'd been allocated such great digs in her first year, even if she had had to share them with, amongst others, an acerbically witted, punky-looking girl who'd scared the life out of her at the start, until Sissy had finally tuned into Renée's sense of humour and realised, thankfully, that she was actually quite nice.

Juliette and Renée were curled up on the couch, watching *Blind Date* on the crackly portable TV Camilla had brought from home. Siobhan was sat on the floor between them, leaning against the sofa, and every now and again she would roar with laughter at something one of the contestants had said, and bang her head on Juliette's legs and go, 'Owww,' and Juliette would ruffle Siobhan's bubble-permed hair affectionately, as if she were a dog. Sissy was sat bolt upright in the single easy chair, looking like a twelve-year-old boy, reading yet another book on the Franco-Prussian war, seemingly oblivious to everything, yet every now and again giggling at one of the impersonations Renée would do of the presenter's accent. As the final ad break finished, Natasha burst through the door, hot and sweaty, Jane Fonda headband luridly pink against her blonde spiky hair, and plonked herself down next to Siobhan to watch the bit where Cilla would say things to the post-date couple like, 'Oh dear, no need for me to be buying me hat then, chuck,' to try to add some levity into the air of mutual hatred.

Just then, Camilla bustled into the room, face shiny with steam, hair pushed back by a tortoiseshell Alice band, stripy shirtsleeves rolled up as if she meant business.

'Supper won't be long, chaps,' she said.

'Thanks, Mum,' said Juliette. 'D'you need any help?'

'Well, if you could peel the carrots that would be super,' replied Camilla.

'Sure,' said Juliette, and got to her feet, despite this being her favourite part of the show; not that Camilla would have minded doing them herself, she loved cooking for everyone – especially when *Blind Date* was on, which she thought was dreadful.

As Juliette made her way into the kitchen there was a knock on the main door, and she assumed it was a friend from one of the other floors, come to borrow something, or simply invite themselves in. She was right, it was Alison, one of the swotty physicists from downstairs.

'Hi, Alison!' said Juliette. Alison just stood there, staring mutely. Peals of laughter sounded from the other room. Still Alison didn't speak.

'Alison, are you OK? What's happened?'

'Is Camilla all right?'

'Yes, come in, she's cooking as usual.'

'Doesn't she know? Hasn't anyone phoned her?'

'Know what? We don't have a phone here.'

'Oh no, I take it you haven't seen the news then?' asked Alison, and she seemed agitated, on edge.

'No, what news?'

'Oh God, sorry, just put the news on, will you? I'm so sorry.' And with that she turned on her heel and walked away, as Juliette stood watching her in bewilderment.

6

East Coast of Australia

Sissy and Nigel's honeymoon, in the earliest days of the new millennium, was very nearly the best three and a half weeks of Sissy's life. She couldn't say she'd *enjoyed* the wedding as such – it had been lovely of course, but she'd become so stressed about all the arrangements, and then she'd hated being the centre of attention, and although everyone told her she looked beautiful she knew she didn't really, that's just what people said to the bride. Her dress had been nice enough, but they'd teased and lacquered her hair until it was like cardboard, and her face had looked as if she'd been crayoned (she *knew* she should have trusted her instincts and done everything herself), and she didn't need to wait to see the photos to know she looked terrible. The food had been OK and the speeches hadn't been *too* humiliating, but no-one had danced much – Sissy was worried that the space had been too big, the lighting too bright, to tempt anyone but the aunts and uncles out – and she'd found herself stressing, convinced people weren't enjoying themselves, wishing the evening would just hurry up and end. It had been a relief to collapse into bed, all thoughts of consummation abandoned; they'd been together for years anyway so it didn't matter, not really.

It was only once they'd arrived in Australia that Sissy had finally begun to relax. She and Nigel spent a week in a fancy hotel on Magnetic Island, where they had their own private terrace, complete with hot tub and sweeping sea views the colour of swimming pools, and where on the beach thirty yards away the sand was soft under their feet and coconuts fell like gifts from a more benevolent universe. And after that they took a trip in a Winnebago up the coast, not knowing where they would stay each night or what the next day would bring, and Sissy had adored it, even more than the luxury of the resort. Nigel made her feel safe, as though she didn't have to worry about everyone and everything for a change, and they found deserted postcard beaches where they set up camp and built fires and cooked fish they'd caught themselves, and she hadn't realised life could be so magical. She found herself falling ever more in love with her new husband, delighting that he was such a decent person, so optimistic about life, so practical and manly, so much fun. It was all too perfect.

So when, near the end of their trip, Nigel had confided over breakfast that he was worried about a mole on his left leg, just above the knee, saying that it had seemed to really grow and darken while they'd been away, Sissy hadn't catastrophised like she normally did (especially after what had happened to poor Camilla while they were at Bristol), and instead she'd felt sunny and positive and had reassured Nigel that it would all be fine. They agreed to get it checked out though, just to be on the safe side, ensure it wouldn't spoil their stopover in Hong Kong. So as soon as they got to Cairns a couple of days later Nigel found a doctor, and she'd taken one look at the mole and sent him straight to the hospital, and that's when the river of dread had started flowing inside Sissy again, the one that had never quite stopped since, not since that sunny afternoon long ago, on the other side of the world.

7

Bristol

Camilla's father had the kind of fall from grace that had the Sunday tabloids whooping for joy, their reporters out sniffing round the corpse like hyenas waiting for the lion to clear off. His story had all the right ingredients for a front-page splash – the oh-so-respectable peer, the dutiful wife, his droning sermons on public morals during the latest election campaign, the handsome rent-boys (with pictures), proof of his particular penchant for wearing rubber and being spanked with a wooden spoon for bad behaviour. For anyone it would be horrific, but for Camilla, in her first year at university and already a minor celebrity around campus due to her famously influential father, it was intolerable.

Camilla hid away in her and Natasha's room for days and days and refused to come out. She lay under her duvet and sobbed, only getting up to shuffle down the corridor to the communal bathroom when she absolutely had to, Natasha on guard to ensure the coast was clear. And even then she would wrap the duvet around herself, as if it were a dressing gown, and it seemed it was her only protection from the world that before this had seemed innocent and sunny, and now was rancid, impossible to navigate. She couldn't even go home, the press were camped outside, and anyway how could she face this man who until now she'd adored and revered, and her poor dutiful mother who must be dying from shame herself.

In the end it was Siobhan who organised a weekend away in her uncle's cottage in Somerset. All six of them went, and no-one remotely knew who Camilla was down there, and they took long walks and drank tea and ate chocolate, and being able to breathe the fresh, unsullied air and avoid the newspapers and the pitying looks was a relief to Camilla. When she got back to Bristol there was a letter from her father, begging her forgiveness, and it was so open and heartfelt she was tempted, which was just as well as the next day he was found dead, hanged in one of the trees he'd planted himself, in the thickening wood on their vast estate.

'Camilla? It's me, Tash.'

'Oh. Hallo.'

'I'm sorry to keep ringing, but I've left you so many messages.'

'I know, I'm sorry I haven't called back.'

'Och, don't apologise. How are you just now?'

'Oh, you know . . .' Camilla trailed off.

'Look, I know this is terrible for you, but we want you to know we're all here for you. Did you get our card?'

'Yes, I . . . I've been meaning to reply.'

'Don't be soft, we don't expect a reply . . . Anyway, we thought we may come and see you soon.'

'Who?'

'All of us.'

'Oh, Natasha, I don't think so.'

'Aye, Camilla. We'll get a takeaway and watch a video or something. You just need a wee bit of normality. Please don't say no . . . Your mother thinks it's a good idea.'

'You've been talking to Mummy?'

'Well, I've been trying to talk to *you* for the last three weeks, ever since the funeral, and in the end she picked up the phone, and she recognised my voice from the answerphone.' Natasha sounded sheepish. She never had been one to take no for an answer.

Camilla didn't know what to say. She was touched that her friend had been so persistent. She hadn't known what to make of Natasha when they'd been put together as roommates – they were so totally different, from different worlds in fact. Natasha was from Glasgow and had an accent so thick that Camilla had struggled at first to understand it, and she'd had bright-blonde, spiky hair that she'd never worn any different since, and she'd been madly into hockey and running and Prince's 'Purple Rain', playing it all the time, and she never seemed to have time to eat anything except Cup a Soups and Pot Noodles. Camilla, on the other hand, had brought her own slow cooker and prepared her evening meals before breakfast, and had an impressive array of stripy cotton shirts and cashmere jumpers, even then. They were the

33

odd pairing of the group, but the strange thing was that although Natasha had been ballsy and ambitious from the start, she hadn't seen Camilla's utter poshness as a threat, just an opportunity to better herself. Camilla had found her guilelessness refreshing.

'So?' asked Natasha. 'Can we come?'

'When?'

'Next weekend?' The question was assumptive.

'Can I call you back, Tash? I don't mean to be evasive, but . . .'

'I understand,' said Natasha, and it seemed her voice was trembling suddenly. 'But if you're coming back next year you need to see us all sooner or later.'

'I – I haven't even thought that far ahead,' said Camilla.

'No, but we have. You can't let this ruin your life, Camilla.'

'It already has.' She said it softly, without self-pity.

'No, it hasn't,' said Natasha. 'You've got us, we're going to get you through this. We'll see you next weekend, bye,' and she put down the phone.

8

Hyde Park

By half past seven the picnic had been set up to Camilla's liking. She had taken charge of the food as usual (fussing around like they were at sodding Glyndebourne or something in Renée's opinion), and even Siobhan seemed to be happier, having finally given up trying to get everyone to move nearer to the water. It turned out that one of the folding chairs was a table so the food had been set out on that, but no-one sat at it as there weren't enough seats for everybody, which Camilla was privately cross about; she'd specifically told them all to bring their own. Some-one had brought an iPod dock, and when Juliette put on Michael Bublé, Siobhan said she adored his voice, so that kept her happy, which was a relief to everyone.

The picnic was eclectic, despite Camilla's best efforts, despite having created a pair of quite magnificent dishes herself – fresh salmon and dill salad with rosti potatoes and soured cream, a raspberry torte – and Sissy having made a passable job of her pasta salad. However, Natasha had come straight from work and had cheated and spent a fortune at M&S, which wasn't at all like her: she'd long since graduated from Pot Noodles and would normally be up until midnight the evening before, she seemed to fancy herself as Superwoman these days. Renée stayed true to form and had provided nothing except three bottles of Prosecco and some shop-bought Scotch eggs, which Camilla just about managed not to comment on, despite Renée having ignored her explicit instructions to make a quiche. Siobhan had brought what was left of the profiteroles and a bottle of white wine. The profiteroles looked quite revolting now but no-one dared decline one, even though they were squashed and the chocolate had half-melted and the cream was thick and yellow – Siobhan didn't have a fridge at work and it had been a particularly hot day.

The sun was sinking gently, and it left behind one of those rare English summer's evenings that were unmatched elsewhere in the world. The atmosphere between the women was more jovial now, thank goodness, and when Camilla announced that the food was ready, even Renée sat up obediently. She poured herself another glass of Prosecco and grabbed a handful of Kettle Chips straight from the packet. Her eyes were shiny.

'How's Stephen, Juliette?' she asked airily, and Juliette still found herself bristling, even after all this time.

'He's fine, thanks,' she replied. She paused. 'How are you? Seeing anyone at the moment?'

Renée laughed. 'Just the odd one-night stand, they're always entertaining, plus the same old thing with Ed. He won't leave his wife, I don't want him to anyway, and we have increasingly mediocre sex the longer it goes on.'

Juliette looked disapproving, although about exactly what no-one was sure, it could have been any number of things.

'Why don't you ditch him and go out with someone nice, Renée?' asked Camilla, as she handed her a plate. 'You might even like it.'

'Well, you know, it's not that easy,' said Renée, and she took another handful of crisps. 'All the blokes I meet these days are either total bastards, or else they think I'm desperate to go curtain shopping and get married and have babies, and so they dump me anyway.' Her voice brightened. 'So I'm quite happy with the occasional night with someone else's husband for the time being.'

'Well, what about his wife, don't you think about her?' asked Natasha, and her tone was stern suddenly.

There was an awkward silence. Natasha took off her shoes to reveal nails that were painted glossy geranium pink, incongruous against her runner's bunions – like a plain girl in a prom dress, Renée thought bitchily. She looked coolly at Natasha.

'I think it's more for him to think about his wife, don't you?' Renée said, and she topped up her glass again so it overflowed, the bubbles chasing down the sides like slalom skiers, before lifting the bottle jauntily and saying, 'More Prosecco, anyone?'

9

Nashville, Tennessee

Renée dyed her fringe pink and flew to Nashville just six days after her graduation ceremony. She was apprehensive – she'd never been to America before, wasn't sure if it would be her kind of place – but Andy, one of her best friends from home, had managed to recruit her into his door-to-door bookselling team. He was taking a group of twelve students, mainly university friends from Cardiff, and he was hoping to make an absolute fortune – it seemed he was operating some kind of pyramid sales model that meant the more people he took, the more money he made. He'd done it the previous year too, and had come back bragging about how he'd made thirty thousand dollars in less than three months, how it was so easy, how people had loved his accent, how complete strangers couldn't wait to let him into their homes, buy his books, serve him iced tea, even feed him lunch most days. Renée wasn't daft. She knew Andy was romanticising the experience, that selling encyclopaedias door to door must be way harder than that, but she didn't know what else to do now that she'd graduated. She hadn't even thought about getting a job yet, she had no money for a holiday, and she couldn't face the prospect of going home to live with her father, in his big empty house near Clacton that was as good as falling down and looked as tired and unloved as he did. She'd shuddered at the thought of the summer at home: silent meals on grimy trays in front of depressing shows like *Morse* and *Murder, She Wrote*, the atmosphere shot with dark resentments that were better left unsaid.

So when Andy had offered to lend Renée the money for the flight (that's how keen he was to have her on his team, sure that with her looks and sassy, irreverent charm she'd be totally brilliant at it) she'd thought *why not*, it was something to keep her busy while she decided what to do with the rest of her life; plus it would help pay off some of her debts.

What had surprised Renée was that it was Sissy of all people who first decided to join her. She never thought Sissy had it in her, or that she could bear to be parted from her lovesick boyfriend for ten minutes, let alone ten weeks. But Nigel was off to stay with his uncle in Sydney, had booked it months ago, before Sissy and he were even going out, and then he was planning on backpacking all the way up the East Coast of Australia with his cousin – and even though Nigel had asked her to come too, Sissy had said it wasn't fair on Brett, that it really wouldn't work with the three of them.

Renée did her best to persuade Natasha to come book-selling too, but Natasha said no way, claiming she could see right through the hype. And anyway, she insisted, she was moving to London to stay with Camilla straight after graduation. She didn't have the time or money to go gallivanting off to America over the summer, she wanted to get on with finding a proper job as soon as possible – she just wasn't prepared to risk ending up broke back in Glasgow, she said.

It was only when Juliette finally caved in to Renée's charm offensive and agreed to come that Renée had felt better about going – until she found out that Stephen was planning on tagging along. Although he'd always seemed nice enough, there was something about him that Renée had never been sure of, and besides, he would only monopolise Juliette as usual. Renée's friend Andy hadn't minded though – the more the merrier, he'd said, presumably thinking of the extra commission for him.

Renée had been irritated enough about Stephen muscling in, but the situation was made even worse when Juliette landed herself a fantastic job on the milk round and decided she wouldn't come after all. She was *really* sorry, she told Renée, but she didn't think she'd be remotely any good at traipsing round knocking on strangers' doors trying to sell them encyclopaedias, and now that she had a job and the promise of money to come, she could afford to go and chill out on a Spanish beach with her old school-friend Katie. Renée just about forgave Juliette, as she knew the real reason (although Juliette hadn't explicitly told her, of course, unwilling to be disloyal to her boyfriend). But privately Juliette had insisted to Stephen that if they were going to end up together, like he wanted, the whole thing stood way more chance if they'd both had some time to date other people first. Stephen had been furious, he wasn't used to being dumped, but for a change sweet, compliant Juliette refused to be swayed – she said *he* could do what he liked, but she was going to consider herself a free agent. She had only just turned twenty-two, she reasoned, she'd only ever had one proper boyfriend before him, and that just wasn't enough for a lifetime.

And so that's how it happened that the unlikely trio of Renée, Sissy and Stephen were squashed together on a United flight from London to New York one drizzly early-summer's morning. From there they would catch another flight to Nashville, where they would meet up with Andy and the rest of the team for their week-long sales training course. Renée had been in a foul mood from the moment she'd arrived at Heathrow, and when they'd boarded the plane she'd insisted on sitting by the window, even though that was actually Sissy's allocated seat, but she couldn't bear to have to sit next to Stephen, with his rugby-playing thighs that were so broad they were bound to encroach into her space. Sissy sat in the middle, tense and irritating, fussing about ridiculously improbable potential catastrophes: picking up every last peanut she'd dropped down the side of the seat in case the cleaner didn't find them and the next person had a child who went on to choke on one; wanting to know exactly where her lifejacket was, just in case; making sure her bag was lodged tight into the overhead locker so it couldn't possibly fall out and injure someone. Sissy was always so anxious about everything, so opposite in nature to Renée that Renée sometimes wondered how they were friends at all. But the thing about Sissy was how loyal she was, and reliable, and just an all-round good person, and Renée had recognised that quality in her from the instant they'd met each other on that terrifying first day of term. And from that time on Sissy had filled a need in Renée, a chronic need to be looked after that Renée did her best to hide but was always there if you looked close enough, stamped forever on her little crumpled four-year-old face on the day her daddy had told her, as kindly as a man raging with resentment can, that her mummy had left and wouldn't be coming home.

Stephen sat in the aisle on the other side of Sissy, and to be fair to him, he just put on his headphones and Renée could forget for a while that he was there. She had never been quite sure what Juliette had seen in him – with those eyes and that hair she was so gorgeous she could do infinitely better, but Stephen was one of those powerful types who always seemed to get his own way. He had set his sights on Juliette, had even admitted to her months later that he would watch for hours out of his window for her to leave her halls of residence, and as soon as he spotted her crossing the car park he would dash from his own room, and run all the way round to the other side of campus, so that just as Juliette was making her way down the main precinct, he'd be sauntering casually in the other direction – and he would be sure to stop her and say hi and get her chatting, until she really felt like she was getting to know him, like he was almost becoming a friend.

When Juliette had confided this to Renée, not sure whether to be flattered or freaked out, Renée hadn't known whether to be admiring or scathing of Stephen's efforts either. One thing she had been sure of though, even then, was that Stephen was ruthless – he would go to limits beyond what other people would, to get what he wanted. It was true that he could be charming, but there was something about him that Renée didn't trust, and sometimes she worried about Juliette, about how she may well even end up with him if she wasn't careful – and if so whether he would quash her eventually. Renée sighed and put on her own headphones and shut her heavily kohled eyes, willing her mind to concentrate on the throaty thrum of the aeroplane's engine, as it headed relentlessly over the never-ending ocean below.

Renée found Nashville freaky. It felt alien, larger than life to her, especially through the prism of jet lag. She was shattered – they had endured two flights, been treated like criminals at immigration, taken a bus to the hotel to dump their bags, and then headed straight downtown to meet up with Andy and the other students in a country-music bar. For Renée it was like stepping back thirty years, back into the movies that she'd watched with her dad as a kid, into a world where people still wore cowboy hats and the men were butch and rugged-looking, and the women's boots were white and studded and their hair was golden and flowing under their Stetsons. The bar was warm and glowing, full of tangerine lights and orange wood, and its walls were plastered with publicity shots of handsome men with fantastic names like Chesney or Kenny or Bud.

Renée felt weird, aloof from life, as she drank bottles of beer and the music twanged with life-lived sadness – almost as if she wasn't there at all. She wondered how Camilla was getting on living back at her mother's in Holland Park (with both her boyfriend James *and* Natasha), whether Juliette was in Marbella yet, what Siobhan was getting up to; but mostly she questioned what on earth she was doing here. Had she made a huge mistake, she wondered. She found the other students nice enough but she was so tired she wasn't really in the mood for talking, plus there was one girl called Melissa who never seemed to shut up, and from first impressions would give even Siobhan a run for her money in ditziness. Just as Renée was about to suggest to Sissy that they head back to the hotel, Stephen, who seemed already to have had one drink too many, leaned in from nowhere and licked her face, big-tongued and slurpy, like a dog, and she realised with revulsion that now Juliette had released him he was going to be after her and Sissy, either of them or both of them.

10

Bristol

Natasha shoved a coat on and popped downstairs to the local newsagents for a pack of ten Silk Cut, although she knew the others would give her a hard time about it. She didn't know why she'd started smoking, maybe she had taken after her deadbeat fag-ashed parents after all, a thought that made her shudder. Despite being barely awake, as soon as she entered the shop the headlines smacked her in the face. Oh *no*, why did they have to dredge up all the same dreadful pictures all over again, just because it was the inquest? Poor Camilla. How could she, Natasha, stop her friend seeing them? Or would it be better to tell her about it, so she was prepared for the new round of whispers and innuendo she'd be subjected to on campus?

Natasha stood hesitantly, full of hatred for the unknown editors of the *Sun* and *Daily Mirror*, but in the end she picked up a copy of each (by the edges, she could hardly bear to touch them) and took them to the counter. She paid for them along with her cigarettes and rolled them tightly, sports pages outwards, rubber gimp masks firmly inwards, before tucking them under her arm. Even though Natasha was still in her pyjamas, originally having intended to go straight home with her nicotine fix, instead she sprinted (the occasional fag seemingly not having affected her fitness at all) to the local park, where she sat on a bench and smoked two in a row as she scoured the papers for any new information from the hearing – but there was none. Thank God, thought Natasha, and she tossed the papers into the bin. As she raced back to halls she decided that, yes, she *would* tell Camilla – forewarned is forearmed, after all. And anyway, Camilla seemed much more herself these days, meeting James had definitely helped, and although he'd seemed a bit insecure, jealous even, at first, he was a lovely guy, and seemed to really adore her. Natasha could even see them lasting the distance.

Oh well, here goes, thought Natasha. She ran up the path, entered through the big old communal front door, took the flea-pit stairs two at a time, stopped outside their door for half a second to brace herself, and then thrust her key into the lock.

11

Nashville

After that first evening, the trainee booksellers never saw Nashville again. For the rest of the week they didn't even leave the hotel, the sales course was so utterly relentless, and on top of the jet lag the effort required to learn how to sell encyclopaedia sets to people who hadn't known they wanted them meant they felt far too exhausted to go out for the evening. Renée still felt disengaged, odd somehow. She had always dreamed of travelling eastwards before, to faraway places like Nepal or India or some remote Thai island, full of spiritualism and culture – but here their hotel was just a modern block next to the highway that might as well have been anywhere. America did make an impression on her though, mainly through its scale, the extremity of things: the two beds in their double room that could comfortably sleep three people each; the throaty clunking of the machine down the corridor that ejected fat glinting ice cubes, tumbling like coins from a jackpotting fruit machine; the tooth-ache temperature of the Cokes from the mini bar (she had never known drinks to be so cold); the improbable proportions of the cars on the freeway; the sleek gleefulness of the morning TV presenters with drawls so sassy they sounded put on; the enormity of the breakfasts and the people who ate them. America seemed souped-up to Renée, as though it had to be bigger, better, colder, hotter, cheerier, louder, just all-round 'er' than everywhere else. She found that she was homesick: for her student flat in Bristol, for her life before graduation, for her group of best friends, but mostly for Juliette.

The training course was attended by hundreds of students, mainly American: eager youths with springs in their steps and dollar signs in their eyes. On the first morning Renée sat near the front of the auditorium, slouched next to Sissy, unable to concentrate, surprisingly close to tears. She watched incredulously as a short puppyish man (hair neatly side-parted, dapper in handmade loafers and an Italian suit) bounced around the stage, drunk on life, telling his impressionable audience how after five wonderful summers with Tyler's Books he was a paper millionaire, *already*, at just twenty-five. Greed wafted through the room, all-pervading, like cooking smells. As the presenter went on to explain to his audience that the volume of books they'd sell that summer would be directly proportional to their future life happiness, Renée wondered what on earth poor Sissy was making of it all – if she felt this bad then surely it was Sissy's worst nightmare – but Sissy just seemed dazed by everything, almost as if she were trying to transport herself back to England, like if she let her eyes glaze over enough then she could pretend she wasn't even there. Most of the other students seemed to love it though, hanging on the presenter's every word, cheering in all the right places, loudly chanting mantras such as 'I feel happy, healthy and terrific' or 'Hey there, beautiful, don't you ever die', which made Renée want to throw up. As the day wore on she even began to feel like maybe she'd landed in some crazy religious sect rather than onto a bookselling course – and when they did finally get a break she barely ate any lunch, which was unlike her.

Renée's mood wasn't helped by the presence of Stephen either. Although he'd apologised for his lecherous behaviour of the first night, and to give him his due had behaved like a perfect gentleman ever since, she still found him grating. In the afternoon session especially he seemed to lap everything up, appearing to love both the role plays (which he performed with sickening gusto with Melissa) and the motivational jingles, generally being loud and annoying. Surely he couldn't really be into this stuff, Renée thought in disgust, as she watched him yelling, 'I'm a fighter, not a quitter' (the truth of which the students might need to remind themselves, if things ever got 'a little tough'), but then she decided he must simply be thinking of the pay cheque at the end of the summer. That was far more likely, knowing Stephen.

Over the course of five torturous days the students were trained like monkeys, as they learned their scripts verbatim, developed their frighteningly positive mental attitude, practised religiously what they would say and how they would say it, with no word changed, no careless deviation, no single opportunity to let the customer off the hook. And the more they went over the knock, the wave, the cheery introduction, all delivered with impeccably fake sincerity, the more Sissy felt sick with nerves, and the more Renée wished she could have gone to Kerala instead.

12

Tooting, South London

Sissy loitered outside in the corridor (long, sky-blue, seemingly endless, as though it were the route to heaven itself), peering through the small square window, steeling herself to go in. It was as if every time she saw Nigel the shock returned, but worse than before. She couldn't believe how quickly things had changed for them – one minute they'd been enjoying the tail-end of their honeymoon, the next they were on the plane, not stopping over in Hong Kong after all, but heading straight back to London and directly into hospital. That had been nearly seven months ago now, she realised with a jolt. Nigel had been in and out of hospital ever since, enduring huge poisonous doses of chemotherapy that seemed to be sapping his soul, making him appear like a shadow-person, a shrunken ghoul from her worst nightmares. His hair, so thick and sandy before, had fallen out almost immediately the chemo started, along with his eyelashes and eyebrows, and although she still loved him she found it hard to look at him now, or at the bag full of sickly brown fluid that lay hanging from his bed, or at his thin, frail hand that could still just about hold hers, gently, as if he were reassuring her instead of how it should be, the other way round.

At the beginning Sissy had had no idea that one tiny mole could be responsible for such devastation. When she'd popped into Waterstones in her lunch hour on her first day back at work, when she'd still been trying to act like a normal newly-wed woman – one who's excited at the life ahead of her, instead of terrified – she had picked out a reference book to read up on his cancer, as she'd known so little about it back then. And after she'd read about the symptoms and treatment for a disease called malignant melanoma, she had turned the page to the outcome statistics without even thinking of the implications, of what it might say. Sissy had stared hard at the 'five-year survival rates', which appeared to range from eleven per cent to ninety per cent, and had felt faint, as though she were leaking every last breath in her body, as if air was seeping out through her pores, not just from her mouth and nose. She had sat down heavily on the floor, not caring what people thought, and had rung him there and then on his brand-new mobile to ask him what grade of cancer he had.

Nigel had been evasive. 'You have to tell me,' she'd shrieked. 'I'm your *wife*!' She'd become almost hysterical by the time he finally confessed over the phone to having something called a Stage 2C, and when Sissy checked in the book on her lap it informed her that a 2C gave him a forty-five per cent chance of surviving five years. Or put another way, it gave him a fifty-five per cent chance of dying. Sissy had remained slumped on the carpet in the corner of the bookshop as the statistics loomed at her wherever she looked, as if they were stamped on her eyeballs, she couldn't shake them away. Eventually a member of staff had come over to ask her if she was OK, and he had looked at the closed book beside her and the misery in her eyes and realised that she wasn't OK at all, in fact was far from OK, and had gone to get his manager.

Standing here now, staring at Nigel through the tiny window, as if he were an exhibit in a freak show rather than her husband, Sissy reflected on how that had been before she'd even known she was pregnant, before she'd had to contemplate life as a young widow-mother-to-be. What was the name for that, she thought idly, is there a name for that? She looked again, saw he was still sleeping, and then she tightened something inside herself, as if she were forcing a dripping tap to stop, pulled her face into a small smile, and entered the death fug inside the room.

Nigel didn't stir. He was on so many drugs that Sissy sometimes wondered if he knew she was even there any more, even when he appeared to be awake, had his eyes open. Nigel hadn't responded well to his treatment, and Sissy hadn't responded well to his illness. She wasn't able to tell anyone (apart from Siobhan, who funnily enough was the only one who'd seemed to realise), but she felt desperate sorrow that her life had been plunged into misery and sickness so soon after the wedding, just when she and Nigel were meant to be unwrapping their presents from John Lewis and looking forward to the rest of their lives together. She'd assumed she would be better at all this, and obviously so had everyone else, but she hid it well. People even kept telling her how stoic she was being.

Sissy had never dared hope for anything amazing in her life before – she'd always been the unremarkable middle child, the plain one with no special qualities, the average student, the nice but boring friend, the girl who made up the numbers; but not to Nigel. He had made something in her sparkle, given her life, courage to be herself, live a little – and when he'd finally asked her out it had all been so phenomenally fantastic she'd felt like the most special girl in the world.

And now he was going to die on her.

What was hardest to cope with was the depth of her anger – at her husband, at the hospital, at the world. She loved him too much to let him leave her, yet she hated him too, for his selfishness, for his failure to get checked out earlier. He had finally admitted after the diagnosis that he'd been quietly worried about the mole for weeks, but had never quite got around to going to the doctor, there had seemed so much else to do before the wedding; and besides, he hadn't wanted to risk spoiling everything. And so in Australia when the mole had started to weep and change shape, more quickly than ever, that's when he'd known he needed to do something – and still he hadn't told Sissy the truth, had claimed at the time that he'd only just noticed it. Sissy felt overwhelmed with loathing – of her own self-pity; of Nigel for lying to her, for letting her down; of her friends and family, the majority of whom didn't seem to know remotely what to say or how to help; but mostly she was filled with loathing of the cancer itself, the creeping malevolent death-force, those multiplying cells so devilishly smart they couldn't be outwitted.

Sissy plonked herself heavily onto the bed, hoping that might wake him, but she was uncomfortable there – her bump was massive these days, and she was so high up she had to dangle her feet, which was making her ankles swell. She put her palm on his forehead, and it felt odd, lifeless. She took his hand and it lay cold and limp, like it was already dead. She waited five minutes for something to happen, but nothing did. She felt like she would go mad. She lumbered herself off the bed again and sank into the blue vinyl armchair next to it, and found she preferred it there. The table that was meant to go over the bed was next to the chair, in her way, and it was cluttered with hospital stalwarts: a box of tissues, a cardboard vomit tray (unused), a plastic jug of water and half-empty plastic cup, a Tupperware container full of grapes that looked soft and over-ripe, an untouched box of After Eight mints (she wondered briefly who'd brought those, she thought people only had them at dinner parties). She scrabbled in her bag and pulled out the review section from Saturday's *Times*, reading the words without taking in any of the meaning, wondering yet again whether Nigel would live long enough to see their unborn child; and as she felt the baby kick, crossly, vibrantly, she was certain it felt the misery in the room and was trying to say, 'Oi, you both, cheer up, don't you forget about me.'

Sissy was about to stand up, go and get another wretched excuse for a coffee from the machine down the corridor, when Nigel opened his eyes and smiled weakly at her. Her heart lifted. She'd always liked his eyes, they'd been easily his best feature, but without his hair and eyelashes they looked googly, and today they were faded and watery and he looked even less alive with them open than when he'd been asleep, if that could be possible. She got up to kiss him, to show him that she loved him still, no matter how he looked, and as she did so she tripped against the leg of the swivel table, and her baby bump brushed against the flimsy plastic cup, and it toppled over, water spilling everywhere, careering crazily across the table and down onto the sheets.

'Oh, sorry, darling,' she said, furious with herself as she took a handful of tissues and dabbed it up ineffectually. Nigel tried to shift upwards in the bed to help her, but the effort made him gag suddenly, so she grabbed the cardboard tray and got there just in time to catch the green-coloured bile that poured out of him, shocking in its vividness, its intensity, his gut the most alive part of him now.

13

Hyde Park

Sissy filled her plate with food, not any of the fancy salads, just the scotch eggs and crisps, it was all she was able to face. She ate without noticing what she was even putting in her mouth, and she sometimes wondered if her taste buds had died along with her husband. People were chatting about their summer holiday plans, but when Juliette asked Natasha what she was up to Natasha seemed angry, accusatory somehow, and instead of looking at Juliette she kept picking at her bunions, which was a revolting habit she'd never grown out of. Sissy felt sad that she wouldn't be going anywhere this year, but she just couldn't cope with the thought of taking the children away on her own, and although she thought it was a little insensitive for everyone else to talk about their trips, she knew that people couldn't keep pussy-footing around her, just because her husband had died. It wasn't any of their faults.

Sissy still made an effort to come to these get-togethers, to keep in touch with everyone, even Juliette, who'd been as good to Sissy as she could be under the circumstances – but she couldn't cope with seeing Stephen these days. Sissy just couldn't understand why Juliette would stay with a man like him. She'd actually quite liked Stephen once, especially when they'd gone to America together. He'd seemed quite decent when she'd got to know him better, beneath the bravado – but things had become awkward when Stephen and Renée had got it together. Although it was true he hadn't technically been going out with Juliette at the time – after all, she'd finished with him, said she wanted to enjoy a bit of freedom – Juliette hadn't been at all happy for one of her best friends to sleep with him instead. Not that it had lasted long: Renée had seemed to go off Stephen as quickly as she'd got into him, which was typical Renée of course, but Sissy always thought it had been more than that. Perhaps Renée couldn't bear to risk losing Juliette's friendship, no matter how much she may have liked Stephen at the time.

Sissy sat quietly watching Juliette and Renée, who appeared to be talking to each other for a change, Natasha having stalked off to dunk her unlovely feet in the fountain, definitely upset about something. Juliette was being cool, distant, and Renée, although chatty enough, barely gave her friend a glance, and their conversation was stilted, over-polite, even though they'd been best friends once. It was ridiculous after all these years – it just made these occasions awkward, agonising even. Sissy didn't know why they both couldn't move on, it was all such a long time ago now, and although they pretended to get along, had never actually fallen out, it was obvious they didn't like each other any more.

The strange part though, Sissy thought, was Stephen's role in all this. She'd never quite understood it. As the years passed he seemed to have changed, gradually lost any kind of morality – plus it was quite unbelievable what he'd do in the name of journalism these days. Sissy couldn't bear him now, and she found that if she saw his smug jowly face appear on the TV she would have to switch it straight off, unwilling to let him into her house, even electronically, after what had happened. God knows how Juliette stayed married to him; she'd been so sweet, so down-to-earth once, but now she seemed tainted by him almost. Stephen acted as though he were above everyone these days, above the law even. Sissy shuddered.

When Natasha came back from the fountain at last, obviously still smarting but with a small, tight smile fixed determinedly across her face, Sissy shifted across to make room for her to sit down, knocking into Siobhan's wine glass as she did so.

'Ohhhh, Sissy!' said Siobhan. 'That's gone all over me! Look what you've done to my jeans.'

'Oh shush, Siobhan,' said Renée mildly. 'It was an accident, it's no big deal. And anyway, you should've been holding your glass, it's too wobbly on this rug.'

'But I'm soaking!' wailed Siobhan.

'Oh, just get over it,' said Renée, more sternly now, which made Sissy feel bad for Siobhan. 'At least it's not red wine – and look at the state of them anyway.' Renée looked accusingly at the long, dark chocolate smear down the front of Siobhan's trousers.

'But that was the last of the Pinot,' moaned Siobhan, trying a different tack. 'I don't like the fizzy stuff.'

Sissy sometimes wondered about Siobhan – her responses were so childlike, disproportionate, and she seemed to be getting worse as she got older, not better. Just what was going on inside Siobhan's head these days? Had she any idea how she came across? Could she simply not help herself? One of these days, Sissy thought sadly, Renée's going to tell her to just fuck off and that will be the end of it, which might be a relief in a way.

Camilla, ever the organised one, got a tea towel from somewhere and started mopping at Siobhan's jeans, but all that did was make the chocolate spread further.

'Ohhhhhh, look, it's making it worse!' said Siobhan.

'Never mind, Siobhan, it'll be dark soon,' said Renée.

'It'll still show though,' said Siobhan, seemingly not getting the irony. 'I've got to get the Tube home, I can't afford to get cabs everywhere, not like *some* people.' And she looked at Camilla in her pearls, but Camilla ignored her, instead just gazed out towards The Serpentine as she took a sip of her drink. Natasha changed the subject, which was unusually diplomatic for her. She seemed to have made a monumental effort to cheer up. 'Hey, has anyone seen *Bridesmaids* yet?' she asked.

'Yes!' said Sissy and Juliette and Renée at the same time.

'Hilarious,' said Renée.

'Shocking,' said Sissy.

Siobhan looked upset. 'Have you all seen it? Did you go together?'

'Don't be ridiculous, Siobhan,' said Renée, not unkindly. 'I went with a friend from work. Why do you always have to be so paranoid?'

'Sorry,' muttered Siobhan, feeling relieved and foolish at the same time. She knew she was acting appallingly tonight, and although the others probably wouldn't believe it, she actually wasn't like this with her other friends or with people from work. There was something about this group, perhaps that they expected so little of her, that she played up to, behaved like the useless under-graduate they thought she was still. Siobhan was well aware she wasn't like everyone else – her life definitely seemed more accident-prone and drama-filled than the norm. But it was as if her friends from college still thought of her as a child, seemed to put her down whatever she did, pick on her really. She felt her eyes starting to prick, and she hastily shoved her sunglasses down from her head, even though the sun had gone. She felt despairing suddenly – she'd got up especially early to make those profiteroles, and she wondered now why she'd bothered.

'Would you like another drink, Siobhan?' asked Sissy. 'There's another bottle of white here, you don't have to have Prosecco.'

'Thanks,' muttered Siobhan. She sat quietly, staring at her nails, which were ragged and had chocolate in them. She took a great slug of the drink Sissy passed to her and then put it down, more carefully this time, holding her hands in her lap now, fingers firmly hidden.

Michael Bublé rather inappropriately started singing 'Feeling Good', oblivious to the tension, but after a few moments of awkwardness his mood seemed to rub off on the group and they started to chat easily enough again, no doubt helped by the fact that they'd got through the third bottle of Prosecco already (everyone apparently having decided to turn to drink this evening as the only way to cope with the atmosphere), with even Juliette giggling despite herself at one of Renée's dating-disaster anecdotes involving a pair of banana-yellow underpants. Sissy had finally perked up and was talking to Camilla about potential paint colours for her living room, about how the samples never looked like they were meant to, so she'd probably end up with magnolia. Renée was lying down yet again, flashing her knickers and eating a scotch egg in between drinking Prosecco, and Siobhan seemed to have seen the funny side of her profiterole catastrophe at last, thank God. Only Natasha still seemed fed up – after her brief burst of sociability earlier she'd gone back to the fountain, and was sat facing away from everyone, kicking viciously at the water.

'Is she OK?' mouthed Camilla. The others shrugged, and Siobhan looked awkward, perhaps blaming herself.

'Maybe she's had a bad day at work,' suggested Juliette.

'Yes, it's so unlike her not to brag about her marvellous fucking husband and genius children,' said Renée cheerfully.

'Sshhh,' said Sissy. 'That's mean.'

'Oh, Sissy, stop spoiling my fun,' she replied. 'What's

life if you can't take the piss out of your oldest friends? Anyway, she needs to be taken down a peg or two every now and again, she's so high and mighty these days – maybe I should remind her of her origins in the Glasgow slums, she seems to have forgotten.'

'That's enough, Renée,' said Camilla. 'There's no need to be rude.'

Renée went to say something, but thought better of it. Instead she got up and walked over to Natasha and to everyone's surprise sat down next to her and put an arm around her shoulder.

'What's up?' she whispered, trailing her fingers in the water, but Natasha wasn't to be placated and shrugged Renée off.

14

Natasha found out about her husband's affair from a text message. It was that simple. One tiny five-word message with two little kisses that popped up on his screen and that she would have avoided if she could have, she somehow knew these days never to check – but as she picked up the phone, thinking it was hers, to put it in her briefcase the message just appeared there, before she'd had time to drag her eyes away, and now it was stuck in her mind, and whatever she did she couldn't make it go away, be unknown again. She couldn't think what to do, it was all so bloody inconvenient. The strange thing was that she was more upset about *the knowledge* than about the deed itself. What was she supposed to do now? Leave him? Confront him? Hit him? They had two perfect little children together, a whoppingly expensive house that relied on both their incomes, shared friends, lives so neatly intertwined that it seemed insurmountable to think about disentangling them. The fact that they hadn't had anything other than irregularly perfunctory, obligatory, lights-out sex for years was something she preferred not to have to think about, and if that meant Alistair went elsewhere for affection, well, what she didn't know couldn't hurt her. She was so busy, with her job, running, the kids, she barely had time to talk to Alistair any more, let alone feel any kind of physical passion for him, and that was OK. She'd been quite happy with the arrangement, before.

And now that text message had gone and ruined it all. It was not so much what it said but who it was from. It made her fucking furious, but bizarrely at the sender rather than at her husband: her betrayal felt greater than his somehow.

Natasha hadn't wanted to confront him, not now anyway, but how could she give him back his phone without him realising she'd seen the message? It was so stupid that she'd picked up the wrong one off the wooden counter top, but they both had the same model these days, the same bloody phone everyone seemed to have – plus she'd been busy doing up her pencil skirt and slipping on her court shoes whilst briefing the nanny on the children's various after-school activities before leaving for her breakfast meeting at the Landmark.

Natasha sighed. Why was her life so perfect on the outside and toxic on the inside? At what point had theirs become a phantom marriage, one where she and Alistair may as well be strangers co-existing in the same house, trying not to bump into each other in the kitchen? She'd loved him so much once, where had it all gone wrong? As Natasha put on her trench coat, she thought that maybe this was the time to confront it after all, maybe it was a sign; and she thought about the conversation they would have and the depressing conclusion they would reach and she felt – what? She stood in the hallway, by the front door with the bright stained glass that the sun was pushing coloured rays through, and tried to analyse it. What was the feeling? Desolation? No. Sadness? Not really. The words that came to her instead were ones such as *anger*, *inconvenience*, *upheaval*, *embarrassment*. Surely she should feel more than that? This was her husband after all. What was she going to do?

And then the solution came to her, how could she not have thought of it earlier? Natasha went back into the kitchen, picked up his phone and simply pressed 'delete', and the message was gone, disappeared into nothing. *He would never know she'd seen it.* Now all she had to do was delete it from her memory, which wasn't so simple, and she wished she could have a cigarette to calm her nerves, but she'd given them up years ago. Maybe a wee glass of wine might do it instead. She knew it was madness straight after breakfast but these were extenuating circumstances, and it wouldn't hurt just this once – the nanny had taken the kids upstairs to clean their teeth and she had another couple of minutes before she absolutely had to leave for her meeting. The wine was so cold it was almost frozen: someone had turned up the fridge too high, and it hit a spot in her brain that didn't quite erase the memory of the interloping message, but it helped her cope better with *the knowledge* for now, just until she decided what to do next.

15

Renée stood alone on the sidewalk in an ordinary middle-class suburb of an unknown city in a different state, anxiously looking around at the houses. At the end of the training course (which had actually only been five days but had felt to Renée interminable), Andy's team had been allocated Cleveland, Ohio as their sales patch, and so they'd all pitched together to hire a minibus to transport them the five hundred-odd miles from Nashville. But now they were here they had nowhere to stay, and most of the students, Renée included, couldn't afford a motel for more than a few days. Even so, she couldn't believe what she was about to do, that this was what the book-selling company advocated *all* their students do, across the whole of America. It seemed bonkers to her now.

Renée had picked a cul-de-sac to try her luck in; she'd been told that people were more likely to know each other in those kinds of streets, be more friendly, but right now she felt exposed, as if she were being watched. The gardens were large and well tended, the expanses of grass brilliantly green, lush with life despite the mid-nineties temperatures, the sprinkler systems poking up like spies. The houses were well-kept too – in fact it was all rather perfect, movie-like, and it felt as if she had seen it all before somewhere, maybe she was having her very own American dream, or nightmare, she wasn't sure which. As Renée hesitated, she felt small and frightened, not at all her usual self, like it was her first day of school perhaps, and the heat from the sun poured into her as if it was trying to cook her. She kept staring at the houses, trying to decide which one to pick first, which one would be the least unwelcoming. She tried to remember her training, how they'd been told that this was all part of the process, part of embedding themselves into the local community, of becoming a loved and trusted part of it for the summer. *As if*, Renée thought, why had she listened to that crap, why the hell was she here at all?

After perhaps two minutes of pacing, where her knees felt hot and unhinged, as though she really could fall over, she decided she just had to get on with it. She picked the friendliest-looking house, the one with a couple of kids' bikes strewn on the driveway, and she marched on slim, wobbly legs up the path, through the neat front yard, and knocked firmly on the door. She stood back six feet, exactly as she'd been taught, and looked sideways down the road: the least threatening position for the door-answerer apparently, the one most likely to grant you an entry.

The knocking set off a terrible racket. What sounded like a pack of dogs started hurling themselves at the door, barking madly. Renée was about to run away when she heard a voice saying, 'Now just you stop that, Betsy, and you too, Growler,' and the door was opened four inches by a harassed-looking woman in a long satin dressing gown the colour of chewed-up bubble gum, as unidentifiable dogs' teeth and paws scratched through the opening.

'Hi, are those your attack dogs?' said Renée. This was one of the stock jokes she'd been fed for exactly this kind of situation, but her voice was squeaky and her delivery was terrible. Renée swallowed hard and continued her patter.

'Er, my name is Renée and I'm all the way from England! I'm on an educational programme here in Cleveland, from the University of . . .'

'Sorry, I'm busy,' said the woman, and shut the door.

Renée stood still for a moment, feeling shocked, violated almost – and then she walked self-consciously through the front yard back to the sidewalk, hoping no-one was watching. She hated rejection, felt it like a punch. She thought of her mother in Paris for an instant and felt sick. She had to keep going. She walked straight to the next house and knocked, firmly, three times. A little kid answered, dragging his filthy muslin behind him.

'Mommy, there's someone at the door for you.'

Renée waited and the roof of her mouth felt claggy, as if she were eating a peanut-butter sandwich. After a couple of minutes a bright, friendly-looking woman with eyes so blue they must have been fake came to the door.

'Hi! My name is Renée and I'm on an educational programme here in Cleveland all the way from Bristol University in England! How are you today?'

'I'm good,' said the woman, but she seemed a little impatient now, as though she knew what was coming.

'I've just arrived in Cleveland as part of an educational programme and . . . and I'm . . . I'm looking for somewhere to stay for the summer. And, er . . . do you have a spare room that I could possibly use?' As Renée said it, she thought she might even keel over with humiliation, even though she'd practised it so many times. The woman smiled kindly and said, 'No, you know what, our spare room is used as an office, so I guess I can't help you. Good luck though, have a great summer,' and as she closed the door Renée could hear her yell, 'Joey, get back up those stairs right now and brush your teeth. We're gonna be late for preschool.'

Renée marched straight to the neighbouring house, refusing to give up now that she'd started. There was no reply at that door, but at the next several the people were friendly enough, in between a couple more door slams, although for various reasons no-one was able to help. Finally she approached the last house in the close, the least inviting one. It was tucked back further from the street than the others, and there was a big shady tree in the front yard and the paint on the windows was peeling. She waited for ages and was about to leave when she heard shuffling inside and several locks being opened, and eventually a man appeared at the door. He was in his late forties, balding, with a big, droopy moustache that seemed old-fashioned somehow, and although his clothes were smart enough his trousers were ever so slightly too short for him.

As Renée went through her patter the man said nothing, just stared at her hostilely. 'So, um, do you have a spare room that I could, um, maybe stay in . . . ?' she finished, her voice trailing off as she saw his face.

'You what?' he yelled. 'What the hell d'you think you're doing? Coming round here asking if you can move in with me? Are you crazy?'

The man's aggression, rather than diminishing Renée, seemed to strengthen her.

'There's no need to shout at me!' she yelled back. 'I'm only doing what I've been told to do. You don't have to be so *rude*.'

'Who told you to? What are you talking about?' asked the man, and after Renée started rambling on about bookselling companies and headquarters in Nashville, and how it was all part of the programme, he seemed to understand, and told her that she'd better come in, and then he led her (quite forcibly, he was obviously angry still) by the arm into a room where the curtains were closed, and it was full of tangly plants and the only light was what seemed to reflect off the white antimacassars. One of the armchairs had a plastic protective sheet on it, and there was a strong fetid smell of cats, although she couldn't see any in the room. Renée was a little freaked out now, but she started explaining how she'd been specifically instructed to go out and knock on people's doors and ask to live for free in their spare rooms, how her friends were doing it too, they were all only following instructions – and as she spoke she felt ridiculous, as if she really had been brainwashed, she was not normally nearly so suggestible.

'Have you any idea how dangerous that is?' said the man. 'How do you know whose house you're going into? Anything could happen.'

Renée privately agreed with him – after all she was sat here now with this weird-looking, raging man in his dingy stinking sitting room – but she didn't know what else she was meant to do. Her host stood up and went over to the telephone table, next to an ancient-looking TV which had a silver film of dust across its screen, and he found a pen and wrote down something on a small square pad, and when he handed the sheet to her it said 'Father Duncan' and there was a phone number, written in scratchy blue ink.

'Give him a call,' said the man. 'Tell him Larry Johnson gave you his number. I can't promise, but he might be able to help you.' He started towards the door and so Renée got up and followed obediently. She thanked him in the hallway, and as she moved out into the sunshine she felt like she'd had a lucky escape, as if the man had just rescued her from something close to madness.

16

Hyde Park

Siobhan is really pissing me off now, thought Renée as she watched Camilla package up the remains of the scotch eggs. She couldn't understand why everyone continued to put up with her, it was almost as if she were a child they'd adopted at university and were all too kind to shake off now. Their over-indulgence didn't even seem to help – in Renée's opinion Siobhan just appeared to get worse behaved every time they saw her. At this precise moment she was moaning on about the fact that they'd been asked to leave the Diana memorial, going on and on and on about how they'd have to pack everything up and that it was so inconvenient, and anyway it wouldn't be dark for ages, why couldn't they just stay where they were, what harm were they doing?

For God's sake, thought Renée, does she really think she's so important that if she complains for long enough they'll bend the rules just for her?

'But we're all settled here,' Siobhan was droning on to the park attendant as the others packed up around her.

'What difference does it make? There are people here who've come from miles for this picnic.' And Renée thought the way Siobhan said the word *miles* she might as well have said *Mars*.

'I'm very sorry, madam,' said the attendant, a sunny-faced young man with a Scandinavian accent and a patience greater than any of the others could bear. 'Those are the rules, I'm afraid.'

'Well they're ridiculous rules – this is meant to be a free country.'

'Just leave it, Siobhan,' hissed Juliette suddenly. 'You're behaving like a child.' The youth looked mortified, as though he didn't want to have caused this friction amongst friends, he was only trying to do his job. Juliette, furious now, pulled fiercely at her rug, causing Siobhan, who was still sitting on it, to topple sideways and knock over yet another glass of Prosecco.

'Owwwww!' said Siobhan. 'Juliette!' She sounded puzzled, hurt even. 'What on earth did you do that for?'

'Sorry,' muttered Juliette, horrified at her behaviour. She didn't know what was the matter with her these days, the problem with her temper seemed to be getting worse. Just yesterday she had yanked, way too hard, her son Noah's arm, hauling him screaming out of the bath after he'd shot her with a water pistol, squirting luke-warm sudsy water into her mouth and all down the mirror behind her. It had set off fireworks where her brain was, and she hadn't fully calmed down until the children were in bed and the guilt had had time to set in. Why couldn't she be a better mother, Juliette thought, her eyes burning. She loved them so much, had tried so hard – she'd read every parenting book under the sun in a bid to do better than *her* mother had managed, but it had obviously been a waste of time – and she was sufficiently self-aware to realise that she was in danger of turning into a bully, one who picked on emotionally retarded adults and little children, instead of dealing with her own issues. She needed to get a grip, before she ruined her poor children's lives too.

Sissy and Camilla helped clear up the spillage, and when Siobhan finally stood up the back of her jeans were wet too now, and the dark-brown stain on the front had crusted where it was drying. She looked a mess. She sulkily followed the others out of the fountain enclosure, muttering on about pointless bureaucracy, to a spot near the cafe, where a patch of grass was just big enough for them all.

'This is fine,' said Renée, and she gave Siobhan a 'Don't you dare' look, and to her credit Siobhan said nothing, despite there being only a very limited view of The Serpentine here. As everyone started spreading out their rugs again, Sissy held hers to her chest, like a shield.

'Look, I hope no-one minds,' she said. 'But I think I'm going to head off now. I'm really tired, and my throat's beginning to feel a bit sore – I think I might be coming down with something.'

'Oh, don't go, Sissy,' said Siobhan, and the slur in her voice was noticeable suddenly. 'We hardly ever see each other these days, let's all just have a good time.'

'Yes, please stay, Sissy,' said Renée. 'At least finish off my scotch eggs before Camilla chucks them at me.'

Everyone held their breath, it was never clear whether Renée was joking or not, but then she cracked a smile, and fortunately Camilla was as gracious as ever.

'Very funny, Renée,' she said. 'I know I can be a trifle bossy at times, but I'm only trying to make sure we enjoy ourselves.'

'I know, and we all love you for it,' cut in Juliette, and she seemed more relaxed now. 'Please stay, Sissy, I want to hear how Nell and Conor are getting on at school. Flo and Jack are fine, but poor Noah's having a nightmare.'

'Sorry, Juliette,' Sissy said. 'I just feel so tired, I don't know what's the matter with me.' Although of course she did.

It was Camilla in the end who persuaded Sissy to stay. She took her by the arm and led her down to the water and whispered to her that this might all be a bit difficult but they hardly ever saw each other any more, and they had a history, a shared past, which Sissy was part of – she couldn't bail out now, before the evening had even got going. Everyone seemed to be settling down, Camilla said, maybe they could all have a good time after all. As Sissy listened, the realisation hit her that Camilla was right, they were *friends*, they'd all been through so much together – and so she walked with Camilla back to the group, and she laid out her tartan rug once more, and she sat quietly in her flowery dress, sipping yet another glass of sparkling wine, looking out towards the ever-darkening water.

17

Cleveland

Bookselling didn't start well for any of them. Stephen had got a dog so mad with his knocking it had flung itself straight through the screen door, ripping an Alsatian-sized hole in it and causing the owner to call the police. The dog's legs had ended up caught in the mesh, so it couldn't actually bite Stephen, thank God, but the wife had chased him off with a broomstick and two little kids on their bikes had laughed at him, which he'd found harder to take in a way.

But, inevitably, it was Sissy who proved to be the most out of her depth, undoubtedly not helped by the fact that they were currently staying in a flea-pit motel, using up all their money, still homeless. She'd obviously been crazy when she'd decided to do this – she thought now it must have been because Nigel had been heading off to Australia, and she'd been distraught at the prospect of the summer at home without him. It had felt like two losses to her – of both her university life and her boyfriend – and so stupidly she'd just followed Renée.

Although Sissy did her best to give at least the book-selling part a go (having absolutely failed to find somewhere to live), it had proved a disaster from the very beginning. Like every Tyler's student, before actively trying to sell any books, she'd been trained to do some investigative work. She was meant to pick a house where it was fairly certain there were no kids: old-fashioned curtains in the windows, primly neat borders, that sort of thing. If she was lucky she'd find a lonely old lady who she'd be able to get talking, as long as she was charming enough – apparently the old dear would be glad of a nice English student to chat to (just start talking about the royal family, she was told, and you'll have her eating out of your hand). The conversation was meant to go something like this:

'Hi, my name's Sissy and I'm on a summer educational programme here in Cleveland and I've come all the way from Bristol University in England. Great to meet you, Mrs –?'

'Smith.'

'Oh, great to meet you, Mrs Smith. You know, you may be interested to know that I'm Lady Di's second cousin.'

'Gosh, are you REALLY?'

'No, no, I'm just joking, but I did see her at a polo game once, and gosh she's pretty in real life.' (*Lots of laughing.*) 'You know, I'm just really looking forward to spending the summer getting to know everyone around here, it's such an exciting programme for the local children. Now, those people next door (with basketball hoop over garage), they have kids, don't they? Great, and they're the –?'

'Joneses.'

'Ah, that's right, the Joneses. And what age did you say the kids were? And the ten-year-old, that's a boy, right? Oh, a girl, and what's her name?'

And the patter was to continue for as long as Sissy could pump sweet, obliging old Mrs Smith for information, and then she was meant to say goodbye and duck into a quiet corner to draw herself a map of the street and detail everything she'd learned – who lived where, how many kids they had, what ages they were, their names, hobbies, etcetera – before she forgot.

Sissy paced up and down the suffocating street, her anxiety threatening to escalate into full-scale panic, until finally she decided on a house that seemed to fulfil the criteria: no basketball hoop, no toys in the front yard, grass with weeds in and slightly too long, the paint on the front door faded and dusty. She clenched her stomach – *come on*, she had to do this, she couldn't travel all this way and not knock on a single door, that would be pathetic. Sissy hoisted her bag, which weighed a ton, further onto her shoulder and teetered up the path. She put down the bag, exactly where she'd been trained to: by the side of the front door, butted up to the house, initially invisible to the person who answered.

She rang the doorbell, but it made no noise and she wasn't sure if it had worked. She stood back six feet, looking sideways down the street, and waited. The house seemed quiet, lonely. She rang the bell again. Just as she was about to give up, the door creaked open a little, and a shrivelled face poked through the crack. Separated as it was from its body, the face's gender was unidentifiable.

'Yes?'

'Hi! My name is Sissy and I'm here all the way from Bristol University in England and I'm –'

'Whaddaya selling?' said the face.

'Uh, um nothing,' said Sissy, flustered now. 'I was just wondering if there are children living next door?'

'What are you, a paedo? Mind your own business. And if you ain't selling nothing, what's that bag doing there? Get outta here, or I'm calling the police.' And with that he, or was it she, slammed the door.

Sissy stood frozen, horrified. Then, as her eyes started swimming, she scrabbled for her sunglasses, lugged her book bag onto her shoulder and started walking, fast, as fast as she could without actually running, cutting through residential street after street, oblivious to the heat now, clueless to where she was going, never looking up from the ground, never slowing, for at least half an hour. Finally she happened upon a deserted grassy park, where she sat down under the single spreading tree that seemed welcoming, almost as though it had been waiting for her, and she took out Volume One of Tyler's handy educational book set and flicked through its pages until she found the history section, which although as a gradu-ate in that subject told her nothing new, was at least something she could concentrate on; and when that inev-itably got too much she lay down and wept, desperate for

Nigel, who was somewhere up the Gold Coast, unaware of her misery, un-contactable.

In the absence of any better options that day, Sissy ended up staying under her tree, periodically shifting round with the sun to follow the shade, reading, weeping, sleeping, for hours and hours, until it was time to go home.

18

Sardinia, Italy

Many years later, Sissy sat on the veranda of an apartment in Sardinia looking out across the low oleander hedge to the bold brash blue of the sea, and the rude red of the flowers sent electricity sparks through her eyes to her brain. It was all too obscenely beautiful, too alive, too vivid for her to believe that she could possibly be here, after the monumental absences, the living death she had endured with Nigel in London. She leaned back against the warm cream canvas of the double deckchair, but the sun felt too hot on her face, she'd never been good in the heat; so she got up and dragged the seat into the shade. She sighed, wriggled her toes, adjusted the seams of her costume, and, finally comfortable, closed her eyes and let her mind meander back, not accusingly this time, but gently, kindly, to the scene in the hospital, the one after Nigel had thrown up yet again from more horrific drug treatments and she'd finally flipped out, stormed out of the room to find a nurse and demand that they call the consultant, *now*. And when Sissy wouldn't take no for an answer, hysterical at last, they had sent for the on-call doctor, who was young and didn't know Nigel at all, and when he turned up he'd just looked at the notes and said impassively that it wasn't clear why her husband wasn't responding to the treatment, it was sometimes just one of those things. But the colour of Nigel's bile, the obscenity of its hue in the face of his impending death, had made Sissy insistent that there was more life in him yet, she was convinced of it. And then she'd broken down and cried her heart out that she couldn't be a widow, not now, not with her baby due in just a few weeks, what was the matter with them, why couldn't they fix him, she *loved* him, for God's sake. She'd caused such a fuss that the fresh-faced doctor became anxious and paged the consultant, so eventually Mr Tatchell had arrived too and they'd all been ferried into the patient's room, and although Nigel was no longer conscious Sissy had screamed that they must be able to bloody do something. She had never been so demanding in her life, hadn't known she even had it in her. Up until then she hadn't asked for anything much, not even from her parents, who lived on the Welsh Borders and had thought Sissy was coping admirably through the crisis, so although well-meaning hadn't visited that often – and Sissy hadn't even thought to ask them to come more. But now, finally, Sissy had had enough, and her anger was spilling out and she didn't care who saw it, and she knew the doctors were only indulging her because they were worried that all the stress might make her waters break, and they didn't want another death on their hands.

Sissy heard a seagull shriek above her head and, looking up, she watched it fly across the peerless sky and land, like a precious object, on a terracotta chimney, and the colours were screamingly vibrant, immeasurably lovely. Her eyes filled with tears, perhaps from the beauty of the view, or from squinting into the sun – or maybe it was something else, the memory of those next critical moments at the hospital, full of drama and passion she hadn't known was in her, and that had changed her life irrevocably. Would everything have been different if she *hadn't* broken down that day? Sissy guessed she'd never know, but it was weird how she still couldn't let it go, now it was over, now that she had room to live and laugh again. It was almost as if the further away she moved from the moment, the more intense her feelings became. *No*. She had to stop going over it. It was time to move on.

Sissy shifted in her deckchair and gazed out to sea. A boat was moving across the water and from here it looked modest, small even, but she knew that up close it would be titanic, probably owned by some Russian oligarch who might have been in jail once for fraud or corruption, but now judged his position in the world by the size of his bank balance or the length of his boat, and never worried about just how he'd made his fortune. *Terrible*, she thought, *how do people like that live with themselves?* It wasn't really her cup of tea, this kind of place, full of gorgeous, exquisitely turned-out people who made her feel dowdy in her canvas shorts and orange Birkenstocks – acutely, obviously English – but really, she was lucky she was here at all, Juliette and Stephen had been so kind to let them come, she shouldn't criticise it. She smiled wistfully, not quite back from the past, as she watched the boat disappear behind the oleander blooms – and then she remembered that the others would be back in an hour or so, she should think about popping down to the supermarket to try to find something not too ludicrously expensive to cook for dinner. She'd go in a minute, she thought drowsily, and then she leaned back against the warmth of the chair and closed her eyes, just for a little while longer.

19

Cleveland

As Larry Johnson's priest friend had sadly proved as
uncharitable as everyone else, much to Renée's disgust,
and all other ideas as yet having come to nothing, Renée
and Sissy still hadn't found anywhere to live. This meant
they had to keep forking out for the motel whilst trying
to sell enough books to pay for it at the same time. It was
depressing. Every day a heat haze seemed to hover over
the endless suburbs, hang around the houses, glinting a
keep-out warning, or so it seemed to Renée, and it all felt
so hopeless she wished that she and Sissy had the money
to just give up and fly home. This afternoon she was tired
and overwrought from another fruitless day of selling,
and she almost burst into tears when she found Sissy
already waiting for her at the spot where they'd agreed to
meet, even though she herself was half an hour early.
Sissy was loitering on the corner, looking like an over-
grown boy scout with her short hair and baggy khaki
shorts and Dr Marten shoes. She was leaning into the
shadow of the last house on the street, and it had a long,

wide front veranda, on which stood a huge wooden swing seat with faded blue and white striped cushions that Renée would have been tempted to go and sit on if she'd been the one waiting – no-one seemed to be in, plus the temperature must have hit one hundred degrees in the sun – but Sissy hadn't, of course.

'Well?' said Sissy. She looked pale. 'How did you get on?'

'Oh great,' said Renée. 'I had I don't know how many people slam the door in my face, and I nearly sold a book.' She grinned. She never had been one to show emotion, it was like she thought it was a weakness. 'What about you?'

Sissy looked vaguely ashamed.

'Oh, Sissy! You didn't even *do* it, did you?'

'Oh, Renée, I couldn't. I tried, honest . . . but . . . but I didn't feel well. I'm sorry.'

'That's OK,' said Renée. She knew how traumatic Sissy was finding everything. Maybe she'd feel better once they had somewhere to live. Renée dropped down onto the edge of the kerb and leaned her elbows on her knees and put her chin in her hands. She sighed.

'So what are we going to do about finding a place to live?' Sissy said. 'Unless we start making some money we can't afford the motel any longer.'

'I don't know,' said Renée. 'But I can't think about it now, I need to get something to drink first – and some paracetamol, this heat is killing me.' She stood up and took Sissy's arm. 'Come on, let's get out of here and go and get a Coke. I think they do free refills at Pizza Hut.' Sissy nodded, and despite her legs feeling hot and useless she forced them to work, and the two friends trudged together down the sun-stricken street, their bags heavy on their shoulders, their feet dragging listlessly, in the direction of the mall.

Although Renée assumed that most Americans in the service industry were only super-friendly because it was the culture to say, 'Have a nice day,' the young woman in the drugstore was smiley and pretty in that rare way that was completely genuine. Her badge informed them that not only was she happy to help (with Panadol, as it turned out) but that her name was Nancy, and she even asked them where they were from – and it was a relief to Renée that someone was interested in her at last, that instead of having to force herself onto others she was able to have a nice chat about what she was doing here in Cleveland, without the conversation containing a currency. Sissy stood quietly as Renée described – nonchalantly deadpan – the book company's despotic training regime, the group exercises straight after breakfast ('Put down the bag, knock on the door, kick the dog,' and so on, complete with matching actions), the hateful motivational mantras, whilst Nancy looked increasingly horrified. But it was when Renée got to the part about having nowhere to live – the expectation that they'd go round knocking on people's doors begging to be taken in, the fact they'd used up all their money on motels – that Nancy became outraged.

'That is just so terrible,' she said. 'You poor girls! So what are you going to do now? Where are you staying tonight?'

'Oh, we're in the motel tonight,' said Renée. 'We're fine.'

'And tomorrow?'

Sissy and Renée looked at each other. Sissy's bottom lip started trembling again.

'Oh, I'm sure we'll find something,' said Renée at last, flashing an unconvincing grin. 'Or there's always the park. At least we won't be cold.' She tried to laugh.

Nancy looked indecisive for a moment. 'Are you in a hurry?' she said. 'Can you wait a while? I think I have an idea.' She walked around the shelves of drugs immediately behind the serving counter, towards the area where they made up the prescriptions, and soon they could see her talking quietly on the phone. Sissy looked at Renée, but Renée didn't dare look back, she didn't want to get her hopes up.

When Nancy returned, her eyes were sparkling. 'I've just spoken to my husband,' she said. 'He's a real-estate agent. He's got a big old house on his books that's been on the market forever. He said you can have that for the summer. It's unfurnished, but apparently it's huge. It would probably fit all of you.'

Sissy started prattling. 'Oh no, really, you don't have to do that. But are you sure? Oh my goodness, that is just too kind, how can we ever thank you?' She looked like she might cry at last, but didn't.

Renée, always the more practical of the two, took over. 'That sounds great,' she said. 'Thank you so much . . . but, er, how much would your husband want us to pay each week?'

'Nothing,' said Nancy. 'Nothing at all. We would be glad to help.'

Renée took a while to answer. 'But why would you do that?' she asked. 'Why are you being so kind?'

Nancy smiled. 'That's how these things work,' she said. 'I know, 'cause my little brother did a similar programme a few years back. And my husband wouldn't do it unless it wasn't a problem.'

As Sissy gabbled her thanks and started on about gas and water bills, mowing the lawn, etcetera, Renée felt the tightness ease from behind her ears, just a little, and although she had no idea if it was the done thing in these parts, she would have hugged Nancy there and then, if only the counter hadn't been in the way.

As time wore on, Renée and Sissy settled into life in Cleveland. The house Nancy's husband had lent them had indeed proved large enough to accommodate the whole team, although the area manager wasn't at all happy for the boys and girls to live together, saying it went strictly against Tyler's company protocol (which was purely in place to protect against potential distractions from the holy grail of encyclopaedia selling, from what Renée could tell). But Renée had put her foot down on behalf of the boys, and the area manager had eventually capitulated, and at least it diluted the effects of having the deeply annoying Melissa living with them, as Melissa, being the only other girl in the team, had of course been granted immediate entry.

Although the house itself was well past its best, it

was passable – neutral colours, serviceable kitchen and bathrooms – except for the fact that it had no furniture, not one piece. The booksellers ate standing up in the kitchen, and in the living room they lounged around on the floor, like in a refugee camp, until someone bought a blow-up sofa in fluorescent pink and they took it in turns to sit in that, although it was horribly sweaty, until Melissa inevitably popped it.

Perhaps unsurprisingly, now Renée had got over the traumas of the first week, she'd also perfected the fine art of bookselling. She'd discovered that she had a natural talent for speaking to people, for worming her way into their houses, for selling them mediocre reference books that their children would barely use. She honed her patter of, 'Is that your attack dog?' when confronted by a chihuahua or anything small enough to obviously not be, along with her introduction of, 'Hi, I'm Renée, I'm Lady Di's cousin,' followed by a laugh and a joke that, OK, no she wasn't really, but she absolutely was all the way from England, and she'd driven the whole way here (just kidding!), and she was so excited to be doing this great project helping all the local kids in the neighbourhood, and she'd had such fun with the Jordans' kids next door, and she was sure that little Johnny and Susie would love the programme too, and anyway, did they have a place to sit down? And at that very point she would break the smiley eye contact and move forward to pick up her erstwhile-hidden book bag, and the momentum would propel her towards the front door, and before anyone could quite work out what was happening she would be over the threshold and standing in the hallway, and then nice Mrs Smith or Jones or Adams would be leading her into their dining room or kitchen (after all they couldn't leave her just standing there making the place look untidy, could they?), and she would sit down at the table and then the kids would sit too, looking super-excited at what this pretty, fun girl with the pink bangs and weird accent was going to take out of her interesting-looking bag. It worked almost every time, once she'd got the hang of it. But it was when she pulled her masterstroke of explaining how she was going to ask the children a question that if they got right would WIN them a set of books, completely FREE, that the kids would be on the edge of their seats, frothing with excitement, and the mom would look a bit guarded, suspicious now, and her smile would fade a little (*oh no*, it must be a con after all) that Renée would say, 'OK, kids, all you have to do is tell me the names of every single American president, and by the way I need them in the *exact* order.' At this point the kids would giggle and say, 'Shucks,' and the mom would look relieved that it wasn't a sting after all, and then Renée would flick straight to the correct page and there they'd be, every last American president from George Washington right through to Ronald Reagan (*now isn't that a terrific book*) — and the kids would be nodding and Mrs Smith would be beaming, and then they'd talk a little more about the section for math (minus the *s* of course), and the great science chapter, and maybe the geography one too; and once they were all nodding and smiling *all* of the time, Renée would very casually pick up her pen and say, 'So this is Rockland

Avenue, right?' and Mrs Smith would smile and say yes, that's right, and so then Renée would nod, 'And you're number forty-eight, aren't you?' and Mrs Smith would agree, yes they were, and Renée would confirm, 'And it's Mrs Smith, isn't it,' and of course that was correct as well, so Renée would continue, 'OK, so it's Tyler's Schoolbooks Volumes One and Two,' not as a question, more as a statement of fact; after all yes, they were Tyler's Schoolbooks Volumes One and Two, and she'd go right ahead and fill that in on her pad too. Next she'd say, 'And shall we add the dictionary, it's so comprehensive it's the only one you'll ever need,' and again there would be no question mark in the statement, just an assumption that the dictionary would indeed be a welcome addition to the Smith family household, and at exactly that moment Renée would look up and smile reassuringly, before confirming, 'So all three together will be just one hundred and seventeen dollars, and all I need you to do is sign right here,' and Mrs Smith would finally acknowledge to herself, although of course she'd known all along, that she was being handed an order form, and she would take the pen that Renée would proffer and sign it, she didn't want to be rude – and besides they were all having such fun – and everyone would be happy, sort of. And *still* Renée would carry on, absolutely word-perfect these days: 'Now the way it works, Mrs Smith, is that I'm taking orders in the area over the next couple of weeks, and then I'll come back and see you, Susie and Johnny (*big smile*), and I will deliver your books to you *personally* at the end of the summer – isn't that great, we'll get to hang out together again. So what I'll do for now is take a deposit, shall we say fifty per cent? No cash? That's fine, a cheque is great,' and Mrs Smith would say OK and go find her chequebook, and Renée would leave soon afterwards with enough money to more than cover the wholesale price the company would charge her for the books; and every Sunday the area manager would drop by to take her deposits off her (minus just enough cash for her to live on for the week) so that she wouldn't be tempted to blow her takings, on self-indulgent nights out, for example, and anyway she was far too tired for those, but instead would be sure to have enough dollars in her company account at the end of the summer to be able to afford to pay for the books she'd promised to deliver to her customers. She'd get to keep any of the remaining funds in her account, of course, plus all the balances she'd collect on delivery of the books, and that would constitute her profit. It was genius how it all worked, how the bookselling company didn't need to risk one single teeny cent on a single one of their students, and yet still made millions.

Renée had become so expert in her bookselling technique that on a good day she often succeeded in sealing the deal at the point she first handed the pen over, but there were some less suggestible people who would be confident enough to object, perhaps say that they were sorry but they couldn't afford them. Renée wouldn't mind though, she was prepared, and she'd smile and say: 'Ah yes, times are tight, aren't they, Mrs Hughes? But what price can you put on a child's education? (*Pause.*) You know, Mrs Smith next door was worried about the cost too, at first, but when she found out that the Joneses at number thirty-eight had got them for their kids she really felt she couldn't let her own children down by putting them at a disadvantage at school . . . Hmm, makes you think, doesn't it . . . ? (*Pause*.) So anyway, Mrs Hughes, all I need you to do is sign right here.' And most people would, after that onslaught. And even if someone did have the mettle to protest yet further, Renée was ready with a perfect guilt-inducing answer to every possible objection, until finally her poor victim would run out of steam and succumb.

Renée grew to so despise the manipulation, the negative energy required for bookselling, that eventually she developed a phobia of the first front door of the day, apparently a quite common phenomenon in the direct-selling business. The strength of the phobia seemed to be directly proportional to how well the previous day's selling had gone, as though she loathed being successful and couldn't bear to inflict herself and her educational fucking books on any more undeserving people for another single minute. Every morning she and Sissy would drive to their allocated area in the beaten-up old car they'd rented off the area manager, and Renée would come over all clammy and faint, and she'd stare with terror at the front yards she'd have to walk through and the houses she'd have to enter, and she'd think of the conversations she'd have to have and the dollars she'd have to take from the people who didn't want to give them to her and often couldn't afford anyway, and she would feel the tears prick obstinately behind her eyes, and it was as if she couldn't move, to even open the car door. Sissy would try not to influence her, would just sit there patiently – after all, her tree in the park, the one she'd resigned herself to spending her days under, writing letters to Nigel or scribbling stories and poems to pass the time, would wait for her. Eventually Renée would either get it together and get out of the car, and Sissy would drive off before Renée had time to change her mind, or else Renée's eyes would overflow with misery and self-loathing, and she would really, really want her mum, although she hadn't seen her since she was a teenager, and besides Simone never had been much of a mother to her anyway. At that point, when Sissy knew it wasn't going to be one of Renée's good days, she would put the car into gear and drive them up to the main road where they could sit in Pizza Hut and drink iced Coke all day, until the air conditioning became unbearable; but even that didn't matter, as Sissy had learned to keep a couple of cardigans in the car for those kinds of days.

Monday had started off as one of Renée's better mornings, maybe not from an emotional wellbeing point of view, but at least as far as selling books was concerned. She had sold two sets of students' handbooks and one cookery book by midday, and had succeeded in largely not thinking, in simply fixing her brain to automatic for most of the time. She'd had just one real failure, at the first door as it happened, which had been opened by a waif-like woman with two scrawny little girls hanging off her legs, wearing matching Barbie pyjamas and peanut butter round their mouths. (The woman had been very nice but alas unbending in her refusal, her kids wouldn't be in school for another two years, she'd said, it might have all changed by then, and Renée had replied with a cheeky smile that trigonometry hadn't changed for thousands of years, but the woman's responses had been equally smart and she wouldn't let her in.)

Renée wasted no time wavering at the doors once she was fully into her stride — knocking, waving, entering, selling — and it had all been working beautifully so far. But right now she was sat in the kitchen of a man who'd said his wife was out at the mall with the kids, and she didn't quite know why but she didn't believe him. He'd seemed so friendly at first, but as soon as she'd made it inside she'd realised there was no evidence of him having any children at all: no scrawled pictures on the fridge, or scuffed sneakers by the front door, no toys lying around — and she'd begun to wonder whether there was even a wife. She just didn't like the feel of him somehow, plus it was so much harder to do her patter without there being kids to play off. And so although at first she'd been smiley and flirty like she usually was with the dads, she felt that he was looking at her a little too keenly as she described the comprehensiveness of the books' content and how it exactly matched the school curriculum, and she was sure he was smiling at her funny, almost like he was in pain — and now he was leaning so far towards her she could smell his stale coffee breath, and his grin had become quite twisted and weird. At the point Renée stoically moved into the order form part of her routine (once she was in full swing she was a true professional) the man grabbed her wrist instead of the pen that she'd offered him, and although he was laughing like he was only joking it hurt her, and as he pulled her to her feet she tried to escape, shake his hand off her wrist, but this seemed to annoy him – and before she knew what had even happened she was down on the cold, hard floor and he was on top of her, straddling her, and his strong, rough hands were fixed around her neck.

20

Hyde Park

Although Juliette and Renée used to be absolute best friends, the nucleus of the group in some ways, things had never been the same since Renée slept with Juliette's boyfriend in America – none of them had ever quite managed to move on from it, even though Stephen had sworn to Juliette that it had only happened the once, and besides he and Renée had both been paralytic. Juliette had always known that Renée adored male attention, as if it proved how attractive she was, made her a better person somehow, but she couldn't believe that she'd targeted *Stephen*. Even now, over twenty years later, Juliette couldn't bear the thought of the two of them together, of where Stephen's lips and hands and, well, everything else had been, it was quite revolting, and she'd very nearly not taken him back – she didn't care that she and Stephen had been on a break at the time, there are some lines you just don't cross. But perhaps it was for the best that it had happened, Juliette had secretly thought, maybe it was a sign that she should make a fresh start. Stephen had had to get

99

super-inventive to make her come round, and of course he had blamed it all on Renée, describing how she had flung herself at him, and, frankly, in Juliette's opinion and from the little Sissy had said about it, it was probably true.

Juliette didn't know what had happened to Renée. Since America she seemed to have changed so much, lost her self-respect, become almost promiscuous if the truth be told – maybe, Juliette thought sadly, it was some weird response to having been raped by that man she'd been trying to sell encyclopaedias to. It must have been so dreadful, and she couldn't understand why Renée had never gone to the police, but Renée just seemed to be so ashamed of what had happened, as if it was all her fault, which was ridiculous. It had taken her weeks to even confess to Sissy apparently, and by then, Renée had argued, there was no evidence, only the man's word against hers. She'd rather just get back to England and forget about it, she'd said, and Sissy hadn't known how to persuade her otherwise.

Juliette sighed as she looked down at her drink, and then across at the men tying up the last of the boats on The Serpentine. She still missed Renée, really missed her, even after all these years – they'd been so close once, like sisters even, and somehow them being here tonight in each other's company, sat together on a patchwork of rugs, not quite touching, unsure how to reach each other again, just made Juliette more lonely than ever. Perhaps if she hadn't got back with Stephen she and Renée would never have drifted apart, and she wondered whether she might even be happier now, with a proper best friend rather than a husband she'd never loved, not really, not like she should do, she could see that now. Not that she and Renée had actually ever discussed any of it of course, it was all so unspoken it was horrible.

Renée seemed to sense Juliette's thoughts, and she turned a little and looked, and Juliette appeared so terribly sad, bereft even, it caused Renée a tiny jolt of anguish, and so she turned back to Sissy and complimented her on her pasta salad, on how it tasted so much better than it looked.

'You cheeky mare,' said Sissy, and it was nice to see Sissy smiling again, she seemed to have lost all capacity for fun since Nigel had died – and suddenly Juliette was smiling too, and it felt almost like old times for a second, and Renée wondered whether they could ever be real friends again. She was sure in that moment that everyone did still need each other in a way. Perhaps their friendships were worth fighting for after all. Maybe all they had to do was try harder.

21

Cleveland

Immediately afterwards Renée had felt too scared, too ashamed to go to the police. She'd been so shaken and tearful she hadn't even thought to call at another house, try to get someone to help her – and as people seemed to drive everywhere in Cleveland there had been no-one walking along the streets to notice her state, just a couple of little kids who stared numbly at her, bewildered by her wailing. She hadn't even known how to get home without the car, and she couldn't possibly hang around for hours until Sissy was due to pick her up. She couldn't bear to talk to anyone. She couldn't think what to do.

She wanted her mother.

Renée bent over double, her head reeling, and vomited into the gutter. Then she stood up, wiped her mouth on the front of her T-shirt, and started to walk – her cries quieting as she moved, until her steps were in time with her snivels – not knowing where she was going, whether she was even going in the right direction, what the right direction was. She tramped relentlessly through suburb after suburb of detached family homes with neat front yards and shiny basketball hoops and massive untapped sales potential, jaywalked over six-lane highways, cut across pin-neat malls and the odd green space where no-one played. The day was stinking hot and her throat was rancid, but she couldn't cope with the thought of doing anything other than moving her feet, one in front of the wretched other, not until she'd got home and showered, had rid herself of the taint of what had happened to her body, of the man's bulk on her, of the vile stench still in her nostrils. Eventually she reached one of the main highways through Cleveland, and at last she recognised where she was, knew she could get a bus home from here, and when it arrived she slunk on and hid at the back, in the corner, like a scolded dog.

The house looked empty as Renée approached it – all the windows were shut and there were no cars in the driveway. She thought perversely how it must have been lovely once – large, well proportioned, set in a generous plot, with great expanses of window that instead of letting light in from the outside seemed to absorb darkness now, so that the house felt unloved, dead. As she opened the front door she was relieved that she'd been right about no-one else being home yet, particularly Melissa (who to be fair probably wouldn't have noticed Renée's state, would just have moaned about her own day). It was only half past three, and even the students who never knocked at a single door, instead found their own tree to sit under for the day, didn't risk coming back much before four, in case the area manager turned up on one of his spot visits. Renée went straight up to the shower and scrubbed viciously at herself with the soap, and then she heaved herself to the very top of the house, to the room she shared with Sissy. Although it was stiflingly hot and furniture-free, it was small and homely – Sissy had brought some pictures from England that she'd Blu-tacked up: that black and white one of the French couple kissing and some moody promo posters of Lloyd Cole and Paul Weller, plus a few Monet postcards she'd bought in Paris. Their sleeping bags were laid out neatly side by side where the beds should have been, and Sissy had even rigged up a string across the corner of the room where their few pathetic clothes hung from wire hangers she'd got from the local dry cleaners. Renée wished Sissy were here now, she felt so helpless and alone, and she lay down in her towel on her sleeping bag and sobbed until her chest hurt, and then she found she couldn't stop, it was as if some long-plugged gash had opened up inside her. She was just so scared, sickened, homesick – but for where? Where was home anyway, now that she'd graduated, now that the safety of three years in Bristol was over? She hated going to her father's house in Clacton, and she hadn't seen her mother since that last trip to Paris, when it became clear to them both that Renée couldn't forgive her mother for choosing her lover over her daughter, and even though she'd been only fourteen at the time there seemed little common ground between them anyway, they were both stuck in different places somewhere between childhood and adulthood, and it had all felt too awkward, fractious.

It had been a relief for Simone to put the child back on the plane at Charles de Gaulle, and then the next year it had seemed easier for Renée to say no, she didn't want to go to Paris this summer, she'd rather go to Cornwall with her cousins, and then after that she hadn't been asked again. It seemed perverse that it was *her mother* she pined for now, but maybe that was the way it worked – that when things were really bad only your mother would do, no matter how useless they may have been before then.

Renée tried to decide how she should handle it. As she lay on her bedroom floor, her revulsion and hatred grew, but she found it was aimed as much at herself as at him. She *knew* she should have listened to Larry Johnson, who'd warned her about walking into strangers' houses, had tried so hard to save her from danger. She should have trusted her own instincts: it had been obvious from the start that last guy was a creep. *It was all her fault.* She started sobbing again.

There was a knock at the door. Renée sat up quickly, wiping her eyes on the edge of her sleeping bag. She checked her watch – it was just before four, still a little early for anyone to be back yet. She adjusted her towel as the door edged open.

'Oh. Sorry. Are you OK?' asked Stephen, retreating a little. 'I could hear you from downstairs.'

'Oh, God, sorry,' said Renée. 'I . . . I just had a really shit day, that's all.'

'Oh no, what happened?' asked Stephen. He hung outside the door as if he didn't want to intrude, she was half-naked after all, but didn't want to leave her either.

He looked like an anxious little boy somehow, and it was endearing.

'Oh . . . oh, you know,' said Renée. 'Just . . . just some arsehole customer,' and she decided in that moment not to tell anyone what had happened, not even Sissy. She knew it was mad, she'd done nothing wrong, but she felt ashamed anyway.

'Look, I was going to have a quick shower and then go for a swim at the lake,' said Stephen. 'D'you want to come?'

Renée didn't particularly want to spend time with Stephen, he still irritated her, but she needed to get out, she'd go mad if she stayed in this boiling box of a room on her own for much longer, and she had no idea when Sissy would be back – Sissy would soon be driving around the suburb Renée was meant to be working in, looking for her, not realising she was home already, and knowing Sissy she wouldn't give up for ages, she'd be beside herself. It could be hours before she got home.

'OK,' Renée said. Maybe a swim would cleanse her, help hose off the revulsion the shower hadn't reached.

'Good. Looks like you could do with getting out. I won't be long.' He disappeared, pulling the door gently closed, and Renée sat there for a while, wondering what she'd just agreed to.

Stephen had a surprisingly good body. He always looked so beefy in clothes, bulky rather than fat, as though he'd been over-inflated, but in his Speedos his skin was smooth and hairless, his legs well defined, his form nicely triangular, almost as if he was on the way to becoming a body-builder but before the steroids had kicked in. Renée was nearly beginning to see what Juliette saw in him, especially as he'd been so kind since he'd found her crying. Maybe finally she, Juliette's feisty, kick-ass best friend, wasn't a threat to him, had shown her sensitive side at last, and on the bus he'd been concerned but not prying, seemingly genuinely interested in how she was, what she had to say for a change.

Renée felt overly aware of Stephen as she stripped down to her bikini, super-conscious of her body and his body, almost as if her hideous ordeal earlier had heightened rather than diminished her sexuality. She tossed her sundress onto her towel and raced down the beach, feeling self-conscious of her pale exposed flesh, towards the waves that she found hard to fathom were not part of a sea or an ocean but were just a lake, a huge landlocked mass of unsalted water where you couldn't even begin to see the land on the other side. As she ran across the sand into the water the splashes felt icy against her overheating body, but she didn't slow down, instead she careered in, as fast as she could, until it was deep enough for her to dive into the waves, and then she put her head down and swam, out away from the shore, breathing hard, doing her schoolgirl front crawl, trying to swim away from the cold, away from herself, from Stephen, away from America.

Finally she stopped, panting, and turned to look back towards the beach. She was surprised at how far out she was, and although Stephen was now in the water too, he was still close to the shore, watching her.

'Are you OK?' he yelled, and she shouted back yes, she was fine, although she wasn't really, not in her head anyway, and as she started to turn back the cramp hit her, hard, as if her left leg were made of wood, she couldn't move it at all, and then as the pain shot down through her spine she panicked and tried to scream, and as she did so she took a mouthful of water and it tasted disgusting, dieselly, and now she was waving her arms frantically as her head bobbed under the waves, and eventually Stephen seemed to understand and started swimming towards her, but he was taking too long, she couldn't be that far out, surely, and she took another gulp of filthy water and then another and she really thought she was drowning now, she couldn't stay up with just her arms, she was tired, the waves were too big, she was sinking, definitely, was this really how it was all going to end, here in this lake after all she'd survived; and then at long, long last there was Stephen, and he grabbed her around the neck and turned her over, and started swimming back to shore, towing her behind him, and she could feel his body hard beneath her even though she was about to pass out, and it seemed to be taking so long, surely it wasn't that far, and then everything went black for a second until another wave slapped at her, and yet they still weren't there, it was hopeless, she knew it now – and then finally, *finally* she could feel the coarseness of the sand grazing against her legs, and her heart felt double its size, pounding outside her chest, and her eyes were glazed and her mind was blank.

22

Dagenham, East London

Terry Kingston emptied the kibble into Humphrey's bowl, placed it carefully on the floor on top of yesterday's newspaper (the *Independent*, 5th July 2011), partially obscuring both poor Milly Dowler's and Rebekah Brooks' faces, and told him to sit. The dog obliged, eager, adoring, awaiting further instructions.

'Down,' said Terry, and Humphrey went to the lino, head between his feet, eyes looking up into Terry's.

'Go on, then,' Terry sing-songed at last, and Humphrey lurched to his arthritic feet and padded over to his dinner. His name tag tinkled against the metal of the bowl as he ate, and Terry found the noise strangely soothing.

'Dinner's nearly ready,' said Maria, from behind him.

'OK, thanks,' he replied. He wondered briefly how his wife still had such a strong accent, she'd been in East London longer than she'd ever lived in Italy. He sat down at the oval dining table, which she'd covered with a transparent plastic cloth, so the wood could only peer through pitifully, as if desperate for air. Two faded stripy placemats sat on top of the plastic, the knives and forks laid out haphazardly either side of them.

'This looks nice,' he said disingenuously, as she put the bowl of gnocchi drowning in an unidentifiable sauce in front of him. He paused. 'By the way, I won't need dinner tomorrow night, thanks. I'll be out.'

'Oh, where?'

'A private job,' he said.

Maria didn't ask more, simply nodded her dark head and started to eat.

Terry couldn't think of anything else to say to his wife. He was annoyed with his client, dragging him into such a sordid business, and he didn't want to tell Maria, implicate her in any way.

'I think I'll clean out Frank and Dean after dinner,' he said eventually, as a way of starting conversation.

'Really, Terry, do you have to talk about such things when we are eating?'

'Oh – sorry, love,' he said.

Terry Kingston adored his pets, almost certainly more than his wife these days, which was a shame for both of them. His love for his animals extended from Humphrey the spaniel, through Snoopy the cat (unremarkable in all but name), onto the pet rats Maria had been horrified by when he'd brought them home a couple of months earlier. Maria hated animals, thought they were dirty and pointless, and she insisted on Humphrey's bowl being placed on newspaper that could be thrown away afterwards, he was such a messy eater it was dees-gusting, she said. But she loathed the rats especially – the sight of their pink eyes and whip tails made her stomach turn like a cranked engine, and she banished them to the spare room, the one where the babies had been meant to go, the ones that had never come, even when they'd been trying. Terry debated now if he should get rid of them, for her sake.

Terry finished his dinner and sat watching his wife. She looked like a little bird, small and delicate, although not pretty exactly, and he wondered again how they'd ended up together. He knew he had a pleasant enough face, but his eyes often looked like they were going to cry, like they might soon be brimming with tears, he suffered terribly from hay fever. Otherwise he was nondescript: average build, average height, mousy wavyish hair, and he prided himself on being the type of person who could meld into the background and just observe, and he found he enjoyed this, it was less stressful than trying to think of things to say.

Terry sometimes wondered whether Maria was as dissatisfied as he was these days, but she always seemed happy enough, and so he never dared broach it, risk having to talk about his feelings. What he did know annoyed her though was his increasing interest in miniature wargaming, the hours and hours he spent painting the figures, and he dreaded breaking it to her that he wanted to go to another convention in Nottingham next weekend. But, he reasoned, she seemed to be pretty busy herself with the choir these days, so hopefully she'd be all right about it. He just needed to pick his moment to ask her.

23

Hyde Park

The skies had darkened over Hyde Park and the picnickers were well on the way to drunkenness now, a most dangerous destination for this particular combination of women. Sissy had tried not to have too much Prosecco at first, having never been much of a drinker, but Renée kept insisting on filling up her glass, and what with all the tension she had eventually stopped objecting. She was relieved nothing serious had kicked off between anyone, although as the evening continued it was an increasing possibility, with Siobhan in particular threatening to cross into danger zones – she'd kept moaning on about her boyfriend Matt, how he would never commit, and how the others were so lucky to have husbands, and then she'd said, 'Oh, sorry, Sissy,' and Sissy could have throttled her. Natasha seemed pretty uptight too, which was unlike her, normally everything was totally marvellous in her world, but she seemed to have the hump with both Juliette and Renée for some reason. And of course Juliette and Renée didn't get on and hadn't for years, so there was that to deal with too. Only Camilla was behaving normally, now she'd got over the presence of shop-bought scotch eggs and the absence of sufficient picnic chairs. Honestly, thought Sissy, this is the last time we should do this, it's just too stressful – we've got to stop living in the past, we've all got our own lives now. She looked out towards The Serpentine and wondered idly whether it was a river or a lake, and what it was like to swim in. She knew people did but it looked dirty to her, unappealing.

'Sissy,' said Natasha, obviously not for the first time; her tone was the one Sissy took with her own children the fourth time of asking. 'Would you like some cheesecake?'

'Oh, sorry, Natasha, no thanks, I'm fine,' said Sissy. 'I'm going to have to think about going soon, I've got an early start tomorrow.'

'Oh, come on, Sissy,' said Siobhan, helping herself to another of her profiteroles. 'Why don't you just let your hair down for a change? You've got to start enjoying yourself again. It would do you good.'

'Siobhan, shush,' replied Renée. 'Don't be so bloody insensitive.'

'Yeah, well, we can't all pussy-foot round her for ever, it's not good for her. And at least she's *had* a husband,' said Siobhan, and she'd obviously had far too much wine now, and not just down her trousers. 'No-one's ever wanted to marry me.'

Everyone was silent for a moment, stunned.

'Well, I'm not surprised with that attitude,' said Renée in the end. 'You are quite possibly the most selfish person I know.'

'I hardly think so,' said Siobhan, and her tone was more sober suddenly. 'I think we all know Juliette's married to the person who wins that prize.'

'Siobhan, shut up,' said Natasha. Her tone brightened, like the school nurse with a sickly child. 'Now, who's going to have this last piece of cheesecake? It's a shame to waste it.'

'Yeah, well, Sissy would still have a husband if it wasn't for Stephen, wouldn't she?' said Siobhan, as though Natasha hadn't spoken, and as she said it she tried to stop herself but her mouth wouldn't cooperate, and she knew she really had gone too far this time.

There were at least three involuntary intakes of breath, and then there seemed to be no breathing at all, and nobody said anything for long empty seconds that even the irrepressible Michael Bublé failed to fill. Sissy downed the rest of her glass in one, and then she stared out at the water again, and it lay still, seemingly breathless too, and she wondered whether everything was slowly dying in her world, and she tried to work out what would be the quickest way to get home, so she could pay off the baby-sitter and go straight upstairs and hide under her duvet, and never come out again.

24

Cleveland

Renée lay on the beach and belched a great flood of lake water into the sand. Stephen was just clambering off her, and she was dimly aware that he had saved her life. She lay still, her breathing shallow and irregular, as she heard other voices now – American, loud, concerned – saying they were going to call an ambulance.

'No, no, I'm OK,' she mumbled. 'I'm fine, I don't need one.' And she tried to sit up and found that she could, in fact she felt surprisingly normal, just a little giddy perhaps.

'Well, let's get you inside and fetch you a drink, and see how you are then,' said one of the voices, and she looked up to see that it belonged to a man with a fierce-looking face, like a wrestler's, and he had long, straggly hair untamed by a baseball cap. He was wearing huge hitched-up jeans and an open shirt, and a gold medallion shone through the hair on his chest, like treasure.

Stephen and the stranger helped Renée up and wrapped her in a towel – even though it was still so hot she felt shivery, which must have been shock, she supposed. A little, sinewy woman in a tiny skirt and cut-off top, with deeply brown tattooed skin, as if she were wearing her hurt on the outside, quietly gathered up the rest of their belongings. Stephen held Renée under one arm whilst the burly man took the other and, as she was propelled between them, she felt like she was floating now, not drowning any more. They walked her one block back from the beach, helped her up some concrete steps and into a big empty bar that looked out over the tops of buildings and the main lakeshore road, towards the drabness of the water. They sat her on a vinyl bench seat, but she was still so cold and shaky that someone turned the air conditioning off and Stephen gave her his T-shirt, which she put on over her bikini, keeping the towel wrapped around her like a skirt. A drink got shoved into her hand, and when she took a sip the liquid was warmly brown and strong-tasting, and instantly the blood in her veins felt a little livelier, as if it were being chased around her body rather than creeping reluctantly.

'Stephen, I'm so sorry,' she said, as he came back from the restrooms, involuntarily half-naked still, towel draped over his brawny shoulders. 'I don't know what happened, I just got such excruciating cramp I must have panicked.'

'That's all right, you don't need to apologise. I'm just relieved I wasn't towing a corpse. I honestly thought you were about to die on me.' He smiled, looking young and nervous, his mid-brown hair beginning to curl at the ends where it was drying, and she thought again that she must have misjudged him. She was still aware of him in a way that she recognised with a shock as maybe the reason why she hadn't liked him much before, and she pushed that thought aside. After all, he was her best friend's boyfriend – they might be on a break but she was sure Juliette would have him back, once they were both home; and she was also sure he would go back, he adored Juliette, who didn't? And why the hell was she even thinking like this after what had happened just a few hours earlier with the stranger in his kitchen? Renée shivered again and took another swig of her drink, a larger one this time, as she tried to process the events of this unimaginable day, tried to work out precisely what impact they had had on her, what she should do. When finally the solution came to her she couldn't believe she hadn't done it. Of course! She needed to go to the police – that's what she should have done in the first place, as soon as it had happened.

Why hadn't she gone to the police?

She stood up, ignoring Stephen's protestations to take it easy, and walked unsteadily to the bathroom where she gazed at herself in the mirror, shaking with cold, or perhaps fear. Her mind was racing. There would be no evidence now, only the faintest of marks on the left side of her neck – it would be his word against hers, and she'd already sussed what the local police thought of booksellers, she'd been moved on enough times, despite having her licence. They probably wouldn't believe her, and even if they did it could just prolong the ordeal – they might want to keep her there, for the court case or something, she might even have to miss her flight home. No, there was no way she was going to risk that.

Renée continued to stare in the mirror, barely

recognising herself, hardly believing she was here. *She had escaped death twice in one day.* She was lucky to be alive. Surely that was enough? She washed her hands again, holding them for ages under the dryer, and then she made her way unsteadily back to the bar, just as Stephen was coming to check that she was all right.

25

Soho

The restaurant was small, charming and candle-lit, the perfect backdrop to the start of an affair. Natasha's husband looked across the table at his companion's lips, as red and vital as newly spilt blood, even in the half-light, and decided she'd looked better before she'd excused herself and gone to the bathroom to apply it – she was well into her forties now and it didn't suit her, aged her even. It didn't matter though – he found he didn't really care what she looked like, or what they ate, or what they spoke about, he just wanted to get her back to his hotel and fuck her senseless. It was quite extraordinary really – that he should be at this table with one of his wife's oldest friends, that she should have been the one to take the first step with him, and he wondered how much the chronic lack of sex in his marriage showed through, in the starvation in his eyes. She must have guessed about that, he was sure Natasha wouldn't have spoken about it to anyone, Natasha was too proud, she wore her life like a trophy – *look at me*, look how far I've come, with my two adorable children, my brilliant career, my handsome novelist husband, my detached house in Barnes, my sub-45 minute 10k runs. Life was just wonderful as far as Natasha was concerned, she would never admit otherwise. Alistair often wondered when he'd first regretted marrying her, and he thought it may have been even before the wedding, once the sex had started to dwindle – around the time the preparations had been fully cranked up: Invite List A minus four months from the Big Day, Invite List B (finalised and mailed minus two months according to acceptees from Invite List A), separate spreadsheets for hotels, menus, flowers, thank-you gifts, transport. She'd made them have weekly meetings, with an agenda and everything, to discuss it. And then immediately afterwards there'd been the baby-making to be getting on with: no more wild abandon, no letting nature take its course, just those offensive ovulation sticks from the get-go, dictating their appointments with passion, purely so she could have autumn or, at worst, December babies – they had so much better an outcome in life, she'd read somewhere. The biggest bang he'd had on his Mauritian honeymoon was on Day Eight, exactly when Natasha would be ovulating, and she'd made him endure abstention for three whole days beforehand to ensure his sperm was top-notch for the conception. He'd nearly bloody exploded. He'd always known she was competitive, and it had served him well in many ways, but he'd preferred her when they'd first met, when she'd channelled it into who could have the most orgasms (her) and finding him an agent – she'd been unstoppable at both in the early days.

'I think I might have the sea bass,' his wife's friend was saying. 'What about you?'

'Um, yeah, sounds good,' Alistair said, and his nostrils filled with fishy smells and his mind crawled with visions of her with her legs apart and him going down there for the first time, like an explorer, and he forced himself back to the little restaurant behind Carnaby Street and told himself, 'Just a couple more hours,' and as he looked at her he thought he might even blow right there with the agony of it all – so he tried to think of something else, recalled his wife bossing the nanny around this morning, going on about the importance of a nutritionally balanced packed lunch, and that settled him down again.

Natasha's friend shifted in her seat and looked shyly down into her wine glass, as if the answer to something lay there. 'So were you surprised when I texted you?' she said. 'I do hope you didn't mind, I just really needed someone to talk to about . . . about . . .' She trailed off.

Alistair thought then that maybe he'd got it wrong, maybe she simply wanted him as a friend, wanted some advice, about writing perhaps. Maybe he'd imagined she wanted the same thing as him, had imagined that she too was after dirty, messy, uninhibited sex with a nice smear of guilt to top it off. He started to feel insanely edgy, like he really needed to get this over with, one way or the other.

'Um, well, of course not. Though I was a little surprised,' he managed. He wondered then, for the first time, as if a revelation, why he had never thought to be unfaithful to his wife before. It would have solved so many problems (and inevitably caused a few others, but he wasn't concerned about those at this precise moment). He must have just got caught up in the frustration of it all, and of course there was the Internet these days and his almost obsessive level of wanking which meant he did it at least three times in the en suite on a bad day. But surely that was better than cheating on her, he'd always thought, not even consciously really – and then he'd got THAT text and it had given him ideas, but maybe he'd misinterpreted it; and now he was stuck here feeling unsure, and he didn't want to sit and eat dinner or chat about anything, large or small, he just wanted to go and fucking finish himself off if she wasn't going to go through with it. Maybe he had some kind of a problem, a little voice whispered, and he looked up desolately, and as he did so she took a sip from her glass, seductively, and her lipstick smeared bawdily, and she reached her foot under the table and rubbed it against his ankle, and as she smiled at him with her smudgy crimson mouth he felt relief gush over him like he'd already ejaculated. 'Shall we go?' he asked urgently, and although she looked surprised she acquiesced and there was no more messing about, thank God, and since then he'd got laid at least once a week, and he thought it was doing them both good.

Less than half an hour after leaving the restaurant, Natasha's friend lay on her back next to Alistair and wondered just what she'd done. She felt wracked with guilt, but more because of Natasha than anyone else. What on earth was she doing sleeping with her friend's husband, no matter how miserable her own circumstances? What had happened to female solidarity? It didn't help that Alistair had proven something of a disappointment anyway – it had been over so quickly for a start. She'd initially hoped he would talk to her about writing, give her some advice, but he hadn't seemed interested, not at all; in fact he hadn't even wanted to stay in the restaurant for long enough to eat, and she felt cheapened now.

Just as she was about to get up, get dressed, try to get the hell out of there, Alistair turned over in the bed and opened his eyes, and as she stared at him, as if he were a stranger rather than someone she'd known for years, he grabbed at her again (his recovery time was miraculous, she had to hand it to him), and this time it was slower, quite nice even, and he *was* handsome, a famous writer, and it did seem to help heal the aching loneliness in her heart – so somehow she agreed to see him on a second occasion, and before she knew it they were meeting every Wednesday, and she dreaded the next time she'd have to see Natasha.

26

Cleveland

Stephen and Renée found themselves getting on better, even becoming friends, after he'd saved her life. They often found themselves seated next to each other at breakfast, it just seemed to happen that way, and the others began to notice, and Melissa even said something once in her normal tactless way, but Renée told her not to be so ridiculous. Sissy seemed anxious about it too, as though she could sense the trouble to come, and Renée privately thought that Sissy was worrying about Nigel, scared that he might meet some nice bronzed girl in Australia. And anyway, Renée knew Stephen was off-limits, plus she didn't even fancy him, he wasn't her type at all. She just got on well with him these days, and what was wrong with that?

The waitress stood patiently in her short brown tunic, beige frilly apron tied neatly, white bobby socks and sneakers over American Tan tights, grey permed hair tucked tidily into her matching cap, waiting for Melissa to order. Melissa's performance had become something of a ritual they all bizarrely enjoyed, in their own ways.

'Have you got muesli?' asked Melissa, studying the menu, which was large and laminated.

'No, ma'am, we have Corn Flakes or Rice Krispies.'

'Ohhhhh, I wanted muesli,' said Melissa. 'I wish you had muesli,' and she said it sulkily, as if the diner not having muesli was a personal slight on her.

'I'm sorry, ma'am, that's all we have. What would you like?'

Melissa couldn't help herself. 'I'd like muesli,' she said.

'Just shut up, Melissa,' said Renée mildly. My God, she's even worse than Siobhan, she thought. 'Do we have to go through this every single day? Just pick something else.' She turned to the waitress. 'I'm sorry about her. I'll have two eggs over-easy please, and some coffee.'

'Same for me,' said Stephen, and everyone else ordered whilst Melissa slumped moodily in her seat. Finally the waitress turned back to her.

'Have you decided yet, ma'am?' she said.

'I suppose I'll have to have Corn Flakes,' said Melissa, with a harrumph. 'If you haven't got *muesli*. And tea please, but not with the teabag left on the side of the cup, in a pot so that the water's boiling, like it should be.'

'I'll see what I can do, ma'am,' said the waitress and whisked the menus away. Renée rolled her eyes at Stephen, and she wasn't sure if she imagined it but he seemed to press his knee against hers, under the table.

The following Saturday everyone was getting ready for a rare night out. It had been Renée's idea originally, and as she'd seemed so jumpy since the day she'd nearly drowned,

Sissy thought it might do her good to get out. She wondered whether Renée would ever be able to recover her selling stride. Although she usually seemed all right at breakfast (when Stephen was there, Sissy couldn't help noticing), Renée had had first door syndrome for the rest of that week and the whole of the next, and had spent hours sitting tearfully with Sissy in Pizza Hut sipping icy drinks with unlimited refills. The waitresses were good though and never said anything, not even when Renée and Sissy paid the bill with a five-dollar note and always took the change.

Stephen took over the evening's arrangements, of course, and insisted on choosing the venue, but Renée didn't appear to mind; it seemed to Sissy that Stephen could do no wrong in her eyes now. They went to a bar in the next suburb, another of those places where everything was old-fashioned and wood-cladded and they played old country tunes on the jukebox, and old men sat silently with just their bourbon for company, and Sissy thought the barmaid had that tired look in her eyes like she'd seen enough of sadness and ruination, but she had two kids to feed so that's just the way it was since her bastard no-good husband had upped and left her. (The truth was actually quite different – the barmaid was very much married, and this job helped pay for their annual trip with the kids to visit her sister in Florida, but Sissy didn't know that of course.)

Renée sat at the bar with Sissy and stared morosely into the bottom of her glass. Sissy tried to distract her with stories of Nigel in Queensland, she'd had a letter that day, but Renée seemed vacant, uninterested, and so Sissy fell silent. The others were standing in a group, laughing at some story Andy was telling about how he'd managed to sell the complete set of Tyler's books, from the toddler nursery rhymes all the way up to Grade Twelve, to a couple who hadn't even given birth yet. Sissy found the story upsetting somehow – that Andy seemed to be mocking these people he'd befriended; that who knows what may happen to them or their child in the next sixteen years or so; that bookselling appeared to be sapping Andy's soul: he seemed more driven by money than ever these days. Renée's melancholy must be rubbing off on me, Sissy thought, and again she felt a stab of panic, that she was in the wrong place, that she needed to go home. But Nigel wasn't in England anyway, and her flights were firm-booked, she wasn't sure she could change them even if she wanted to; and so she had settled into her days under trees, dreaming, drifting, reading, writing, to pass the time. It was only sometimes that it hit her, the head-filling, heart-emptying loneliness, though usually when she was in a crowd rather than on her own.

She turned to Renée, who looked like she might cry herself.

'Are you all right, Renée? What's wrong? You're not at all yourself these days, I'm worried about you.'

'I'm OK,' said Renée. 'Apart from hating bloody bookselling.' Sissy didn't look convinced, so she added, 'I'm sorry, Siss, I don't know what's up with me really.' She felt tempted, for just a moment, to tell Sissy about the man, the horror of the attack, how close she'd been to perhaps being killed, but she stopped herself. She still couldn't face talking about it, not even with Sissy.

'Well, nearly drowning can't have helped,' said Sissy. 'You're just so lucky Stephen saved you.'

'I know,' said Renée. She hesitated. 'You know, I'm not sure he's as bad as I thought.'

Sissy looked across at Stephen, beefy arms stretching the sleeves of his too-tight T-shirt, head thrown back with laughter, and she tried to think that perhaps Renée was right, now his initial desperation to get his own back on Juliette for daring to dump him had faded, and he'd stopped trying to get off with them both. But she didn't like the way he was showing off now, it was almost like he thought he was David Hasselhoff or something since he'd saved Renée's life. It was funny how Stephen instilled such mixed emotions in people, she really couldn't work him out.

'Well,' said Sissy. 'You'll always be grateful to him, that's for sure.'

'I know,' said Renée, and she took a swig of her drink as Stephen turned and caught her eye, and when she smiled at him he seemed to puff up even further, like a snake who'd just eaten a mouse. But Sissy was wrong; Renée would not be grateful to Stephen for always, not at all.

27

Hyde Park

The atmosphere was poisonous now, and not even the languidly liquid disappearance of the sun, turning the park into a cooler, more peaceful place, could rescue the evening. Renée and Juliette sat stiffly next to each other and didn't appear to be speaking at all any more, there may as well have been a fence between them, and poor Sissy looked as though she was going to faint with the stress of it all. Natasha was sullen (as she had been for much of the evening) and Siobhan was trying to paper over her appalling insult of Juliette's husband, having dared to imply that Stephen somehow had had something to do with Nigel's death. To break the impasse Natasha started tidying up, grimly, as if she were picking up dog-shit – tipping the remaining quarter of Sissy's pasta salad into an M&S bag she'd designated for rubbish without even asking Sissy whether she wanted to keep it; scraping plates like they were potatoes to be scrubbed (or perhaps children to be bathed); scrunching used napkins with unnecessary force into tight mucky balls that were tossed into the carrier bag too, not bothering with recycling, just chucking the empty wine bottles in with the mess; flicking stray flakes of sausage roll towards Siobhan, perhaps deliberately.

It was Renée in the end who said it. She tried for a chummy tone but it came out strangled, and although it was clear she was suffering too, she was drunk enough to not care about the consequences.

'Look, girls, I'm sorry, but I'm just sick of this atmosphere. If it's going to be like this every time we see each other we might as well not bother trying to get together any more.'

'All right, Renée,' said Natasha. 'I don't think we need to discuss it here.'

'Oh, but I disagree,' replied Renée, more airily now. She emptied what was left of the last bottle of Prosecco into her glass. 'Here's as good a place as any. Why do we all pretend we still get on for a start? Who's to blame for this whole *horrid* situation? Is it just the passing of time, the natural growing apart we can't seem to accept, or is it something more, more . . . *sinister*? Siobhan, you seem to think Stephen's responsible for all this, why don't you start?'

'Shhhhush, Renée,' said Siobhan. 'I said something out of line, I take it back.'

'Ah, but maybe you shouldn't take it back,' said Renée, and her eyes were flashing warnings, and no-one had ever seen her like that. 'After all, it's true, isn't it, Juliette? Stephen killed Nigel, didn't he?'

Juliette stared at her former friend. 'Don't be so utterly ridiculous, how on earth can you say such a thing?'

'Because it's true!' said Renée. 'If it wasn't for Stephen, Nigel would be alive now, Sissy wouldn't be struggling on her own, she'd still have a husband who loved her, way more than yours ever has. But Stephen fucked it all up through his greed and selfishness. He's such a fucking cheat and liar, as well as a –' She stopped.

Juliette looked horrified. 'What the hell are you trying to imply, Renée? Don't *you* start now, please, not after Siobhan's outburst.'

'What has become of you, Juliette?' said Renée, and she said it quietly now, almost as a caress. 'Where has your sweet, beautiful heart gone?' Juliette looked broken for a second, and then she looked away, towards The Serpentine, which appeared calm and serene as it faded into the night.

It was Natasha's turn to speak, to break the loneliness of the silence. 'Leave her alone, Renée. I don't think you of all people have the right to lecture anyone on morals.'

'Well, I think I have more right than most of you,' yelled Renée, inflamed again. 'Just take a look at your husband for a start.' Everyone gasped as Renée blushed. She carried on hurriedly. 'Sometimes I think Siobhan's the only one round here who's at least honest, who says it like it is.'

'I think you should be quiet, Renée,' said Camilla quietly, but it was too late. The incriminations continued on in the downy dusk, where the air was soft and summery and there were no strangers to inhibit them, where the alcohol had finally dislodged stuck feelings, like years' old plaque set free by mouthwash. Sissy sat, feeling dizzy, on her auntie's rug, bought as a wedding present in a far ago, happier time, staring at her ankles below her hideous flowery dress (why hadn't she just worn shorts like she'd wanted to?), and they appeared to be swelling, trying to drown the bones out. She wanted the screaming to stop, she didn't much care what they were saying any more, she didn't care who was to blame, after all maybe *she* was, and anyway Nigel was dead, none of this would bring him back, no matter how loud any of them shouted.

28

Barnes

Alistair had just come back from the en suite feeling a little better, but he still couldn't bear to even sit down at his desk, let alone make contact with the keyboard. The room was large and bright and looked out onto their garden which backed onto the common, so the view was sunny and cheerful and Natasha had thought it would be a wonderful place for him to write. In London yet out of it, she'd said when they'd been to look at the house with the weaselly prick of an estate agent who Alistair had always felt like punching. Alistair hated the room now. It made him feel trapped, locked in an airless hostile space with just the deeply irritating Shouty Mouse and Rude Rabbit for company. He thought if he had to do this for much longer it would drive him insane – but his agent was breathing down his neck, threatening that if he didn't come up with Volume Six soon the publisher would be taking back part of his latest advance for breach of contract. As if. Alistair Smart, king of children's fiction, author of the bestselling series about behaviour-challenged furry creatures, a poor

Tourette's-ridden mouse and an autistic rabbit. Child psychologists had queued up to fete him, he had made 'different' children feel normal, had created tales of such moral fortitude he'd helped parents and children alike gain empathy and understanding for these all-too-common conditions. His writing was acerbically, charmingly witty. He was a modern-day Roald Dahl, a fucking hero!

Alistair finally stopped pacing, sat down and clicked onto one of his favourite porn sites, and as he watched two big-breasted girls cavorting in baby oil he felt his desire build all over again. What the hell was wrong with him these days? Just how much sperm could one man produce? He heard a noise on the stairs and quickly flicked over to his email, and swore he was going to get rid of their housekeeper. He loathed her being around – even when Natasha was at work and the kids were at school he felt like he had to be on his guard, behave himself, almost as if he were just visiting, in his own fucking home. There was always someone in the house to intrude on his loneliness – the cleaner, the housekeeper (what was the difference between the two, he wondered idly), the gardener, the nanny. And how much did they all bloody cost?

The idea came to him in an instant then, and he kicked himself that he hadn't thought of it before. That's it! He'd get a lock for his office door. Then he could browse lesbian porn and wank to his heart's content without even leaving his desk, whenever he was bored rigid (quite literally, he sniggered, always the master with words) or stuck on Shouty Mouse's latest tedious adventure he couldn't give a shit about.

Alistair was so excited by his idea that he thought he might go to Homebase right now, so he could buy a lock and a drill and fit it himself; it couldn't be that hard, surely. That would give him something to do. He was about to get up from his desk in a rare burst of energy when his email refreshed and two new ones appeared: the first from his agent which he ignored, and then one from some-one called Smartfan, entitled: HELP ME ALISTAIR. Alistair was used to getting fan mail, mainly from seven-year-olds, saying things like: 'Dear Alister Smart, thank you so much for riting Showty Mous, he has mad me so hapy that I am not the only won lik him, love Oli-ver,' or, worse, from gushing mothers saying, 'You have made my darling Lucy one happy bunny (pardon the pun!), she no longer feels so isolated by her condition, and you have made me one very happy mummy!! Thank you so much, and please keep on writing your wonderful books.' They made Alistair want to puke.

This email however seemed a bit too shouty (he couldn't bring himself to snigger again), too desperate, to be just another fan letter, and although he usually left this kind of correspondence to his agent's assistant Xavier, he found himself opening it: he didn't dare go back on the Internet while Mrs Cole was outside hoovering, and he couldn't face even looking at his hopelessly overdue manuscript today.

Dear Mr Smart,

I am a budding new writer and I have written a new chil-dren's book about a boarding school for dogs. All the dogs have different characters and the book is the first in a series that deals with all sorts of issues for the 'Tweenie' market, from bullying to how to cope with not having the latest must-have possessions, to realising you might be gay. I haven't sent it out to any agents yet because I would so love to have your view of my book first, and perhaps even a quote to put on the cover. You are the absolute champion of children's issue-based fiction and I have admired you for many years, from when I was a behaviour-challenged child myself. I am nineteen years old and this is my first novel.

Yours excitedly,
Lucinda Horne

Normally Alistair ignored these kinds of emails, but there was something about this one: was it her name, or maybe her age (totally legal) – he still hadn't quite settled down in the trouser department – or was there something interesting about her story? He opened the attachment and started reading about Bottersley Dog School, with its three houses, Barkers, Howlers and Sniffers, and its key characters Fluffy, T-Bone and Wowser, and as he whipped through the chapters he found the story surprisingly compelling, and so he settled down lengthways on the sofa under the window, bare feet up and over the end of it, and he felt himself relax for a minute, and then tighten – and then he felt his heart rate whoosh as the idea came to him, devilish and fully formed.

29

Cleveland

The music in the bar was loud and twangy, and although it wasn't the type that people usually dance to, there was so much pent-up energy in the room that before anyone knew it Stephen was pulling the girls up and twirling them around as if they were in a salsa bar in Rio – Juliette had dragged him to classes in their final year at Bristol and he was surprisingly adept at it. Sissy had mildly protested and gone bright red, but hadn't actually stopped him when he'd grabbed her, she must have been drunk for once; and although the dreadful Melissa complained loudly when they accidentally barged her during a particularly complex over-the-head manoeuvre, once it was her turn she joined in with gusto, giggling up at him, even smooching a little, until he pushed her off with an expert flick of his wrist that sent her spinning away from him towards the bar, where the barmaid with the dead eyes looked on inscrutably.

Renée was sat in the corner, propped on a high bar stool next to Andy, drinking steadily, and she found she couldn't stop herself from watching as Stephen twirled Melissa (who right now was griping and moaning that he was hurting her back, and then as she came up from an admirably athletic backwards lunge was mooning at him with her silly simpleton face). Since the day at the lake, almost two weeks ago now, when Renée had felt Stephen's solid flesh beneath hers as he towed her out of the waves she'd been aware of him in a way that surprised, no, not surprised, *shocked* her. She tried not to think of Stephen in that way, she wasn't the type to steal other people's boyfriends – and of course she'd never much liked him before, let alone found him attractive. It was bizarre.

Renée tried to force her mind away from strange thoughts about Stephen, but combined with the drink the effort of doing so seemed to make everything worse somehow, mixed everything up, distressed her again. Suddenly, almost as if he were there, she remembered the stranger on top of her, saw the twisted look in his eyes, smelled the sour stench of his breath, felt the hairy sweat between his legs, the hardness, of him, of the floor . . . and now she was back in the lake, stinking water filling her mouth, lungs burning, Stephen's thighs beneath hers, waves slapping at her face, remonstratively . . . and to drown out these sensations, try to stop the spinning in her head, she took another deep draw of her beer. She shuddered. When would she ever feel normal again?

Renée knew within herself, somewhere locked and fragile, that this peculiar mindset wouldn't simply go away, couldn't be cleansed by the water of Lake Erie, by pretending nothing had happened – or by becoming attracted to *Stephen* of all people. She tried to process it. Just how had the man's attack left her? Naked and lacking in self-respect, that's what. She bitterly regretted not having gone to the police, but it was too late now. *But what if he does it to someone else?* It would be her fault if he did, she'd be as culpable as him in a way. She stared at her hands and willed herself not to go and wash them again, they were getting so dried out. She shivered, although it was hot in the bar.

'Are you OK, Renée?' asked Stephen, as he walked over and stood casually next to her in the dingy light, having managed to shrug off Melissa at last, who was now propped further along the bar droning on to Andy about the inadequacies of American food establishments.

'Sure,' said Renée, and she looked sideways at him and smiled, and then she felt nervous so she looked down again, back into her beer. 'Enjoying swinging the girls around, are you?'

Stephen laughed. 'It started off as a joke, but Melissa seems to think she's on bloody *Come Dancing*.'

'That girl is so unbelievably stupid,' said Renée. 'It's like there's a part of her brain missing or something.'

'That's a bit harsh,' said Stephen. 'You're not jealous, are you?'

Renée coloured, and they both stared into their drinks now. Stephen shifted as Andy roared derisorily at something Melissa had said, although she hadn't meant it to be funny, throwing his head back, narrowly avoiding knocking into Stephen's drink. Stephen budged up and Renée could feel the comforting warmth of his arm against hers.

She thought about moving away, about creating some space between them, but she stayed there, not quite knowing why.

'Remember, he's Juliette's boyfriend,' she told herself, but the thought drifted away and her brain replaced it with another: 'She finished with him, they're not together any more.' She looked into his eyes and they were large and deeply brown, like muddy puddles, kind even. She smiled shyly at him, and Stephen moved in a little more then, until his leg was pressing against hers under the bar, and they remained like that for ages, half-enjoying, half-dreading the physical contact, the possibility, as the music blared around them.

30

Hyde Park

In a park in central London on a perfect summer's evening it was a close call who could become the most hysterical. Amongst the candidates was a woman who was tired of her marriage to a man who was not only overbearing but had just been called a *murderer*, in effect; another whose husband was dead; one who had recently found out hers was having an affair with one of her supposed best friends, who happened to be right here too, apparently unaware that her secret was out; one sobbing drunkenly about having been raped years ago; one who was horrified at how their friendships were unravelling, finally; and a sixth who usually managed to be the most melodramatic without having to try too hard, so was feeling a bit put out, unused to this level of competition. Siobhan was confused. Her skinny jeans were ruined, she was mortified by her outburst about Stephen and what it had set off, there was a sick feeling in her stomach that Matt still hadn't called her – and she was far too drunk to deal with any of it. She leaned over and picked up a glass near Sissy, she had no idea whose, and drank the contents straight down, although she knew that wouldn't help. Camilla was getting up, trying to be all mumsy and sensible, draping her jumper over her shoulders, slurring on about how they should all go home; and Siobhan had a sudden dread of the evening ending, despite how horrifically it was turning out, of going home to her empty flat and her absent boyfriend and her over-fed cat Norris – and all she wanted was for the others to look after her, like they used to. She started bawling, mainly because she was pissed and couldn't think what else to do. It was dark and the park was nearly empty now, and the sounds seemed to travel further than they should, ringing out rancorously across the water, as if they would reach over the grass and through the trees all the way to the Bayswater Road.

'Oh, just shut the fuck up, Siobhan,' said Natasha. 'For God's sake. If it wasn't for you and your big mouth none of this would have happened.' Siobhan looked stunned at Natasha's outburst, how *dare* she speak to her like that. Natasha looked across at Sissy, who appeared to have deflated, was slumped with her head on her knees on her fancy woollen rug, shoulders shaking gently.

'And just look what you've done to poor Sissy,' Natasha added, as if for emphasis.

Siobhan lost it then.

'Look what *I've* done to her,' she yelled. 'I've done nothing! Sissy wouldn't even be a widow if it wasn't for Juliette's lying bastard of a husband, and she knows it.' Even Siobhan looked shocked at what she'd said, for a second – and then her tongue ran away with itself, as if it were operating unilaterally and had decided there was no going back now. 'In fact both of your husbands are repulsive,' she yelled at Juliette and Natasha. 'Stephen should be in bloody prison' (at which point Juliette put her head in her hands and started weeping), 'and Alistair thinks he's such a big shot just because he's a children's author.' Siobhan stared down Natasha, inflamed after years and years of her put-downs. 'And *you* – you always have been a social climber. And now you're so wrapped up in your fancy job and posh house and flash cars and private schools you seem to think you're above everyone else these days. And you're not.'

'You're just jealous,' snorted Natasha. 'You are so ludicrously hung-up that you've never managed to hold down a relationship, or get a decent job. It's always the same when I see you. If you didn't bitch and moan and go on about yourself so much maybe you wouldn't be so bloody lonely.'

Siobhan was standing now, looking like she might even punch Natasha, and she was so furious that she was debating whether to just bugger off and go home, flag down a cab on the bridge and leave the lot of them, this was unbearable. In the end it was Sissy who spoke.

'Please can we stop this,' she said quietly. 'None of it's going to bring Nigel back, and I'm sure no-one did anything deliberately. Please let's not make everything worse by all screaming and shouting at each other. All I want to do is go home, *please*, let's just get packed up and go.'

Sissy stood up and shook out her rug, and even in the

fading light it was clear that tears were running down her cheeks and she looked small and hunched, like a little girl who'd been smacked by her mummy. No-one spoke as they packed up and the atmosphere was sullen, brittle, utterly irreparable; and each woman was aware that her life would never be quite the same again, not after this, although at that point none of them realised in what way.

31

Cleveland

Sissy looked over into the corner of the bar, where the lights were dimmest and the music was loudest, and she didn't know whether to feel annoyed or anxious. What the heck was Renée thinking? She really was going too far now. Stephen had found himself a bar stool and was sat next to Renée, his dirty mid-brown head bent close to her sleek dark one, and even from here Sissy could see that their feet were intertwined underneath the counter. What on earth would Juliette say? The funny thing was that Sissy had asked her, back in Bristol, if she was worried about Stephen meeting someone else over the summer, and Juliette had replied that she might even be quite glad if he did – what would be would be, she'd said – and Sissy had wondered at the time if Juliette would ever get back with Stephen, she'd seemed almost desperate to be free of him.

'What *would* upset me, though,' Juliette had continued. 'Is if he got off with one of my friends – but you're far too in love with Nigel, thank goodness, and Renée doesn't even like him.'

'Juliette!' Sissy had said, shocked. 'That's not true; of course she does.'

'Darling Sissy,' Juliette had replied. 'You're so sweet and that's what I love about you. But Renée's not keen on Stephen and never has been, and if I'm honest that's always made me ever so slightly wary about him too. I do tend to trust her opinion, deep down.'

'Don't you think it might be that . . .' Sissy had stopped.

'What?'

'Oh, nothing.'

'Come on, Sissy, what were you going to say?'

'. . . Don't you think . . . she might be . . . a little bit jealous of him?' Sissy had said finally.

'What on earth do you mean?'

'Well,' she'd floundered. 'You do see him quite a lot.'

'Oh,' Juliette had said. 'Do you think so? (*Pause.*) I suppose I do . . . Oh God, I feel awful now.

'Anyway,' she'd continued, changing the subject. 'Let's see what happens over the summer – and with any luck I might meet a hunky Spanish waiter in Marbella.'

Just as Sissy remembered the end of this conversation, she saw in the orange glow Stephen lean in and caress Renée's face, and Renée stop and look at him, as if trying to make up her mind what to do; and now she was laughing at something he'd just said and they were almost rubbing faces, and although Sissy tried not to look she was almost transfixed; and now, no, oh my God they were, they were fully, full-on, mouth-open tonsil-munching snogging, and she could see his revolting darting tongue, and he was wrapping his arms around her clumsily, like a bear – and, oh no, now he was standing up and virtually dry-humping her. It was disgusting.

Melissa noticed next, and started going, 'Urghh, have you seen Stephen and Renée?' When they realised everyone was watching, they stopped snogging for a while, and Stephen sat back down on his stool with his hand in his lap, as if he were concealing something; but after a little while they started laughing and smooching again, until eventually Stephen stood up and hoisted Renée off her seat too, and Sissy noticed that she staggered a little – and then they left, and didn't come back.

32

Hyde Park

Terry Kingston was fed up with prowling around in Hyde Park, like some kind of cottager, chasing after a group of middle-aged women having a *picnic*, for God's sake. It seemed obvious to him that his client's wife was on a girls' night out, and a pretty tame one at that, rather than taking part in any clandestine extra-marital relations – for tonight at least. Terry was tired and wanted to go home, get back to painting his fusiliers, he needed to finish them before the convention in Nottingham the following weekend. It had been more difficult to observe the women since they'd moved from Diana's fountain; there was no obvious place for him to sit here, plus it was getting late for him to still be in the park alone, he'd look like a ruddy pervert if he wasn't careful. He'd ended up having to hide behind a tree near the cafe, meaning he couldn't actually watch them any more, but he could see along the path to the bridge, would know if anyone came or went – and although he could no longer hear the detail of what they were saying, it was pretty obvious no-one was having much fun. What are women like, he thought to himself. Why oh why had he ever married one, he'd have been so much happier with just his pets and his pastimes for company. And then he felt a flash of guilt about Maria — she'd been good to him over the years, it wasn't her fault how he felt about women — and this train of thought led him morosely to wondering about Eileen, smug in her new life in a suburb of Liverpool, and he debated whether he should try to get in touch with her. She must be getting on now, it would be too late one day. Perhaps he should at least try, he thought, she was his mother after all.

Terry shifted on the patch of grass he'd made his seat for the past hour and looked at his watch for perhaps the twenty-fifth time. He'd been specifically told to wait all evening to see where she went afterwards. His client was convinced that she wouldn't be coming straight home as she'd said — she always got in so late from her supposed girls' nights out these days — and so Terry was stuck here. It was tedious, normally he wouldn't take on a domestic job, creeping around in the bloomin' bushes like this, but he was doing it partly as a favour, plus his client was very hard to say no to.

The dark was descending quickly now, and what little of The Serpentine he could see streaming away towards the bridge appeared blackly thick, like liquid mud. There was hardly anyone around — just a wiry, middle-aged woman with over-sized headphones and well-defined muscles who jogged elegantly past, her breath effortless, like a Kenyan marathon runner's; and twenty minutes later a couple walking along the bank arm in arm, chatting comfortably, as if they were still in love.

Terry was sleepy. He rested his head against the tree and felt himself almost dozing off in the lazy summer air. He was tired of listening to all the bitching and moaning, glad he couldn't make out the exact words – apart from the occasional louder one every now and then (*murder* he was sure was one, which had woken him up, and surely *rape* another). And then it went quiet suddenly, as though someone had told them to shush. He yawned. His eyelids started to stretch involuntarily downwards, his long lashes fluttering indecisively, as though debating whether or not to succumb to sleep – and then he flicked them up again, briskly. He'd been startled by a scream; well, not a scream exactly, more of an anguished roar, as if an animal had grabbed a woman's baby perhaps, and was running off with it. He shrank into the shadows as a woman came careering past, sobbing. He watched as she threw herself down by the side of The Serpentine, her identity unclear in the darkness, and despite himself he felt a pang of sympathy as she knelt at the water's edge and keened, head between her knees. What the bloody hell was going on? He thought he'd been hired simply to find out if his client's wife was having an affair, and now it seemed he'd stumbled into a potentially more explosive situation.

Terry stood up and hopped from side to side, like a little boy who needs the toilet, trying to decide what to do. He sat down again, and waited. After a few minutes, he heard voices coming closer to him, and he shrank back into the bushes as he heard one of them slurring, 'My

God, I can't deal with any more of this tonight, let's just leave her to it.'

'But d'you think she's OK?' said another voice, timid, anxious-sounding. 'She's hysterical . . . how's she going to get home?'

A third voice cut in then. 'That's up to her. I really am past caring.'

'But she's right by the water,' the timid voice said. 'And she's drunk . . .'

'She'll be fine,' said the first voice. 'And anyway, I've just about had enough for one night. If she does fall in she can bloody drown for all I care.'

The timid voice went to object, but the first voice said, 'NO. Let's go, she'll be fine, there are loads of cabs up on the bridge. I need to get home now, I just can't cope with anything else this evening. It's all too awful.'

Terry pressed back into the undergrowth as the women started leaving. He counted five of them – although one was quite a long way in front, walking fast, as though she couldn't wait to get away – but it was too dark to be sure from here whether his target was amongst them. Perhaps it was *her* who'd run off into the night – he wouldn't put it past her, he'd always known she had some kind of screw loose, like most women. One of the group seemed to be limping, and another two were carting an enormous picnic basket and carrying folding chairs across their backs, like bows and arrows. They were nearly at the bridge now and he could see the outlines of four of them, a good hundred yards from him. It was probably safe for him to start following now. He hesitated again. Maybe he should double-check it wasn't his target down by the water after all, just in case – his client would give him hell if he lost her, and it would only take a minute . . . but there again he might lose the others then, up on the road. *Oh God*, what should he do? After a few more agonised seconds Terry finally made up his mind, and he came out from his hiding place, glanced swiftly left and right, and moved carefully along the shadows.

33

Cleveland

Stephen and Renée staggered home from the bar along the deserted sidewalk next to the busy main road, arms draped around each other, stopping continuously to snog, then carrying on walking, still kissing and laughing and stumbling. Even through her drunkenness Renée felt oddly euphoric, and it was as if the acute sadness of the past weeks were twisting and lifting, spiralling away from her, leaving her free again. She realised now that part of her distress had been pure unbridled loneliness – she'd felt isolated and disorientated anyway since graduation, but it had got so much worse since the attack. She'd obviously been missing college life, her friends (especially Juliette), the home they'd made in Bristol which was now for ever gone, even her mother in Paris who she never saw anyway – and it felt so good to be held tight and safe again. It wasn't sexual as such, it was more a feeling of being alive, of being important, relevant again in the world, at least to someone.

As they reached the house and started dragging themselves up the driveway, Stephen went in for an overly ambitious embrace, causing Renée to stumble, and they finally, inevitably, lost their footing. They collapsed together onto the packed red dirt, and the dust flew up accusingly.

'Owww,' laughed Renée, but she didn't get up, just lay there winded, knickers on show, her knee burning and sticky. 'Are you OK?'

'I'm fine,' said Stephen, and as he nuzzled into her she could feel the grit sticking to them both, like breadcrumbs on schnitzels. They continued kissing but Renée was uncomfortable now, the stones were digging into her; so she pushed Stephen off and straddled him instead, leaning down and teasing that she was filthy, that she needed a shower first. She hauled herself up and managed to pull him to his feet too, which was no mean effort, and although he went to grab her again she told him he'd have to wait, and then she ran giggling upstairs to the bathroom, and locked the door.

34

Hyde Park

Even as Terry crept closer, he still couldn't be sure whether the woman by the water was his target – clouds had drifted in, obscuring the moon, and with her head between her knees like that it was difficult to be certain. His eyes were watering now, one of those bushes must have set off his hay fever, and he couldn't help rubbing at them which just made it worse. He was feeling increasingly agitated – the longer he hung around here the more likely it was that he'd lose her if she *had* left, was with the group after all. His client would give him hell. He had to be quick. He moved a little closer. As if on cue, the moon came out and she lifted her head and looked up.

Shit! It wasn't her. She must be with the others after all. He was going to lose her. He ducked away and legged it past the reed beds towards the bridge, his heart hammering in his ears.

Terry was relieved to find he was in luck – the women were moving so slowly, weighed down as they were by their picnic paraphernalia, that they were still on the path. As he got nearer he slackened his pace and edged along carefully, discreetly following them. The arguing had stopped but he could hear soft crying now, although he wasn't sure from whom. No-one was speaking, and the fury in the air, even from a distance, felt tangible, like dust. They were almost at the bridge and he could see four of the women clearly, a good fifty yards from him still. Just as the first one made it onto the stone steps there was a noise: a thud and then a loud, undignified splash, resonating into the night. They stopped.

'What was that?' one of them asked, the timid one, Terry thought.

'It must have been a bird,' someone else said.

'Don't be ridiculous, that wasn't a bird,' said a third voice. 'It must have been her.'

They all stood still, weaving a little. There was silence, no splashing, just the dull thrum of the traffic along Kensington Gore. Precious seconds passed.

'We need to go and look,' the woman with the timid voice said, and she spread fear into the air.

They listened again, but it was quiet still.

'It's nothing, come on,' said a voice, and it sounded impatient, panicked almost.

'Maybe we should check.'

'I've told you,' said the second voice. 'I'm not going back, I'm going home. She'll be fine, I'm telling you. And I didn't even hear anything if anyone asks me; ten more yards and we'd be up on the road with −' Terry didn't catch the name.

'I can't believe you!' slurred a new voice.

'Well, what are you going to do? Call the police?'

'Yes, maybe I will.'

There was more silence then, as if they were all hesitating, not sure what to do next. Finally, one of the earlier voices spoke and said, 'Well, I don't think we can do anything now. It must have been nothing, we would have heard her screaming otherwise. Let's go.'

And it was like an unspoken pact, a group brainwash, a decision made, and as if connected by a long, invisible rope, they slunk drunkenly up the steps together, heaving picnic baskets and rugs and chairs. Just before the last woman reached the road, she turned, seemed to stare in his direction – *shit*, had she seen him? – but then she shook her head and shuffled after the others into the night. The whole thing had taken less than a minute. Terry hesitated himself now, his instinct telling him to go towards the water – and then he thought of his client, of his client's temper, of his, Terry's, fee, and he came out from his hiding place, and he looked up and down the bank seeing no-one, nothing, just moonlit nothingness. He went to hurry away from The Serpentine, after the women, and then he remembered himself, someone could be *drowning* down there, and so he turned and ran back towards the water's edge, and as he stared down into the stillness, willing himself to see something, a ripple, *anything*, he reached into his jacket pocket, for his mobile phone.

Part Two

Part Two

35

Bristol

Late on a sultry summer's afternoon a quarter of a century earlier, six undergraduates were enjoying an impromptu (if rather culinarily unsophisticated, despite Camilla's best efforts) picnic in a beautiful historic park with views across the city, less than ten minutes' walk from the halls of residence where they'd all been thrown together, and, for the next week at least, still lived. It was nearly the end of their first year and most of them were hungover from a party the night before, but Natasha had suggested it, saying it was the last weekend they'd all be together before the summer, and in any case, she'd said, it was far too nice to be indoors.

Although still not anywhere near her old self since her father's suicide, Camilla had perked up a little at this (which had been Natasha's intention), and had miraculously rustled up egg sandwiches and some chocolate Krispies. Meanwhile everyone else had raided the communal kitchen, with Natasha grabbing a slab of jelly (that she was now eating cube by cube, which normally would have made Camilla apoplectic), and the others cobbling together some on-the-turn fruit, a lump of Cheddar cheese and an open tub of Philadelphia that Renée had stolen out of the fridge, and an ancient-looking packet of crackers they'd discovered behind the boxes of cereals in the larder. Sissy had been the most proactive and had dashed out and bought some crisps and soft drinks from the newsagent on Queens Road, although she'd refused to buy Natasha the cigarettes she'd requested, saying, quite firmly for her, that she couldn't possibly take part in helping one of her best friends get cancer.

In the absence of proper picnic rugs (not even Camilla was that organised in the early days), Juliette and Renée had dragged along their university-issue blankets for everyone to sit on. Siobhan had brought her portable stereo, and Madonna was now tinnily belting out 'Like A Virgin' (the cover of which Siobhan was apparently modelling her latest look on), and although everyone winced at the sound quality no-one had the heart to tell her. They were all drinking Moscow Mules out of plastic cups, even Sissy, who didn't much like alcohol but felt she should make the effort, especially as Renée had gone to so much trouble, having mixed up a huge batch in the kitchen and transported it in giant-sized empty Fanta bottles. The cocktails looked murky, distinctly unappetising – at best like melted Coke floats, at worst not worth thinking about – but at least they seemed to be hitting the spot.

'Well, this is nice,' said Renée, kicking off the patent leather Dr Marten boots that she'd worn all year, whatever the weather, and hitching up her black ra-ra skirt.

She blew her fringe out of her eyes, which she'd recently dyed purple although the rest of her hair was black. 'I'm going to miss you lot in the summer. It's weird that we won't see each other for weeks,' and although her voice was full of its usual bravado the others could hear the faint crack in it, and could tell that she meant it.

'Well, don't worry, you won't miss me, Renée,' said Juliette, plonking herself down next to her. 'Seeing as I'm coming to stay at your dad's for a week. I'm looking forward to it — I've never been to Clacton.'

'And nor would you want to under normal circumstances,' said Renée. 'It's a total dump; I've warned you. And my dad's a right miserable git.' Her face darkened. 'Sometimes I wonder how I'm even related to him . . . Oh! Sorry, Juliette.'

'That's all right,' said Juliette. She turned her face into the sun and closed her eyes. Her hair was pulled up messily in a scarf she'd tied in a great bow on the top of her head, presumably to better show off the huge black cross that dangled from her right earlobe.

Everyone looked awkward. Natasha flashed looks at Renée not to say any more, as Juliette continued to sit there, face tilted upwards, soaking up the sun, as if opening her eyes would give her away.

'Juliette, are you OK?' asked Siobhan after a while, and she put a skinny arm around her friend's shoulder and Juliette leaned into her, for just a moment — and then she pulled gently away and composed herself. She changed the subject, slightly too abruptly.

'Camilla, have you worked out what you're doing in

the summer yet?' she said. 'Are you sure I can't persuade you to come to Renée's with me?' She put her forefinger to her dark, glossy lips. 'Hmm, Clacton or Provence . . . ?'

Camilla smiled but didn't answer. 'Seriously, Cam,' Juliette continued. 'D'you think you will be able to persuade your mother to go to France?'

'I hope so,' said Camilla. 'I'm sure it would do her good, she loves the house so much, but of course it'll be the first time without Daddy, and she'll have to face all the neighbours . . . I do wish I could invite you all, it's so beautiful there, but under the circumstances . . .' She trailed off.

'Don't be ridiculous, Cam,' said Renée. She tried to lighten the atmosphere. 'And anyway there's always next year – except knowing Siobhan she'd probably forget her passport.'

Siobhan grinned good-naturedly, her imperfect teeth flashing white in the sunshine. She pulled the tartan braces attached to her Levi's down off her shoulders, presumably so it was easier to sit. 'Don't worry, I wouldn't,' she said. 'Auntie Camilla would pack for me, wouldn't you, Cam?'

'Knowing you she probably would,' said Renée. 'Somehow you manage to get us all running round after you. I'm so surprised you're not blonde.'

'Hey, don't be blondist!' said Natasha, but with her short, spiky mop she wasn't really the type of blonde Renée was referring to.

'I know!' said Sissy, the Moscow Mule talking. 'What about everyone coming and staying at my parents' house? The countryside is gorgeous where they live, plus they're going on a trip to Lourdes in August, so there'd be plenty of room for us all. I'm sure they wouldn't mind,' and as she said it she realised that they'd be so shocked at their middle daughter making any demands on them that she really had no idea what they would say.

'That's a super idea,' said Camilla, pushing her hair band back, a nervous habit she'd picked up lately. 'I'd like to come, if I can manage it,' and because it was the second thing Camilla had shown any interest in in ages (the picnic being the first), Sissy did end up asking her parents, and although Sissy's older sister had the hump about it – they had never let *her* have the house to herself when they were away – her parents had said yes. So that's where the six of them did go for that last week of August, which was fortunate, because all through the summer Camilla had been dreading the thought of going back to Bristol, of having to bear the humiliation all over again, with a new batch of freshers pointing her out, whispering about her. She'd even drafted a letter to her tutor, withdrawing from her course. But as soon as she'd got to Sissy's in Shropshire, everyone had immediately fallen back into their familiar patterns, their complementary roles (Siobhan scatty, Natasha nervy and driven, Sissy unfailingly sweet, Juliette sensitive and fragile, Renée sassy and sardonic, Camilla the mother hen) and they had laughed and danced about in their pyjamas to their favourite Wham! and Wet Wet Wet and Prince albums; or else curled up with a bottle of wine to Sissy's *Best of Frank Sinatra*; and Camilla had known that she'd get through it all with the support of this eclectic bunch of girls – they were her best friends in the world now, and would be forever.

36

Chelsea

Camilla stood splashing water on her face in the 'hers' sink of the marble en suite bathroom, her head feeling like it might even explode. The children were downstairs already, having breakfast. Now they were in their teens they were largely self-sufficient in the mornings, but even so Camilla would normally be down there fussing around them, trying to force them to eat porridge, make sure they had their PE kit, and they would chastise her crossly, complaining that they were fourteen and sixteen, not four and six, and James would tell them not to be rude to their mother, they were lucky they hadn't been packed off to boarding school like every other male in her family.

Camilla felt devastated this morning. She had been so excited about the picnic, about seeing everyone again – it had been much too long since they'd all got together – but last night had been horrendous, and she knew that James had been deeply perturbed by her arriving home not only drunk, which was unusual in itself, with hair band askew, pristine white jeans trashed, but *sobbing*, which was absolutely unheard of. She vaguely recalled staggering into the bedroom, wailing that she'd had the worst night of her life, but she couldn't remember now exactly what she'd said to James, and then she'd just fallen into their antique French bed and passed out. She'd been horrified when he'd asked her all sorts of terrible questions this morning: about Renée nearly drowning, and being raped, and someone being killed, by *Stephen*, had she said? What on earth had Camilla revealed to her husband?

Camilla was aware that she hadn't been so hysterical since her father's death, when her friends had done everything for her, been everything to her – perhaps that was why she'd become so distraught last night; maybe the fact that the ties had been severed at last was triggering some new wave of grief for her father.

Camilla felt heartbroken as she acknowledged that things would never be the same again. What had happened to her old friends? They seemed to have changed so much, particularly Natasha, who although she had been Camilla's fiercest protector once, seemed so cold and brittle now. Privately Camilla had thought for ages that if Natasha would only spend more time at home with her family, rather than obsessing about her career, maybe her children wouldn't be so badly behaved and her marriage (in Camilla's opinion) wouldn't be in trouble.

Camilla turned off the tap and buried her face into a thick white towel. She was grateful to James now, that he'd insisted he didn't need to go into the office today, could work from home instead, keep an eye on her. Even if her group of best friends had just been decimated, at least she still had her husband, her children – and even through her current despair Camilla knew that, unlike some of the others, she would be all right, that ultimately her family's love would be enough.

37

Bristol

On a cold, frosty morning, more than six months before their impromptu end of year picnic, Renée knocked gently and, hearing no answer, slowly opened the door to Juliette's room. Her eyes took a while to adjust to the half-light, but soon she could make out the melee of clothes and papers and textbooks strewn on the floor, like the wind had got to them, and the lump in the single bed, one cold-looking foot protruding from the pink gingham duvet.

'Oh, you are there,' she said. 'I thought you might have stayed at Stephen's last night.'

'No, he tried to get me to,' said Juliette, turning over and yawning. 'But I need to do an essay today, so I wanted to get back.'

'Why didn't he come too?' asked Renée. 'After all, you two are officially joined at the hip these days.'

Juliette looked uncertain for a second, unsure whether Renée was joking or not. It was still only halfway through the first term and she hadn't quite worked out Renée's sense of humour. 'Oh, you know,' she said, stretching her arms above her head. 'I hate sleeping in a single bed with him, he's such a lump, so I sent him home.'

'Oh, well done,' said Renée, and she smiled to show she was being kind rather than sarcastic, she knew she could sometimes come across the wrong way.

'And anyway,' continued Juliette. 'I thought it would be nice to spend some time with my flatmates. I feel like we hardly get to see each other any more.'

'Well, and whose fault is that?' said Renée, and this time it did come out more harshly than she'd intended: Juliette had the right to have a boyfriend, even if she did lack quality control in picking them. Renée changed the subject.

'Are you going to the Economics seminar this morning?' she said. 'Can I borrow your notes? I'm not going, I need to finish my sodding Psychology assignment.'

'Sure,' said Juliette. 'Although I don't know why I bother, I never understand a word of it. I don't think maths is in my genes.' She stopped and looked lost suddenly, as if she'd forgotten something important. Renée spotted an opening. She sat gingerly on the end of Juliette's bed and hitched up her black bustier, which Juliette secretly thought was an odd wardrobe choice for a freezing Tuesday morning. Renée picked at her heavy bead necklaces with her black-painted fingernails.

'Listen, I saw this thing in the *Guardian* yesterday, there was this article about how to track down your birth mother. I think it's quite easy.'

'Renée, please, I told you before, I don't want to,' said

Juliette. She shifted in the bed and sat up against the pillows, resting her head awkwardly on the bare wall behind. Renée went to speak again but Juliette stopped her. Sometimes she wished she'd never even told Renée that she was adopted. Renée seemed quite obsessed by it somehow, unable to believe that Juliette showed so little interest in the identity of her birth mother. 'Why should I?' Juliette had said, on more than one occasion. 'She obviously didn't want me, so why bother trying to find out who she was?' Renée had told Juliette not to be so hard on herself, she didn't know that her mother hadn't wanted her, there were all sorts of reasons women had their babies adopted – and anyway, Renée had thought, it was less of an insult to be given up at birth, before her mother had got to know her, than to be left at four years old for a lover in Paris. Now *that* was a rejection if ever there was one, not that Renée ever voiced the comparison of course.

'But it might really help you, Juliette,' Renée said now.

'Help me with what? Honestly, I'm fine as I am. Please, Renée, she's my mother, not yours.'

'Sorry,' said Renée. Her face flushed a little.

'I'll decide if and when I'm ready, thank you very much,' said Juliette, but she sounded softer now, as if she knew Renée meant well. 'Look, I know *you* think there's one, but *I* don't feel like there's a gap in my life. In fact my life feels quite full enough right now without anyone else getting involved in it.' She swung her legs out of bed and they were blue-mottled, like a baby's. Her pink-eared rabbit lay forlornly on the pillow, abandoned.

She stood up and tugged at her T-shirt, which had a cartoon dog on its front, pulling it down over her bottom (sending the dog upwards), and then she bent right the way over and shook her hair, so dust and dandruff flew up and danced in the sunshine drenching through the thin curtains.

'Ugh, I need a cup of tea,' she said.

'I'll make one,' said Renée, and she fled to the kitchen, which even by student standards was a bit of a dump, especially for the likes of Camilla.

Alone in her room, Juliette moved through one hundred and eighty degrees to stand up straight, and behind the shimmering auburn curls there were fat sparkling tears forming at the very edges of her eyes – although of course they were gone by the time her friend returned.

'D'you ever wonder what she's like?' asked Renée. It was a week or so later and she was lying curled up at the bottom of Juliette's bed, as had become her wont, the edge of the duvet folded over her feet against the winter cold. Juliette was still in the bed, even though it was nearly midday and she should have been at a Psychology lecture, and she was propped up against the wall with a mug of sweet milky tea under her chin. A deluge of clothes lay flung across the floor, and it was impossible to tell whether they were clean – just tried on and carelessly rejected – or actually in need of washing.

'Yes, sometimes, I suppose,' said Juliette. She seemed in a more reflective mood than usual, happy to talk about it for a change. 'It's just very weird, knowing that there's someone out there who gave birth to me and then . . .' She stopped.

Renée couldn't help herself. 'Have you thought any more about tracking her down?'

'Oh, no, what would my mum and dad say? I'm sure they'd think of it as some kind of betrayal.'

'I'm sure they wouldn't,' said Renée. She thought again of her own mother then, who'd done the same thing in effect, had relinquished her too, although it had taken her a few more years to do it. Maybe that's why she and Juliette were so close – they both had 'abandonment issues', and it was weird how that had never occurred to her before. They were similar in so many ways, it was uncanny.

'What do you think she looks like?'

'How would I know?' said Juliette, but she didn't say it crossly as such, more as a matter of fact, which Renée took as encouragement.

'She must have been beautiful,' she said. 'Look at that hair she's given you.'

'Shush,' said Juliette. 'I hate my hair.' And she did, although she had tumbling corkscrew curls the colour of ginger biscuits that people always stared at, because combined with her dark lashes and deep-green eyes she was just so unimaginably stunning.

'Maybe she was a film star,' Renée continued. 'Maybe she was Chantelle Dauphin, she's about the right age. *Yes*, you look just like her. Maybe she was over here filming when you were conceived, and then she thought she'd have you adopted by an English couple.'

'Don't be so silly,' said Juliette, and although she tried to smile Renée knew she'd gone too far now. She shifted a little on the narrow bed, away from Juliette's foot, which had been poking her in the ribs, and as her head hit the wall the pain was concrete, unpleasant.

'Why don't you at least think about it, Juliette,' she said gently. 'I'm sure it would do you some good – maybe it's the not knowing that upsets you . . .' Juliette didn't answer, but Renée saw a spark of acknowledgement in her friend's eyes. 'And I'd be happy to help you if you liked – it'd be far easier than doing it on your own.'

'I don't know, Renée, I'll have to consider it,' said Juliette. 'And even if I did do it – which I'm ninety-nine per cent certain I won't by the way! – even then I'd only do so if you agreed to us going to Paris next summer.' She paused, and her own tone became softer. 'Surely it would be good for you to see her, Renée, she is your mother after all.' Renée almost recoiled from the word. 'And . . . and we could go shopping,' Juliette continued, flustered. 'Drink *cafés au lait*, hang out in the Louvre, chatting up French boys – just so we could practise our French, of course. It would be amazing.'

Renée's face hardened under her bleach-tinged fringe, which Juliette secretly thought looked odd against the black of the rest of her hair. She'd preferred it when it was all one colour.

'We'll see,' said Renée. 'But I've told you what she's like – even if she did offer to put us up she'd probably charge us for breakfast.'

'Well, please will you think about it?' said Juliette. 'We

wanted to go inter-railing anyway, it would be mad not to start in Paris, and it might even go better with your mother than you think.'

'I don't know about that – you haven't met my mother,' said Renée, and her tone wasn't quite as jokey as she intended.

'I haven't even met my own,' her friend replied, and Renée wasn't sure how to respond to that, Juliette had seemed so vulnerable before – but then Juliette started to giggle, and as she did so she slopped her tea onto the duvet and kicked her feet in mock-rage, sending Renée sprawling off the single bed, onto the blue-striped nylon carpet.

38

Balham, South West London

Nestled in an otherwise smart residential street and emerging from the darkness like a shipwreck, Sissy's house was most definitely letting the side down in this corner of the capital. Weeds grew through the paved-over front garden, the recycling bins were stacked untidily in full view of the street, and the single ornamental rose bush that had been planted by the previous owners was sprouting two unsightly runners that would have taken less than thirty seconds to remove with a decent pair of secateurs (as Charlotte next door had been tempted to do many times, if Sissy wouldn't ever be bothered, but her husband had just about managed to restrain her). Balham, previously the dull poor relation of Clapham, had recently acquired such a level of chi chi-ness that Sissy felt like she didn't really belong there any more, with her scruffy house and clapped-out car and charity-shop wardrobe. She'd tried to placate herself that looking after two children on her own and trying to do up the inside on a shoestring (even with Siobhan's help, which although well-meaning was sometimes a little disruptive) was all she could manage right now. Anything beyond the front door would have to wait for the moment.

This particular day was destined to be as glorious as the previous one, meteorologically at least, but Sissy didn't notice. She sat numbly in her kitchen, staring blankly out to the back garden, which was worse than the front if anything: the grass knee-high on the children (it grew so *fast* at this time of the year, how could she possibly keep up), the borders jungly, the swing wonky and rusting. Nell and Conor were still asleep, thank goodness, but there again it was only seven minutes past five. Sissy hadn't been able to bear lying in bed for a single second longer and so she'd got up, made herself a camomile tea, put on Classic FM – tried as best she could to calm her nerves. The clock hands dragged themselves around, and it was unbearable. What time could she try ringing her? Six? Six-thirty? She thought of the picnic last night, of the row they'd all had, of the accusations that had been flung around like confetti, of how her friend had run off in hysterics and everyone had let her go. Sissy couldn't believe now that she'd just walked away too, had left her there alone, in that state. It was no excuse that she'd been drinking herself, what kind of friend was she? It was a terrible enough thing to do in its own right, and that was *without* Sissy having heard the splash. What could have caused it? It must have been a bird, surely her friends had been right. Sissy kept thinking of all the birds it could have been – a goose perhaps? A seagull? They were big, would make quite a splash – and they came up the Thames as far as London, didn't they? She tried to convince herself that everything would be fine, that once it was a decent enough hour to ring, her friend would answer – resentful, definitely, hungover, certainly – but alive. Yes, six o'clock, that's as long as Sissy could wait, that's when she would call, and too bad if she did wake her up.

39

Bristol

Juliette abandoned her essay and scrabbled in the bin for the leaflet Renée had left in her room, feeling like she was cheating on her parents, even unscrunching it. She found she couldn't help herself though – Renée had seemed to unleash in her the desire for knowledge at least, if not reconciliation. *Who was she? Where had she been born? What name had she been given? Who was her real mother? What did she look like? Who was her father? Had her parents loved each other once? WHY had her mother given her up?* It was very strange, almost like now the questions had been asked, they wouldn't go away, couldn't be un-asked, although she didn't dare tell Renée that of course – before she knew it Renée would be rushing her off to find out, given half a chance.

Juliette looked again at the leaflet. She needed her place of birth, her adoptive parents' names, some proof of ID and five pounds in cash. That was it, to make a start at least. That was all it took. There was only one problem: Juliette didn't actually know where she'd been born, had never even asked her parents, which was odd now she came to think of it. Why hadn't she asked? Had the subject just been completely off-limits, or had she simply not been interested? Or maybe she'd asked when she was younger and been brushed off, so had given up. It was weird. It seemed even odder now, to ring up her mother and ask about the weather and her jam-making and the Women's Institute, and, 'Oh, and by the way, Mum, where did you get me from?' Argh, why had Renée ever stirred this up? Usually Juliette tried not to think about any of this much, and frankly she didn't have the head space for it at the moment – they had their end-of-term assignments due in soon, plus Stephen was taking up so much of her time these days, monopolising her in truth.

Juliette got up from her desk and walked over to the window and gazed out across the roof-tops. She couldn't believe that she lived here in the best part of this wonderful city, with such brilliant new friends, a doting boyfriend, doing a course that she loved; she really should be fantastically happy. But instead she felt a growing sense of detachment, depression even, and she was vaguely aware that the space she had here, away from her family, had given her the freedom to question who she really was. She moved across to the mirror next to the bed. Where *had* she got these extraordinary curls from? What if it turned out her birth mother really was a film star? She looked at her nose sideways in the mirror. It did have a conk to it, exactly like Ms Dauphin's. Don't be so ridiculous, she told herself, it's just Renée putting ideas into your head. She thought again of Somerset House, of how London was only an hour and a half away by train, of how she and Renée were planning a trip there anyway to stay with Renée's aunt for the weekend. Maybe it wouldn't hurt to ask Mum, she thought. It's such a simple little question, surely she wouldn't mind. She could pretend it was to do with her course, having to research her birthplace or something, she didn't want to upset her mother unnecessarily. Yes, that's what she'd do, next time she rang.

'Hello, darling, how lovely to hear from you! I thought you weren't going to call until Saturday.'

'Yes, I know,' said Juliette. 'But I was walking past the phones on campus and they were empty for a change, so I thought I'd just give you a quick ring to see how you and Dad got on on your gardening trip.' (This was a rare lie, she'd been queuing for over forty minutes at exactly the same spot where a couple of months earlier she'd been befriended by a solid-looking rugby type, Stephen he'd said his name was, who she now seemed to be going out with, although she wasn't quite sure how that had happened.)

'Oh, you're such a sweetheart,' continued her mother. 'Yes, Wisley was super, thanks. It was terribly cold, but I'd made a Thermos of homemade soup, leek and potato, the cafes are so expensive in those places, and that kept the chill out.'

'Great,' said Juliette. 'And how's McGee?'

'Oh, he's fine, darling. He's eating at last, thank goodness, and he's taken to chewing your father's slippers again, so he must be on the mend. Anyway, how are you? How's your course going?'

'Oh, it's good, Mum,' said Juliette. She paused, she couldn't think what to say.

'Juliette, are you all right?' said her mother. 'Is something the matter?'

'No, nothing, Mum, honestly.' The phone started beeping: her phone card was about to run out. She had to be quick. 'Mum, we're doing a project as part of Psychology.' She stopped again.

'Ye−es,' replied her mother, aware now that something was definitely up. Surely Juliette wasn't homesick, she'd seemed so happy when they'd spoken the other day.

'Well, we're meant to research the town where we're from, where we were born, I mean, and . . . and, well, I . . . Mummy, I don't know where I'm from.'

'Oh,' said her mother, and her voice changed, still warm but wary now. 'What are you asking, Juliette, dear?'

The phone beeped again. Juliette spoke urgently.

'Mum, where was I born? Can you tell me?'

Her mother replied and then the phone cut out and between the beeps Juliette wasn't sure whether her mother had said Acton or Clacton.

40

Barnes

It was Friday morning, five to eight, and Natasha had been back from her run for well over ten minutes. She was standing in her kitchen now, fuming, absolutely bloody furious with everyone, but she was dimly aware that that was easier than being angry with herself. Every time she rang it, Juliette's mobile went straight to voice-mail, and no-one was picking up the home phone either, although Natasha knew Juliette should be there, it was still too early for the school run. Surely one of her many domestic staff would be there by now, why weren't they picking up either?

Natasha let Juliette's home phone ring for the ump-teenth time – it didn't seem to go to answerphone, instead just kept ringing and ringing until finally a loud, continu-ous parp-parp would signal that even BT had had enough of waiting, and then Natasha would call it again, dogged as ever. She debated whether to simply get in the car and go round to Juliette's – find out where she was, what was going on, so that everyone could get their story straight if something terrible *had* happened – but the traffic would be awful and she needed to be at work on time today, she had a board meeting to prepare for. As Natasha stood staring at her mobile, ready to hurl it across the room in frustration, another idea came to her. Perhaps she should steer clear of everyone for the time being, it might make things worse. Hopefully she was just catastrophising anyway, but if there was still no news after the weekend she could always go to the police then. *She* hadn't done anything wrong after all, not really, and then if anything terrible had happened to her friend – whose mobile still went straight to voicemail (*that's because it's waterlogged, at the bottom of The Serpentine*, said a little voice she tried to ignore) – she, Natasha, would be in the clear. Natasha flinched, both from guilt at even thinking such a thing, and from a noise she'd just heard in the hallway. The kids were still upstairs with the nanny, and the cleaner hadn't arrived yet. *Alistair*. Christ, she could do without seeing him this morning – she'd snuck out of bed while he was still pretending to be asleep, his back to her, hostile as ever. Anyone would think it was *she* who'd had the affair, and the thought made her sad about her marriage for a second – until she remembered to be mad with him all over again. The sounds faded, thank God: he must have heard her too. She knew she needed to confront him soon though – they couldn't carry on like this, it wasn't good for the children. The kettle finished boiling and Natasha made a strong instant coffee, no milk, three sugars, and when she drank it she wished desperately that she had a cigarette to go with it, although she hadn't smoked in years. The coffee was too hot without milk and it burned her mouth, and the sensation, that her tongue was rough and sanded, stayed with her for the rest of that terrible day, like an imprint of wrongdoing.

41

The Bristol to London train

The 17:35 service was crowded with a mixture of people –
commuters, day-trippers, students – and the carriages
had been incorrectly labelled, so everyone was sitting in
the wrong seats and passengers were having to stand up
again although they'd already got settled in for the journey, resulting in much clutching of disrobed coats and
scarves and hats to chests, and inelegant struggles with
Walkmans and glasses and books and already unfolded
newspapers, as people tried not to but inevitably dropped
things. Although it was freezing outside, the train itself
was hot and airless, almost feverish in its atmosphere – it
was Friday evening and people were in that specifically
jolly mood of work being over for a while, and what with
the carriage mix-up strangers were being forced to interact more than they usually would, rolling their eyes at
each other good-naturedly, saying things like, 'Bloody
British Rail', and even offering to swap seats in an abnor-
mally magnanimous fashion.

Renée and Juliette were sat crammed in by the door

next to the buffet car, which kept opening and closing, giving rise to the occasional whiff of toilets, and Juliette found her mind was racing, absolutely bloody motoring, faster than the train even. She sat pondering all sorts of important issues: wondering what mark she'd get for her Economics assignment, it had been so rushed in the end; trying to picture what kind of train designer would put the toilets right next to the food, surely that was unhygienic; questioning who had chosen the vile green pattern for the seat covers, was it the same person, or would that be someone else's job; noticing that Renée seemed to have put on a little weight lately, was looking fuller around the face, or maybe it was just the effect of her new orange fringe; observing that the guard in the buffet car had that faraway look in his eyes, as though he were on a journey somewhere, which of course he was, and what must it be like to trundle from one side of the country to the other serving coffee and sausage rolls as your job; and what was his accent, it was so distinctive but she couldn't place it, where did he actually live, east or west, or maybe in-between, Swindon perhaps. Juliette thought of absolutely anything she could, anything that might stop her looking at every passenger who passed by her seat and thinking, 'That could be my mother' or 'Maybe that's my brother' and she wondered again what was going on inside her head these days. Why were all these questions and fanciful theories surfacing now? Was it just that twenty years of self-denial had dammed up, like water reaching a frozen waterfall, unable to go anywhere, and now the sun had come out and the waters had started to melt, just a little, until the onwards force had become inexorable and the water had started fully flowing again, down into the icy river, waking her up from herself. Don't be so bloody pretentious, she thought. All she planned on for now was having a look – and even if she found it, which was unlikely anyway, just a little peep at a birth certificate wouldn't make much difference, surely? And even if she did find that she wanted to carry on further in her search she'd wait, for months or years even, until she'd worked out how to talk to her parents, made sure they were all right about it. No, there was no harm in just having a look. And besides, surely she'd need to know one day – if she was ever planning on having children of her own she'd want to find out if there were any genetic issues beforehand. The thought made her feel faintly queasy. She didn't think she'd be cut out for motherhood somehow, she'd always found little children hard to relate to, alien almost.

'You all right, Jules?' said Renée, glancing across from her *Marie Claire* article about ten ways to say no to your man without him losing interest.

'Yes, I'm fine, thanks,' said Juliette, forcing a smile.

'You'll like my Auntie Linda. She is one feisty woman.'

'Where did you say she lived?'

'In Camden, not far from the market.'

'Oh,' said Juliette. She couldn't recall having been told that before, surely she would have remembered. She wondered what kind of place Linda had – the only time she'd been to Camden it had just seemed full of dirty-looking people with parrot-red mohicans and rings through their noses, or else drunks with uniformly grey beards and filthy overcoats, like they'd been dipped in ash, or dread-locked hippies straight off the plane from Goa in tie-dyed trousers with the crotch around their knees. She thought it seemed an odd place for an auntie to live, and one who was a doctor at that. She thought of her own Aun-tie Deirdre and Uncle Peter in their neat semi-detached house in Amersham, and decided Linda sounded nothing like them.

'Did she ever get married, or has she always been sin-gle?' asked Juliette.

'Hmm, I don't think marriage is her thing,' said Renée.

'What do you mean?'

'Well, you'll see,' laughed Renée, and Juliette felt even more uneasy then. It all felt a bit much – going to some-where as edgy as Camden, staying with an odd-sounding stranger, *taking the first step to maybe finding her mother*. She leaned back against the seat and shut her eyes and willed herself to feel the vibration of the train, the steady clackety-clack that grounded her again, made her feel more normal, and as she did so the buffet man said, 'Two coffees, there you go, sir,' and she realised with a jolt that he was from Birmingham, just how could she have missed that.

42

Hyde Park

Terry Kingston seemed like a dodgy sort of bloke to PC Ryan. What was he doing hanging about by The Serpentine cafe at this time of night? How could there possibly have been a splash but then no other noise, as he was claiming – surely if some drunk woman had gone and fallen into the water he would have heard a commotion, or seen some splashing, would have known where it had happened at least?

PC Ryan was fed up. It was his wife's birthday the next day and they were meant to be going away, down to Ramsgate for the weekend, and he wanted to get home on time tonight of all nights, so he could get up early and not be tired and grouchy for a change. He walked up and down the river bank (was it actually a river, he wondered, does London have other rivers apart from the Thames?) although he knew there was no real point to it – if she really had fallen in at around 22:35, as Terry Kingston had said, then that was over twenty minutes ago, there was no way she'd still be alive by now. He sighed. He'd probably have to call in the frogmen, which meant he wouldn't be getting home for at least a couple more hours. He thought he would try one last time.

'Mr Kingston,' he called.

'Yes,' said Terry, and as he came over he looked timid and frightened, his sallow face twitching, suspicion pouring out of his eyes like magician's smoke.

There's something not right here, thought PC Ryan. But if he'd pushed her himself, why on earth would he have called the police? Surely he'd have made a run for it?

'Are you absolutely certain that a woman fell into the water?' he asked.

Terry hesitated. His mind crawled across the facts as he knew them, like a beetle over dung. Six women. An annual reunion. One of them suspected by her husband of having an affair. Terry assigned to discover whether it was true. A row, a humongous one at that. Accusations flying, too numerous, too hysterical, too incoherent, too muffled mostly to understand. Someone having been *raped*? Someone's husband being *murdered*? Just a load of hysterical nonsense, surely?

Terry knew it was better to say nothing about any of it. It could get messy. He regretted now that he'd even dialled 999, it had obviously been too late to save her if she *had* ended up in the water – whether she'd fallen in, or jumped deliberately, or even been pushed, whatever might have happened to the unfortunate woman. She'd be dead by now, and the thought filled him with dread. Implicating the others wasn't going to help either – as they'd said themselves, they could simply deny they'd heard anything. Thirty seconds later, fifty yards closer to the road, and they really wouldn't have heard it. Even if there was CCTV here, and Terry wasn't sure about that – although it was sodding well everywhere else – no-one knew that they'd heard the splash.

Someone does. *You.*

Terry felt increasingly panicky. This was a mess. He'd definitely be implicated, if it turned out she had died. His client would get dragged into it, and that would go down unbelievably badly, would cause him, Terry, all sorts of problems. And conversely, what if she hadn't fallen in at all, what if it *had* been a bird, like one of the women had suggested? This could all be a blinking wild-goose chase. He might even get done for wasting police time.

Terry became more furious with himself, the more he thought things through. He *knew* he should have turned down the job, no matter how much money he'd been offered – he could sniff trouble a mile off on this one. What the heck was he going to say to the police? What explanation was he going to give as to why he'd been in the park? He'd be the prime bloody suspect, he was sure of it, if there really was a dead body in there. Well, if it does come to that, Terry thought, I'll have to sing, regardless of who I implicate, after all *I've* done nothing wrong. That will get me off the hook at least.

But would it? Terry knew that his client was clever, too clever to mess with, too powerful, in with the right people these days, a stitch-up could be just what he needed to keep his own nose clean – and, after all, there'd never been any love lost between them over the years.

'I said, what were you doing in the park, Mr Kingston?' asked PC Ryan, and his tone was definitely accusatory now.

'Um, well . . . it was a nice evening,' said Terry, his palms sweating and his heart pounding, much like at key moments during war-games conventions. 'I . . . I thought I'd go for a walk.'

'And you live *where*?' asked PC Ryan. He was sounding even cockier now that his colleague, a little round Asian man (was there no minimum height for police these days, Terry thought idly), had joined him, and PC Ryan obviously fancied himself as the senior of the two.

'In Dagenham,' said Terry.

'And so on a summer's evening you come all the way from Dagenham to Hyde Park, on your own, just for a *nice little stroll*?' The sarcasm was unbridled.

Terry didn't know what to say. It was too late to admit he'd been lying, so he decided he'd just have to go with it for the moment. He felt sick. He *knew* he should have left it, simply followed his target as he'd started to do, made sure he got his money, kept his client off his back, and be done with silly drunk women who ran around shouting and screaming and drowning themselves.

'Yes,' said Terry in the end, and that one little word was the official beginning of his nightmare.

43

Camden, North London

Outside the Tube station it was noisy and dirty and full of people hanging around, looking either like they had dodgy business to do or nowhere better to go. Juliette wished she hadn't put her purse in her rucksack now, she felt vulnerable with it zipped into the outer pocket, readily accessible for anyone to steal. She kept swaying from side to side as she walked, the bag following an awkward semi-circled arc, in an attempt to make pickpocketing her too tricky, but people were getting hustled and jostled, and someone even told her to mind the fuck where she was going. She struggled to keep up as Renée marched confidently through the throng, seeming to know the way – left out of the station, straight up a grotty, litter-lined street, past an unappealing pub with a horrible little courtyard teeming with black-drainpiped people with gravity-defying hairdos and painful-looking piercings, over the dankly pungent canal, until after four or five minutes they turned right into what seemed to Juliette like another world entirely, one of smart Georgian terraces and lit-up Christmassy trees. The house they were looking for was just a few doors up, on the left, and the door they knocked on was painted pale pink, the colour of a fairy's costume. They waited for maybe twenty seconds, and then there was a deep, loud, 'Coming', and the door was thrown back so the warm air could come gushing at them, as if to say hello, and on the breeze drifted the smell of percolated coffee and freshly baked cake.

'Hallo, Renée!' said Auntie Linda. 'And you must be Juliette! Come in, welcome. Don't worry about your shoes, just get yourselves inside out of the cold.' She was small but stocky, neatly oblong, her white T-shirt tucked into hitched-up Levi's, bottoms turned up neatly to show off her polished Dr Martens. She beamed a smile across her oval face, and it sent her forehead creasing up towards her cropped dark hair, and the skin around her eyes darting out as if to meet her ears. Her nose was straight and her lips were thin.

'Hello,' Juliette said shyly – she had never met a lesbian before, not properly anyway. She shrugged off her rucksack in the hallway and untied her granny boots, and followed Renée and her aunt into the kitchen at the back. The room was small and cosy with painted floorboards and an old pine dresser full of floral crockery, and the table was covered in a polka-dotted oilcloth, surrounded by mismatched chairs with chintzy seat pads – and Juliette couldn't believe that Linda was so boyish and yet lived in such a pretty house, in so delightful a street, a mere stone's throw from the revoltingness of Camden, and which according to Renée she'd bought, owned, all by herself.

'Now, what would you girls like – tea or coffee?' asked Linda.

'Oh, tea please, Auntie Linda,' said Renée.

'Um, yes, the same for me, please,' said Juliette.

'Milk and sugar?'

'Uh, yes, please, thank you. Oh actually, no sorry . . . just milk please. I have sugar with coffee but not with tea.' Juliette was embarrassed by her gaucheness, she wasn't usually like this. But now she was here she was wondering whether she was making a huge mistake after all – taking on way more than she could handle, and betraying her parents to boot. She could hardly change her mind now though, Renée would probably go mad.

Renée was asking how Linda's job was going, and Juliette thought it was amazing that Linda worked in A&E, Juliette couldn't even cut her own finger without fainting. People like Linda tended to make her feel inadequate somehow – she seemed to have such a strong sense of purpose, a belief in who she was, in where she was going. Juliette thought she'd never feel like that. *You won't know where you're going until you know where you come from*, said a voice inside her head. She felt sad then, in Linda's charming little kitchen, with its warmth from the oven and optimistic glow; like an outsider, which of course she was. It was obvious that Renée and Linda were related: they had the same straight nose, same colouring, an easy familiarity. Juliette wondered whether maybe she had a real aunt somewhere too, even a load of cousins perhaps, people that looked like her, had similar mannerisms – and she wished suddenly that she *knew*. Perhaps Renée had been right to push her into this, after all. And as Tracey Thorn sang softly in the background, comfortingly melancholy, Juliette finally acknowledged that no matter how good they'd been to her, Cynthia and Giles weren't enough, could never be enough. She sat quietly, sipping her tea, doing her best to smile politely, as her thoughts spiralled inwards – and maybe because she felt as lonely as she ever had, at last she made up her mind.

44

Hyde Park

PC Ryan had called his sergeant, and his skipper had initially told him to just have a bloody good look round first – if this odd-sounding bloke was now saying he wasn't even sure someone had fallen in the water, they didn't want to waste time calling in the frogmen. It all sounded very strange to Sergeant Hunter from what PC Ryan had said. Flasher type calling 999, saying he'd been enjoying a stroll in the park when he heard a woman fall in the water, now saying that perhaps he'd imagined it, that maybe it was a sodding bird instead. What the heck were they dealing with here? In Sergeant Hunter's experience it sounded most likely that this Kingston bloke was an attention-seeking weirdo, but in theory he could also be a murderer – or else he could actually be telling the truth and there really had been a tragic accident that he'd happened to witness. It was all a bit annoying, as he wanted to go off shift and get down his snooker club for a few frames and a couple of well-earned pints. Typical, he thought, it was only when he'd got something planned that anything interesting happened – usually it was just routine stuff like domestics or burglaries. He decided he couldn't take any shortcuts on this one though, not when there was potentially a body involved, just in case.

'Call up more units,' said Sergeant Hunter. 'Get a load of officers down there with torches. Call India 99, and the Marine Support Unit, I suppose. We can't take any chances.'

Terry Kingston stood in his cheap grey suit watching PC Ryan's bumbling response to this barrage of requests across the radio waves, and although he didn't know what India 99 was, he could pretty much deduce everything else, and he knew that he'd well and truly had it now. The skin between his top lip and nose was moist and the twitch in his hands had grown into a full-scale tremble. He desperately wanted to be at home, in front of his miniature armies in the bedroom cum office that Maria never came into, ever, with Humphrey curled at his feet and Snoopy purring on the easy chair behind him, the rats whirring madly on their wheel to nowhere. He badly needed to relax, badly needed not to be here, and he wished he could just leave now, make his way home so he could get back to his Prussian general, which needed one final coat of varnish before it was finished.

'Er, do you still need me?' he said.

PC Ryan looked perplexed, not knowing what to say to this – he couldn't let his would-be murderer just wander off, could he?

'Um, well, can you wait for a while, just until we've completed our search,' he said finally. 'We may need to take a statement from you – if we do find anything,' and he said it in such a way it was clear he thought that this was all a complete waste of everyone's time.

Terry acquiesced meekly, and went and perched on a stone step outside the cafe, and as he watched the park fill swiftly with officers searching in the bushes, torches bobbing, and a van turn up with a load of scuba equipment in the back, and heard the ominous thrum of the helicopter overhead, he put his head in his hands and wished with all his heart that he had never called 999, even if she had bloody drowned.

45

Juliette's mother looked across the table at her husband, or at his hands more precisely, which peered elegantly around the edges of *The Times*. She had debated whether to tell him, in fact had put it off for over a week, but she knew she couldn't risk him finding out through anyone else. She coughed delicately, but Giles didn't appear to hear her, just carried on reading the paper, occasionally tutting, the newsprint rustling quietly. She normally liked to leave him alone at this time, just after breakfast, in that brief moment of peace before he had to leave for work, but for some reason she found she couldn't put it off any longer.

'Giles,' she said. 'Giles, darling . . . *Giles!*'

'Oh, sorry, dear,' he said finally, angling the paper downwards, so he could look over the top of both it and his reading glasses, at his wife.

'I need to talk to you,' she said.

'Yes, dear,' he replied, and waited, and when she didn't say anything, he hoisted the paper up a little, perhaps about to start reading again.

'Juliette wants to trace her birth mother,' Cynthia said, as if it were one word, one fast uninterrupted stream of letters, and this time Giles sighed and laid the newspaper flat on the table, its edge soaking up the remains of the milk from his cornflakes in the shallow beige bowl.

'Oh,' he said. 'Oh.'

'Exactly,' replied Cynthia, staring at him. 'What on earth are we going to do?'

'I don't know,' said Giles. 'What can we do? We knew this would probably happen one day.'

'Yes, but not now,' said Cynthia. 'She's not long been at university, she's not ready for it.' She stood up and paced back and forth, as though the room was too small for her. Then she stopped and leaned against the Aga.

'Well, what's happened?' asked Giles. He shifted uneasily in his seat, and resignedly closed his newspaper and folded it in half. 'How do you know she wants to? Did she actually tell you? Maybe you've got it wrong.'

'She rang me last week and I knew there was something up, she sounded funny, and it wasn't even the right day to ring. But she kept chatting on and I was even quite pleased that she sounded interested in my boring old WI stuff, and I assumed she was just a bit homesick – and then she came out with this story about needing to research her origins for an assignment, but it was obviously rubbish . . .' Cynthia's voice started to break a little. She sat down again, looking desolate.

Giles took his wife's hand across the table, and the sleeve of his crisp striped shirt got a smudge of newsprint on it, just above the cufflink.

'It's all right, dear,' said Giles. 'What did you tell her?'

'The truth. I told her where she was born. I didn't know what else to say . . . What can she do now?'

'I'm not sure, dear. But she can certainly go to Somerset House and look up all the births on the day she was born, until she finds her own certificate.'

'And then what?'

'I don't know, Cyn. I suppose once she knows the name though, she can go about trying to trace her.'

Cynthia looked down into the dregs of her coffee and it was strange, they seemed to have settled into a human shape: two eyes, a sad downward mouth, the exact opposite of one of those yellow smiley faces that were everywhere these days. She couldn't look up at her husband again, she knew that if she saw the kindness in his eyes she'd be unable to stop the tears coming. Cynthia was a reserved woman – she hardly ever cried, and if she did it was usually in private. She wasn't ready to let out her emotions about this, not even to her husband. Maybe Juliette wouldn't even go through with it in the end, and they could all forget about everything again for a while. As Cynthia sat there gazing at her diamond-ringed fingers, she knew she was being over-optimistic, like she always used to be, every single relentless month, yes, every single one, until every single bloody hateful month it had come (and she was sure it had been all her fault, not poor Giles'), until eventually it had stopped for ever, and she'd thanked God that she'd been blessed with Juliette instead.

46

Hyde Park

Elijah Carlson was excited. His daddy had just said they could go on the boats after all – he had definitely clocked that if he nagged his parents for long enough one or other of them usually caved in in the end. And his mummy had already promised him an ice cream, so there was that to look forward to too – he wasn't going to let them forget about that, no way José.

Elijah's excitement didn't last long however, once his brief sense of triumph had dimmed. As they stood waiting for their boat, he thought the water looked brown and dirty on closer inspection, and actually rather scary; and then when the little boat turned up it was all old and decrepit and there was water in the bottom of it, like it was leaking; and when his dad got in it rocked wildly, and as he was a large man they wouldn't all fit in anyway – and so Elijah decided that maybe he didn't like the look of rowing, after all.

'Right, in you get, sweetheart,' said his mother.

'No,' said Elijah. Now he'd spotted that his father's big fat bottom was already wet he definitely didn't fancy it *at all*.

'Come on, Elijah, darling,' she said. 'D'you want to hold Mummy's hand?'

'No!' he said.

'What d'you mean, no?' said his father. 'I've just bloomin' well paid for this. Get in.'

'I don't want to any more,' said Elijah, snivelling.

'Oh come on, angel, it'll be fun,' cajoled his mother, as she stood next to him on the bank in her high heels. She tried to push him gently towards the boat.

'Noooo!' screamed Elijah, and as she went to take his podgy arm he made such a commotion everyone looked over. Perhaps they should leave it after all, she thought, this was becoming embarrassing.

'Elijah,' said his dad, in a low voice, as patiently as he could manage (although it still sounded unmistakably tight, not far off temper-losing pitch). 'If you get in the boat we'll take you to get a milkshake after.'

'As well as an ice cream?' said Elijah, smelling an opportunity.

'No, not as well, either or,' said his father.

'Then *no*!' said Elijah, folding his arms defiantly. Other people were still looking over, with a definite whiff of parental superiority now. Elijah's mother really couldn't cope with yet another scene, they were meant to be having a nice Sunday afternoon as a family, and she was sure her son would enjoy it once they'd got going.

'Oh, OK, Elijah, just this once,' she said quietly. Her husband threw her a look and shifted crossly in the boat, and as Elijah stepped in jauntily, his fear miraculously dissipated despite the new rocking his father had just created, she caught the tell-tale shape of his tongue poking through his right cheek, and she saw the victory in his eyes.

47

Barnes

Even though she'd given up years ago, Natasha lit up a cigarette (from the pack of ten she'd bought whilst out for her morning run) as she pored over her board presentation, unable to concentrate. It was Sunday afternoon, three days since the picnic, and she knew things weren't looking good now. Where the hell *was* she? Maybe she'd gone back to a friend's house that night, had been too upset to go home, and perhaps now had gone away for the weekend – which was why there had been no answer when Natasha had gone round earlier. But even if that *was* the case surely she'd have charged her mobile by now, posted something on Twitter at least? Another possibility, Natasha thought hopefully, was that she'd passed out on a bench somewhere and been picked up by the police – she must have been paralytic to have run off into the night like that, she wasn't usually that rash – but if that had happened wouldn't they have let her go by now? Normally even Natasha wouldn't hope that someone she knew had been arrested, but it was a hell of a lot better than the outcome she kept trying not to think about, the one where the reason her erstwhile friend still wasn't answering her mobile was because she wasn't able to, was because she was lying cold and dead at the bottom of The Serpentine. It was like a nightmare, like something you saw on the news that happened to other people.

Natasha knew in her heart now that it wasn't a bird that they'd heard, it was a bloody big woman-sized splash. But if that was the case why had there been silence afterwards? What could have happened? Surely if it *had* been her she would have splashed around, screeching for help?

Natasha's heart thumped as she redialled the number, but still it cut to voicemail, and Natasha cursed the cheery, ghost-like voice, and then the horrors, circling in her head like buzzards around a dying carcass, all got too much for her, along with the cigarette smoke, and she ran to the bathroom and retched endlessly into the toilet bowl.

48

Hyde Park

Seven-year-old Elijah was a clever little boy. Not only did he have his mummy and daddy firmly wrapped around his little finger, he'd soon got the hang of rowing a boat too, quickly realising that he could send his parents into even more of a spin than usual with just the little boat's right oar. It was all such tremendous fun – skimming the surface of the water with the paddle so a mini wave could form, and then if he changed the angle just a *teeny* bit, the water could travel the length of the oar and soak his mummy (eliciting a plaintively ineffectual, 'Oh, Elijah!'); banging the top of the water so that the noise was hollow and eerie, water spraying everywhere like an aquatic firework while his dad yelled, 'Stop that, you little bu—' before just about restraining himself; or, perhaps best of all, simply digging the oar vertically into the water, so that the boat started to rotate and his dad would start ranting that they weren't bloomin' well going anywhere.

'Elijah, just stop that,' said his dad, for the hundredth time. 'Otherwise I'll take that oar off you and I'll row the ruddy thing on my own. Look, we're heading right for the bank now – *be careful* or we'll flippin' well hit it.'

'Sorry, Daddy,' said Elijah, as he lifted up the oar and drove it towards the bottom, exactly as his father had just told him not to. His dad roared at him and Elijah grinned happily, desired outcome achieved, and then he shoved it in again, just for fun. As the oar stabbed down into the tea-coloured water for perhaps the fifth unapproved time, Elijah felt it hit something, and in his young brain he assumed quite sensibly that it was the bank or even the bottom. But when he looked over the side he saw through the murk long trailing hair tangled like weeds, and one hollow eye gaping at him hopelessly, and a flash of colour, and although when they finally got back to shore he was eventually bought an ice cream, his parents never did get him his milkshake, and as he grew older his behaviour worsened if anything, and he never, ever stopped seeing that image.

49

Wandsworth

On the morning after the picnic, Juliette's home phone kept ringing but she ignored it. Instead she sat motionless at the oak kitchen table nursing her mug of tea, staring into its contents, trying to look beyond the surface at what lay beneath. She'd barely slept the night before, and she'd obviously drunk way more Prosecco than she'd realised: her head was throbbing and she felt empty, as though her stomach had been hoovered perhaps. She tried to fathom just what she and the others had done the previous evening. Had they been totally insane, abandoning their friend like that when she'd been so drunk, especially near water, *and especially once they'd heard a splash*? What if it had been her after all, what if she really had fallen in, had drowned, was *dead*? It was too horrendous to contemplate. OK, they may just have had an almighty row, but no-one wanted anything bad to happen to her, they hadn't wanted her to *die*, for God's sake.

Juliette felt devastated. She knew she could never see her university friends again after this, whatever the outcome – getting together had become increasingly fraught over the years anyway, for all sorts of reasons, but last night they had mined a new seam of hatred and envy, of poisonous secrets uncovered, of tragedy beckoning and maybe having occurred. She'd discovered things that were surely too hideous to be true, things that made her sick.

Radio Four blared obliviously in the background, going on about a double-dip recession, and it made her think idly of a fairground ride, a roller coaster that left your stomach in the downward bit, before it swept upwards again, away from it, leaving you screaming with terror.

Noah slunk back into the kitchen, although she'd sent all the children upstairs to get ready, unable to cope with the noise levels this morning. He stood there silently, staring at her, dangling his revolting-looking bear by one arm beside him. His pyjamas didn't match and there was a dark patch on the front of his trousers, Ireland-shaped. Juliette looked up from her tea. She tried to stay calm.

'Noah, sweetheart,' she sighed. 'Have you wet yourself again? I thought I told you to go upstairs and put on your school uniform.'

'I haven't, Mummy,' said Noah, trying denial as a tactic this morning.

The panic was rising in Juliette's throat.

'Yes, you have! Please don't lie to me, Noah.'

'Sorry, Mummy,' he said, taking a conciliatory approach now, but rather than help it seemed merely to enrage her. Juliette let rip, with less provocation than usual.

'Well, sorry's not good enough, is it? *Not* wetting your trousers is good enough. *Getting ready* for school is good enough. Anyone would think you were still three years old.'

Noah looked as if he might cry at this onslaught, but he didn't answer, just stood there silently, teddy trailing, eyes wide, the patch in his trousers getting bigger.

'Oh, for goodness sake,' said Juliette. 'Just get into the toilet, will you,' and she stood up and dragged him by the arm towards the downstairs cloakroom, and he started screaming now, and she couldn't stand the noise, so she shoved him in and pulled the door shut, leaning heavily against it, so he couldn't get out. She closed her eyes and tried counting to ten, but by the time she got to six she heard a sound, and when she opened them Flo was standing there.

'What?' she said crossly.

'Mummy, are you being mean to Noah again?' asked Flo.

'No, I am *not*,' said Juliette. 'He just can't stop wetting his trousers. It's disgusting.

'And what do you mean, again?' she added, realising what her daughter had said. She felt inflamed with shame. 'That's a *terrible* thing to say.'

Flo stood looking at Juliette, and somewhere in her nine-year-old brain she was aware that her mother's temper and Noah's incontinence were quite firmly related, but she knew better than to say anything more, she was lucky Juliette's reaction hadn't been worse. Noah sat silently on the toilet seat behind the door, his Spiderman trouser bottoms around his ankles (he found he needed to do a poo as well now for some reason), and as he kicked his legs the word kept repeating in his head, over and over, although he tried his hardest to stop it. The phone started up again and even the sound of that changed into the word, and it went on and on, through the hallway, echoey with its high ceiling and fancy light fittings and solid parquet floor, as his mother still didn't pick up – *bring bring*, *bring bring*, disgusting, disgusting, disgusting.

It was nearly nine now and the phone went unanswered yet again (much to Natasha's continued fury, she knew that if anyone could help sort out this mess it was Juliette, she was the one with connections), but in Juliette's defence she was oblivious to the ringing this time rather than deliberately ignoring it, having sloped back to bed where right now she had a plump Canadian goose-down pillow over her head. Although she'd tried to make amends with Noah earlier, once she'd finally coaxed him out of the toilet, he'd rebutted her attempt and bolted straight past her up to his bedroom and hidden under the duvet. She'd followed him upstairs and sat on the bed, tried to hug him, tell him she was sorry, that it was her fault not his, but he'd turned his stiff little body away from her which had made her cry again. She was a useless mother, the worst in the world, despite loving them so much. Perhaps she shouldn't even have had children, it wasn't fair on them – how could she have hoped to be any good at it, she obviously hadn't had a single maternal gene passed on to her by her bitch of a mother. This line of thought had been almost as distressing as imagining her friend at the bottom of The Serpentine, or thinking about the terrible things her husband was alleged to have done – it was hideous, everything was turning into a never-ending horror show. And so when the nanny had finally turned up, Juliette hadn't been able to bear for Didi to witness her hapless parenting, see her red-rimmed eyes, and she'd rapidly made her excuses and disappeared off to the spare room, where she'd slept last night, unwilling to share the marital bed with Stephen after what she'd heard about him.

As Juliette shifted in the bed, her bones felt heavy, like they were trying to burrow into the mattress, which was soft and pocket-sprung and ludicrously comfortable, but the comfort somehow made her feel like an imposter, like she shouldn't be there, like she should be lying still and drowned herself.

Drowned. Surely not, *no*.

Juliette lay still, too anxious to move, the pain in her head nuclear now, trying to quell the dread. Finally, in desperation, she removed the pillow and sat up a little, tried to study her surroundings, take in every detail – apparently it was a form of meditation, Renée had told her once, back when they were friends – and besides she hardly ever came into this room, had forgotten how nice it was. She concentrated hard, noticing how the curtains at the bay were thick and silky and hung all the way to the floor, pooling luxuriously; how the chaise longue in front of the window was upholstered in dove-grey velvet that seemed to absorb the shadows thrown from the monstrous crystal chandelier hung high above the bed; that the gorgeously thick sheepskin rugs slung casually across the linen-white floorboards were perfectly positioned to keep visitors' toes warm as they stepped out of bed. She admired the fireplace, which was large, white marble, with arty black and white photos of the apparently happy family arranged across the mantelpiece, below the muddy-hued artwork of a naked man and woman abstractedly embracing (is it from Habitat, she remembered Siobhan asking once, guileless as ever, unaware it was worth a fortune). Juliette sighed to herself – she did have good taste, at least in home furnishings if not in husbands, she'd give herself that.

It seemed calmer downstairs now, the kids having stopped screaming at last, Didi a miracle-worker as always. Maybe she'd get up in a minute. But the feeling of doom, of fear and recrimination, just wouldn't go away, so when the home phone started up, yet again, Juliette dived further under the covers and lay there, luxurious between the Egyptian cotton sheets, cold and shaking.

50

Sardinia

Sissy had fallen into a deeper sleep this time, and when she awoke her face felt hot and tight, as if she'd maybe had a facelift. Delighted squeals that carried in on the hot breeze from the carport below were almost certainly what had roused her, and as she shifted in the double deckchair she heard the key in the lock and two little children come stomping through, flip-flops thudding, sand going everywhere, she was sure of it – how many times had she told them?

'Hello, Mummy!' cried Nell, her eldest, as she ran onto the terrace. 'We went snorkelling and I saw a huge fish and it came swimming right by us. It was brown,' she added proudly.

'I had a ice cream,' announced Conor, and she could tell, there was chocolate all round his face.

'Did you have a lovely time, my darlings?' said Sissy, her head aching as she scooped them towards her. Nell snuggled in whilst Conor wriggled away, giggling.

'I think they did,' said her husband, coming out onto

the balcony after them. He must have gone into the kitchen first, to fetch a tall glass of water that was now shimmering in his hand, like a mirage in the sunlight.

Sissy turned and smiled up at Nigel. He looked blondish and fit, larger than life through her sunglasses, and it seemed almost impossible that they were here in Sardinia, on holiday as a family, celebrating ten unbelievable years of life after cancer. She was so grateful to Juliette and Stephen for lending them their holiday apartment, she'd never known Stephen to be so generous before, at least not without expecting something in return – maybe she'd misjudged him after all. He'd been delighted for them, according to Juliette, calling it an absolute bloody miracle, and it was he who'd suggested they borrow the apartment, saying it was only sitting there unused at the moment. They'd been reluctant to accept, but Stephen had insisted, saying he needed someone to give it a trial run now it had finally been done up.

Sissy knew she would never understand what had caused Nigel's journey back from the very edge of death. She often found herself going over that pivotal day at the hospital, the one when she thought he was actually about to die on her, fail to hold out long enough to even see their baby. She never stopped wondering what had saved him. Was it her outburst itself, the heart-wrenching, long-overdue outpouring, irrefutable proof at last of her love for her husband, of rage and bewilderment that he would simply fade away, unchallenged, that he would leave her without a damn good fight at least, and with the doctors just stood around watching, doing nothing? Or was it the new drugs the doctor had put him on, their barely legal experiment on the half-human she still called her husband? Or perhaps it was simply a miracle, as her parents had always thought, a benevolent gift of life sent to them by almighty God himself. She guessed she'd never really know, and anyway it didn't matter now – she had him back and she'd always be grateful for that. He'd even rallied enough to see their daughter on the day she was born, just a week later – Nell had been delivered in the very same hospital, and they'd taken her straight over to the cancer ward when she was less than an hour old, and Nigel's joy at meeting his daughter had had even the stoniest of ward sisters dabbing at her eyes. And when, five years later, they'd eventually had a son too, it was all so fantastically miraculous that Sissy swore she would never take anything for granted ever again.

Sissy squirmed to the edge of the deckchair and, her bottom firm against the wooden strut that held the canvas, hauled herself out of it. As she stood up, the banging in her head worsened and she felt perversely weightless, spinny. It was clear she'd had far too much sun. What time was it, how long had she been asleep?

'Please could I have some of your water, Nige,' she said. He passed it to her and as she leaned against the railing she laid the cool of the glass against her forehead and then against the top of her chest. When she drank it the water was over-chilled and her teeth twinged, and it hurt the back of her throat as she swallowed.

'Are you OK?' said Nigel. 'How long were you in the sun? You're very red in the face.'

'I fell asleep,' said Sissy. 'The sun must have come around – I was in the shade before. So much for me trying to give my skin a rest.' She seemed anxious now, and they both knew that it was Sissy who suffered most these days, worrying about every last mole on her or Nigel's freckly body, or the slightest fever one of the children got – and she still found it hard to go to the beach, but the kids loved it, so usually she managed, as long as they were in full sun suits (which looked odd on these beaches, no-one else wore them). But today, because the weather had been due to be so hot, she'd said she fancied just a quiet couple of hours writing her diary on the balcony, and Nigel had understood.

Nigel took Sissy's arm and led her inside, helped her onto the bed. By now she'd started to feel sick and her insides felt watery, as if they were being liquidised. It was gone five, Nigel had told her, so she must have been asleep in the sun for over two hours, and now she was lying down she felt like she couldn't ever get up again. Her limbs felt heavy and independent, as if they belonged to someone else. The children had the TV on and the Italian voices were fast and high-pitched, and there was laughter from a live audience of excitable minors, and although Nell and Conor would have had no idea what was being said they were being swept away on the outré vitality of it, and laughing in all the right places.

When Nigel came back in to check on his wife he was alarmed to find she could hardly lift her head now. He either needed to keep her cool and get her to drink lots of water, or else he would have to get her to a doctor – he'd already spotted the signs of heatstroke, his cousin had had a mild dose of it all those years ago in Australia. Nigel turned the air conditioning to full, and the unit swept up and down rhythmically, blindly squirting out cold air, but the room was so hot the air had warmed up again by the time it reached her. He grabbed a couple of towels and soaked them in the sink, then he wrung them out like he was strangling someone and took them, still dripping, into Sissy and placed them on her forehead and over her body, but she was no longer reacting to him. Her face was red like soup and burning up, and she seemed barely conscious. As he raised the glass of water to her lips, her head was bowling-ball heavy under his arm. It was alarming how quickly she'd deteriorated since he and the children had got back – at first she'd seemed just flushed and a bit groggy perhaps. He'd already been debating whether he needed to call a doctor, but when he saw her eyes start to roll towards the back of her head he knew he couldn't delay any longer, and he yelled at his daughter to bring him his phone.

51

Balham

On a sunny Sunday afternoon, at the height of an unusually balmy British summer, Sissy's decorating was going even more badly than usual, mainly because she felt like she was in danger of actually going mad. Since Thursday night she hadn't been sleeping at all well, and she'd had that familiar feeling of dread that she'd harboured for so long about Nigel, and everything else for that matter, but it seemed that it was worse than ever today. As well as her desperate worry about her friend's safety, about whether she was alive or dead, she kept playing over Renée's meltdown last night at what had happened in America, and she wondered how Renée had coped all these years, carried on as if everything was normal – and how she, Sissy, had been oblivious. No wonder poor Renée had become hysterical last night. And on top of all that the kids were playing up and Sissy couldn't quite deal with them at the moment, so she put down her scraper to turn on the Disney channel while they ate their tea – it wouldn't hurt just this once. After messing about with two remotes for what seemed like ages the TV finally sprang into life, causing Sissy to shriek so loudly that both her kids turned their wide sad eyes on her, and Conor said over his boiled egg, 'What is it, Mummy?'

Sissy didn't need to listen to what the newsreader was saying. As soon as she read the caption, 'Live, Hyde Park', and saw the white police tent and the grungy brown of the water, she knew they'd found her. It had actually happened, she really had drowned – and as Sissy flicked the channel frantically to a re-run of *Top Gear* she felt as faint as she had on holiday in Sardinia, the time she'd nearly died of heatstroke.

Her poor, poor friend. *Siobhan was dead!*

Sissy felt the grief as if she'd been punched in the stomach, hard. When Nigel had died it had been too quick, too unbelievable to take in, so her feelings had been stuck for days, weeks even, her brain unable to comprehend what had happened. On this occasion she'd been prepared for death, had dreaded it, whilst also hoping desperately that Siobhan would turn up at her desk on Monday morning with a comical tale of a wild weekend. It had happened before – but not this time.

Sissy tried to think logically through her grief and panic. Siobhan had drowned, was dead. But not only that – she, Sissy, *had left her to drown*. What on earth had been wrong with her? How had she convinced herself that it wasn't Siobhan, a great big splash like that? She *knew* she should have gone after her. Why hadn't she? *Why?* She'd let her friend drown, had just jumped in a cab and gone home to bed, leaving her helpless and dying at the bottom of The Serpentine. They'd all left her, Sissy tried to remind herself, it hadn't just been her – plus she'd been drunk for once. Surely it wasn't anyone's fault. The splash must have sounded like a bird, they couldn't all have been wrong – but inside Sissy knew she was as complicit as the rest of them.

Sissy sat down on the faded sofa and dropped her head between her knees to try to stop the roar in her head. The children sat mutely watching *Top Gear*, even though Nell especially didn't like it, all the cars looked the same to her. A new thought came to Sissy now, and it made her feel physically sick. She accepted she was at fault morally, was sure of that, but what exactly was she culpable of in the eyes of the law? Obviously it wasn't murder – but did her inaction constitute some kind of crime, even manslaughter perhaps, through negligence or something? Would she be arrested? As she tried to control her panic, aware that the kids were watching her, she remembered a couple of the others flippantly saying that if anything had happened to Siobhan they'd just pretend they hadn't heard the splash – but they wouldn't really do that, surely? No, they would all have to go to the police, file a report, admit that they'd *abandoned* her, and gone home.

Sissy's thoughts began unravelling further. What if she even ended up in prison over this, left the children without a mother *or* a father? She started panting, hyperventilating almost, and although she'd thought she would never cry as hard again as she had over Nigel's death, she'd been wrong. Her children looked desolate, already aware, as children usually are, that there was yet more sadness and heartbreak to come in their poor young lives. And as Sissy sobbed, she remembered all over again that Siobhan was *dead*, and she cried even harder – for her lost friend, for Nigel, for her children, already so damaged – for what the fallout from her madness that night might ultimately prove to be.

Sissy could bear no more. She jumped up, stumbled from the room and ran upstairs to run Conor's bath, leaving her children to finish their tea alone at the second-hand dining table, shocked, but safe for now, in the capable hands of Jeremy Clarkson.

52

Barnes

Alistair Smart was getting extraordinarily fed up with his wife now. Over the weekend she'd been even more of a bitch than usual – moody, monosyllabic, forever shouting at the boys. She'd even bloody taken up smoking again, and in the house too, what the hell was wrong with her? Even when Rebecca from next door had popped round to invite them to a barbecue the following weekend, Natasha had seemed unable to put on her normal 'everything's-fucking-marvellous' front, and Rebecca had left nonplussed, assuming Natasha and Alistair must have had a row.

Unknown to Natasha, there was another reason Alistair was so uptight – he hadn't heard from his lover all weekend, she just wouldn't answer her phone, and nearly a week had gone by since he'd had sex (well, proper sex, with a woman anyway), and he'd realised how addicted to the real thing he seemed to have become of late. Even relentless wanking just didn't seem to do it for him any more.

Alistair thought he may as well pretend to do some

writing, mainly to get out of his wife's way – plus he had a nice sturdy lock on the door now, so his web browsing was that much more relaxing, although it did lack a certain frisson which he missed a little. As he made his way up to his sunshine-filled office overlooking the common, with its cheery fucking pictures of beach huts and camper vans that Natasha had chosen and made him want to vomit, his naked little toe caught on something, and when he looked down he saw that the stair carpet was threadbare, unravelling in fact. They desperately needed a new one. Alistair smiled to himself. Once his little arrangement with Lucinda Horne (Horne by name, horny by nature as it turned out, landing as she had in his inbox like manna from heaven) was sorted, he wouldn't need to worry about paying his half of the ludicrous mortgage, or about replacing the car or the carpet, or even about paying for winter trips to Courchevel or the Caribbean – just to complete the alliterative landscape of their financial future. (*Yes! He was a writer, an artist at heart, he hadn't lost it.*) Although no money had actually come through yet, it was definitely on the cards, the deal was about to be done, worth absolutely loads his agent had assured him; and it was such a relief to have got his publisher off his back at last.

'You little bugger,' Sebastian had said, when Alistair had presented him with three full volumes of *Bottersley Dog School's Woofy Adventures*. 'I thought you were going to give me one almighty heart attack, winding me up like that, giving me the impression that you'd done absolutely sod all for eighteen months. This new stuff is going to *fly* off the shelves, kids aren't going to be able to get enough of these characters, it's like Harry Potter with dogs, but without the magic.' Alistair had looked at his agent witheringly at this point, but he knew better than to say anything – and to be fair to Sebastian, he was on the cusp of landing Alistair a quite sensational deal, one that would enable him to carpet the entire sodding street if he wanted to. It was bloody miraculous.

The whole thing had been managed so neatly, so seamlessly, had turned out to be a complete doddle in fact. It seemed that little Miss Horne was so in awe of the great Alistair Smart she would have agreed to pretty much anything. He'd been generous, he felt – a full thirty per cent to her, seventy per cent to him, and besides, sales would be absolutely huge with his name on the cover, far more than she'd ever hope to achieve on her own. So he was doing her a favour really. They had met to discuss things at the Holiday Inn at Brent Cross – she was coming down from Stevenage and was scared of driving in central London, and to make sure there was no chance of them being overheard he had booked a room, and when she'd walked in she'd been so cutesily pretty, so child-like, but with the most voluptuous assets, that he felt himself explode inside; and having spent years and years being faithful to his wife (and *for what?*), managing his extreme sex starvation as best he could, he found that having already taken one lover it was just too easy to take another. Lucinda had been so impressed by him, so naive and giggly, and although in truth it did creep him out that she'd grown up with his stories, was one of his original fans (she even had a signed photograph from 1997, she'd told him), once they'd agreed terms in principle, which only took one cup of room-made tea and a shortbread finger, he found that her age and immaturity didn't put him off after all, in fact it was a bloody great turn-on, and it most definitely hadn't stopped him pulling her down with him onto the just-too-convenient bed, and as she squealed delightedly he'd groaned and then come, all over her amazing tits.

'*Alistair*,' said his wife, for maybe the fifth time, and as he turned and looked at her she stared at him open-mouthed, slack, like a rubber band that has been pulled too tight, and then she nodded mutely towards the flat-screen TV on the wall behind the kitchen table, and he looked vaguely at the news, but he was so mesmerised by thoughts of the marvellous Miss Horne that he had no idea why his wife wanted him to watch a body being pulled out of The Serpentine.

53

Somerset House, Central London

Juliette felt like a child again as she stood in the middle of the vast building, clutching the knowledge (adoptive parents' names, recently learned place of birth) inside her head, the fee (one folded-up five-pound note) tight in her fist, and her passport (complete with de rigueur terrible photo) deep inside her handbag.

Now Juliette was actually here at Somerset House she felt an uncomfortable obligation to go through with the search – Renée would never let her leave at this point, not without at least trying. Renée was doing her best, but she couldn't hide her ridiculously over-the-top excitement, and it saddened Juliette that it almost seemed like entertainment to her friend, as if Juliette's past of rejection and abandonment was some kind of treasure hunt, with the fantastic prize of a mummy at the end of it. She privately thought that Renée ought to sort out the issues with her own mother rather than keep chasing after hers, but she tried not to be upset with her, she knew Renée meant well.

At the enquiry desk Juliette was timid; there were

other people around, and she felt ashamed somehow. But once she'd half-whispered her reason for being there, one of the clerks came straight round from behind the counter and led her towards a private room that smelled of furniture polish and stillness. Renée gestured to ask whether she should come too, but Juliette shook her head apologetically, suddenly aware she needed to do this herself – and that seemed to upset Renée, almost as if she were being left out of the best bit.

'So, let's see,' said the clerk, peering over the top of his glasses as he settled into his chair behind the massive desk. He wore a burgundy cardigan with a grey bow tie, like a friendly old uncle, and Juliette started to feel a little better, despite a twinge of guilt about making Renée stay outside. 'Your adoptive parents' names, please.'

'Cynthia Jane Greene and Giles Arthur Greene,' said Juliette, and although she had spent all but the first few weeks of her life with her adoptive parents, here in this wood-panelled room they felt as unreal, unconnected to her as long-dead movie stars.

'And your place of birth, dear.'

'Acton,' said Juliette, as confidently as she could manage. The man was perceptive and looked at her, gently inquisitive.

'Or maybe Clacton,' she admitted, and as she said it she thought for the thousandth time how strange it would be if it did turn out she'd been born there – after all, that was where Renée was from. The man looked puzzled.

'I'm afraid I'm not a hundred per cent sure,' she added lamely.

'Oh. Well, we can always check Clacton too if we need to.' He coughed. 'Erm, I don't suppose you know which Acton?'

'Er, no . . . *oh no*, is there more than one?'

'I'm afraid so, my dear, there are four or five, I think.'

Juliette looked crestfallen. 'Shall we try the one in London and start from there?' he said. She nodded gratefully.

'And may I see your ID, please?'

Juliette handed over her passport. The photo was from when she was thirteen and she'd had great silver braces on her teeth and a velvet hair band taming her hideous hair, and she remembered the horror she'd felt when, after what seemed like a lifetime, the machine had spat out the photos, as if in disgust, and Juliette had begged her mother to let her take them again. But Cynthia had just smiled and said they were fine, not in a mean way, but in a way that made Juliette feel unconnected with her mother, not misunderstood exactly, just *un*-understood. She wondered whether her real mother would have acted in that way, and then she thought, well, maybe she was dead, or a hopeless alcoholic, or so deadbeat her daughter wouldn't have had a passport at all, would never have gone anywhere. And then she thought she might be about to be one step closer to finding out, and it made her feel light-headed, faint almost.

'Are you all right, my dear?' said the clerk.

'Oh, yes, thanks,' said Juliette. He wrote down some details from her passport and she handed him the money, which was crumpled and ancient-looking now; she didn't know why she hadn't just kept it in her purse until she'd needed it. The man got up from his chair and walked across the room, to where there was a wooden ladder, and she noticed with a start of sympathy that he limped a little. He climbed slowly, seemingly unable to bend his left leg properly, and Juliette thought he looked well past retirement age, was perhaps even in his seventies, and she worried he might fall. He reached one arm up, looking ever more precarious, and after running his finger along the length of identical-looking volumes he eventually selected one of the giant leather ledgers. As he pulled it down he seemed to only just avoid dropping it, and she was anxious as she watched him one-handedly descend the rickety-looking ladder with this over-sized book that maybe contained her mother (not literally obviously, but it almost felt like that, like she was there in the room with them) tucked awkwardly under his left arm, and as he sat down behind the desk again Juliette found that she seemed to have forgotten to breathe. She felt like she might even take off, literally flutter away with nerves.

The clerk opened the ledger about two-thirds of the way through, and as he let the pages fall there was a dull thud that vibrated through the table, across to Juliette. He licked his fingers and thumbed backwards a few pages and then stopped, seemingly having found the right one, and then he ran his forefinger down the records, as though his skin itself could read. It was excruciating. Eventually his finger became stationary, and he looked up over his glasses again, into her frightened face.

'Well, you were right the first time,' he said with a kind

smile. 'I've found the record here.' Juliette's eyes welled involuntarily.

'I'll leave you now, to have a look yourself,' he said. 'Just come out when you're ready.' When he got up he appeared to be limping slightly less than before, and as he passed her he squeezed her shoulder, just for an instant, and she was grateful to him.

54

Dagenham

In a grim little pebble-dashed house in East London, a wheel was spinning frantically. Frank, or was it Dean, was in need of some exercise, and he ran like his life depended on it, getting nowhere of course, as if he were trying to exorcise the miserable reality of his pathetic little existence – and it was only as Terry Kingston watched him that he realised that that was all he, Terry, did too. He was no better off than a caged white rat with mean pink eyes and a long kinked tail, spinning his own metaphorical wheel – trapped between his faintly grubby detective work, his solitary obsession with painting miniature figures of Prussian fusiliers in their exact colours, and his dispiriting marriage to a woman he had nothing in common with. He sighed, but in truth he did feel a little better today. It was Sunday afternoon and the sun was shining and he had heard nothing more from the police, thank God, so maybe it was going to be OK after all. Surely if there had been a body they'd have found it by now? The whole thing had been humiliating certainly, and he was still worried he might be charged with wasting police time – he could tell they thought he was some kind of pervert, so they'd be bound to try to throw something at him – but surely that was better than a woman being dead and him having done nothing about it? Or worse, a woman being dead and him being accused of *murdering* her. He shuddered.

Terry Kingston was a surprisingly principled man, and in other circumstances might have led a very different life – he'd just taken a couple of wrong turns here and there, and that's all you need to screw your life up, isn't it? And so Terry was insightful enough to realise that despite his situation, his moral compass was still essentially intact, and that comforted him a little, even made him feel slightly superior to those braying women in the park, who despite their veneer of respectability had carried on like fishwives, and all seemed to be having affairs from what he could tell – and who were so hypocritically selfish they'd been prepared to leave a so-called friend for dead.

The telephone rang downstairs, which was unusual. No-one really called that number any more, people tended to get them on their mobiles these days, and Maria had managed somehow to get their home number delisted, so they no longer got call-centre workers haranguing them about changing their energy supplier or installing conservatory blinds or saving starving people, thank Christ. As the phone rang and rang insistently, Terry knew what it would be about, and he fretted that perhaps something had happened, after all. He couldn't face talking to the police right now though, and Maria wouldn't answer, as she was out – at choir as usual, he presumed. But when his mobile went a minute later Terry knew he couldn't delay for any longer, otherwise he'd have them turning up on the doorstep before he knew it. He sighed.

'Hello, Terry Kingston,' he said, in his best telephone voice.

'Mr Kingston,' said the caller. 'My name is Sergeant Hunter. As you may have seen on the news a body has been found in The Serpentine river in Hyde Park. We'd like you to come in for questioning.'

Terry said the right things and made the necessary arrangements. As he put down the phone and picked up his paintbrush he felt anxious again, now more than ever, as well as irrationally annoyed at Sergeant Hunter, with his chirpy manner and supercilious air of authority. Surely if he'd been down there fishing a body out of it he should have known that The Serpentine wasn't a river, it was a sodding lake.

55

Somerset House

Juliette wondered how just some smudgy old ink, written nearly twenty years earlier, could be so critically important to her, how the old-fashioned curl of those letters could potentially reshape the direction of her entire life. There it was. Proof. Yes, she had had a life before adoption, she had been borne by a flesh and blood woman, the stork hadn't brought her, it had all really actually happened. *Her mother had abandoned her.* Hammersmith Hospital, Acton, 23rd April 1967, given names Amanda Lily. She was shocked to see she'd had a father too – and *my God*, what a father: he wasn't 'unknown' like they usually were, like she'd been expecting him to be.

Juliette sat for ages trying to make sense of what she saw. She was vaguely aware of Renée loitering outside, obviously desperate to come in, but although Juliette felt for her friend she willed her away with her mind and the set of her back, and it seemed to be working for the time being. This was her moment, her moment of truth. Renée would have to wait.

Potts. The name was familiar but she couldn't think why. Was she famous or something? Who was Elisabeth Potts? She'd never heard of her, had she? *Pots and pans.* What did it mean?

Juliette sat in the quietness of the room for more long, slow minutes, her mind locked in a peculiar state somewhere between racing and blank. Just before she stood up to leave at last, she looked again at the two words that had struck her most, despite all the revelations of the morning. *Amanda Lily.* And that's when her tears came. The one thing her mother had given her, apart from life of course, and they'd taken that from her too.

56

Wandsworth

In the end it was Renée who got in her car on Sunday afternoon, an hour after she'd seen the headlines, and drove round to Juliette's – if she wasn't ever going to come to the sodding phone she'd just have to visit her in person. When Juliette finally answered the door, she was in tracksuit bottoms, and a tuft of her hair was stuck up in the air as if she'd gelled it like that for a joke, and the bags under her eyes were definitely over the luggage limit, metaphorically speaking. She stared hostilely at Renée, but Renée wasn't in the mood for histrionics, and instead pushed past her former friend and stomped into the cavernous kitchen to put the kettle on. Juliette came in and slumped into one of the white Eames chairs at the dining table. She put her head in her hands, avoiding eye contact. The atmosphere was poisonous, like methane.

'Where are the kids?' asked Renée, meaning *where's Stephen?*

'At a friend's house for the afternoon. Stephen's at work.'

They were both relieved.

'Has anyone contacted you yet?' asked Renée.

'No,' said Juliette.

'What about Stephen? Have you said anything to him?'

'No.'

'Have they named her yet?'

'Not that I know of.'

'So what do we do now?'

'I don't know,' said Juliette, and she looked up at Renée, and for a second it was as if time had turned backwards and none of the stuff with Stephen or with Juliette's mother had ever happened. They were still simply two best friends gossiping over a cup of tea in their university flat share. When the moment passed – and it was over in an instant – both of them felt hollow, lonely again, devastated for their dead friend, scared for themselves.

'D'you think this room's bugged?' asked Renée then, and she sounded panicked.

'What on earth do you mean?'

'Well, what with Stephen's job . . .' Renée's voice fell away, embarrassed.

'Don't be so bloody silly,' said Juliette, but for some reason she felt nervous too now, and as it was such a lovely day they both moved instinctively, without speaking, through the sliding glass doors that ran the width of the kitchen, as big as the windows in a car showroom, and out into the garden, which their gardener George had worked miracles on this year. The scent of the summer roses hung in the air, sickly almost, and they sat together on the bench under the cherry tree at the end of the garden, unspeaking at first, as they silently mourned their lost friend, their lost friendship.

'D'you think anyone else heard?' Renée said eventually.

'What do you mean?' said Juliette, speaking into her sweatshirt as she kicked ineffectually at a weed growing through the concrete between the paving stones, hell-bent on living.

Renée lowered her voice, although no-one else could possibly have heard them.

'Well, Natasha said that we should just leave her, and that if she ended up drowning we'd just say we'd already left, hadn't heard the splash. That's pretty incriminating.'

'No, she did not,' said Juliette.

'Yes, she did,' insisted Renée. 'You heard her too. Why are you lying?'

'I'm not lying,' said Juliette, and maybe she even believed it herself; perhaps she'd been married to Stephen for too long.

'Well, what if someone heard us talking?' persisted Renée. 'We can't say we didn't hear anything if someone witnessed that we did.'

'I *told* you,' said Juliette, but she wasn't cross exactly, more resolute. 'Natasha never said we should leave her. She never said anything.'

Renée was confused – why the hell was Juliette trying to protect *Natasha* all of a sudden? Finally she got it. Even if someone had overheard them, it had been dark; they wouldn't have been able to tell who said what. But did that make any difference? The fact that *someone* had said it damned them all, didn't it? They had all left her, to die as it turned out. They were all despicable.

'Juliette,' said Renée, and she was stern now. 'We have got to work out what we're going to say to the police. We'll have to speak to them eventually, we were the last people to see her alive. And we'd all just had a bloody big row. It's not looking good.' She stared at the ground, at the edge of the lawn where George had uncharacteristic-ally missed a bit with the strimmer, the few stray blades rising sharp and defiant, glaringly green above the paving stones.

'Well, I don't know what you want *me* to do,' said Juli-ette. 'Get Stephen to keep it out of the papers or something? Talk to his mates at Scotland Yard?'

'Don't be so fucking ridiculous,' said Renée. She waited but Juliette said nothing more. 'Well, I'll just have to talk to Sissy and the others then, but if it does all come out *I'm* not going to lie about what anyone said.'

'Is that a threat?' said Juliette, and she pulled at her bel-ligerently sticking up hair, tried to tame it like she was trying to tame her temper.

'I don't know,' said Renée. She hesitated, aware that she should probably leave it there, but this was likely to be her only chance.

'D'you think it *was* an accident though?'

'What on earth do you mean?'

'Well, some of the things that were said between us . . . I mean, some people wouldn't want any of it to get out . . .'

'Oh, don't talk such utter shit,' said Juliette. 'If you mean Stephen, he'd have had to push *you* in, not her, you're the one who made all the vile accusations. You are such a total drama queen, a complete raving fantasist. You always have been, look at what you were like about tracing my mother, thinking we'd have some beautiful reunion, become like the fucking Waltons.' She couldn't keep the bitterness from her voice.

'No, I am not!' said Renée. 'It's not my fault Elisabeth's like she is. I don't know why you've always blamed me.' Juliette went quiet, just kept her gaze focused on the ground. Renée tried again.

'Listen, I swear there was someone there the other night, watching us. I could feel it, and then when we were leaving I think I saw someone, crouched behind a tree.'

'So who was it? Stephen?' said Juliette, sarcastically. Renée said nothing, just looked away, towards the house.

'My God, I don't *believe* you,' said Juliette. She felt almost hysterical. 'So now you're saying Stephen just *happened* to be loitering in a bush in Hyde Park and *killed her*, as well as, according to you, *killing Nigel* and –' She stopped. 'You've got a cheek coming round here, after the things you've said about my husband.'

'I'm not saying it was Stephen. I just think there may have been someone else involved.'

'Well, it doesn't make any difference then, does it? If it turned out someone did kill her – my God, I can't believe I'm even saying this – it doesn't matter whether we heard anything or not.' She suppressed a sob. 'We couldn't have stopped it.' There was a long, painful, death-throe silence, before Juliette kicked viciously at the weeds again and said, 'I think you should go now.'

Renée knew that was it, there was nothing more to be said. She stood up from the bench and steadily walked the length of the garden, past the raised vegetable beds, the slide, the trampoline, the goalposts – all screened cleverly with bamboo fencing or evergreen hedging – past the gravelled herb garden with the Rodinesque centre-piece, through the half-open sliding doors into the gleamingly chaotic kitchen, across the book-lined Victorian hall, and out the matt-black-painted door into the front garden full of artfully tasteful topiary. It was only when Renée reached the street and the safety of her car that the really ominous feeling left her, and she knew that all she could do now was tell the truth, she'd done her best, and if you'd done no wrong and you told the truth what harm could possibly come to you?

57

Sissy stopped scraping hopelessly at the wallpaper, which was several layers deep and mostly stuck solid, resistant to home improvement, as she heard the trill of her mobile. Dried-up bits of paper littered the living-room carpet like worn-out confetti. She pulled out the phone from her jeans pocket and, seeing who it was, answered on the sixth ring.

'Hello,' she said, pushing her hair out of her eyes and heading out to the hallway, which was still grimly dark green, where the children wouldn't hear. 'Yes, yes, I know, it's just so awful, I just can't believe it . . . OK, I agree, it's our only option . . . Yes, I think we should go in together. If the others want to deny it then that's up to them . . . All right, I'll wait to hear from you then . . . Yes, I'm OK (*sob*), I just feel so terrible for her . . . OK, bye.'

'Who was that, Mummy?' said Conor, looking up from playing with the cat as she re-entered the lounge, which was looking worse than ever. Sissy hadn't known why she'd attacked the wallpaper like that, but she'd felt she had to do something, had to keep busy instead of sitting around feeling helpless and distraught, scared out of her mind. She kept replaying events from three evenings before, and it was driving her insane. *If only I'd trusted my instincts, gone home when I'd wanted to, before everyone started arguing, maybe nothing would have been said, maybe she wouldn't have run off. If only we'd gone back when we heard the splash. If only she wasn't dead.*

'Who was it on the phone, Mummy?' Conor repeated, and he sounded fearful now. His little brow was furrowed under his sandy hair, and he reminded her of his father, and the pain was acute. He tickled the cat's tummy as he stared at her.

'Oh, no-one, darling,' Sissy replied.

'Was it the hospital? Are you going to die, Mummy?'

'Oh, darling, of course not,' said Sissy, horrified.

'Well, who is then?'

'No-one darling, no-one's going to die,' and as she said it she comforted herself that she wasn't actually lying, the dying bit had already happened. 'I just have to go out a bit later, there's been a little accident.' And as she said the word accident, she kicked herself, wished she'd chosen a different, less emotive word.

'Will Auntie Siobhan look after us?' asked Nell, who'd stopped playing on her 3DS and was stood facing her mother, blocking the kitchen door, her stance taut and unbearably adult.

'No, darling,' said Sissy, suppressing a sob.

'Who will then?' she persisted.

'I'm not sure yet, darling. Someone nice.'

'I don't want someone nice. I want Auntie Siobhan,' said Nell.

'I want Daddy,' said Conor, and he pulled the cat to him and hugged the hell out of it (which Coco rather stoically put up with, she was used to it), and then he burst into noisy tears.

58

Belgravia, Central London

As soon as Terry arrived at the police station, he'd been unceremoniously arrested and bundled off to a cell, as if he were nothing more than a common criminal. They'd said they weren't ready to interview him yet, despite him arriving on time for his appointment, and it seemed they were entitled to lock him up in the meantime, even though he hadn't actually been charged with anything – which was a ruddy disgrace in Terry's opinion.

The cell was small and dirty and stank of urine. Terry felt trapped, desperate, as he paced up and down, unwilling to sit down on the rank-looking bunk. As he waited for what seemed like hours, he felt more and more hemmed in, as if the room were shrinking. He found that he couldn't stop thinking of poor Frank and Dean, caged not as a one-off travesty, because they were falsely under suspicion of something (no, not just of something, *of murder*), but instead were interned for ever – and he hated the thought and debated how he could set them free. Would they be able to even survive in the wild? he wondered. Would they know how to find food? Was there an organisation that could help him do it, the RSPCA perhaps? He knew he was being ridiculous, he had far more serious things to worry about than his pet rats' wellbeing, but the more he paced, the more concerned he became, about all of his animals now, fretting about whether Maria would feed them if he was kept in overnight, God forbid – not because she was cruel or anything, just whether she'd think to, know how to, know who got which food and how much, even if she did remember. He needed to ring her.

Terry hauled his brain back to his own predicament. He tried to work out what was going on, why he was being held here, what might happen next. He needed to be prepared, know what to say. He needed to *think*.

Terry wound his mind around the facts, as though he were there again, as if the evening was happening right now. He is in Hyde Park, near The Serpentine. He has his client's wife under surveillance. He hears an argument. He hears a splash. Her so-called friends leave, despite hearing it too. He dials 999. The police find nothing, are annoyed with him for wasting their time. Three days later, a body is found, by a small boy in a boat apparently. They think it may be murder. It appears that he, Terry, is the prime suspect, even though he's the one who called the police in the first place. He's locked in a cell at this very moment, waiting for them to interview him.

Terry fast-forwards, imagines what he will say. He tries to calm down, think clearly, assess his options. He doesn't know what to do. He goes round in circles, getting tangled in the details of the lies he could tell. Sweat breaks out across his smooth top lip, and his tongue feels dead. He worries about everything and nothing: his pets, what Maria will think, what his client will say, what really happened that night.

And then finally, eventually, it comes to him.

Yes, that's it.

He'll tell the truth at last. He has no other option. He'll confess that he was being paid to trail a woman whose husband was convinced she was having an affair; that *that* was why he was there, not for a nice evening stroll after all. He'll confess that his target was Juliette Forsyth, a woman possibly familiar to the more dedicated readers of *Hello!* magazine. He'll admit that his client was the illustrious Stephen Forsyth, and he might even confess the truth of their relationship, as it would probably come out in the end.

What would the police do? Would they believe him? What the heck was going to happen? Terry put his head in his hands, to stop it from moving involuntarily from side to side as if in denial, to stop his hands from trembling like an addict's. He wished he had a paintbrush, a figure, some tiny intricate detail to tackle . . . an insignia perhaps. That always helped steady his hands, steady his nerves. He looked down at his shoes, his leather-soled smart shoes – he'd dressed up for the interview, almost looked quite handsome in fact, although he didn't know why he'd bothered. *So I don't look like a creep, a murderer*, he acknowledged now. He wasn't sure if he'd been successful. He didn't know if they'd accept his story, telling the truth didn't always pay, not when people like Stephen Forsyth were involved.

Terry sank down on the filthy bed at last and put his head in his hands. He stifled a sob. All he'd done was try to do the right thing, save someone's life, and now here he was, locked up like one of his poor pet rats, his own life about to be ruined.

59

Somerset House

Renée was hovering outside the door, debating whether she should go in. But something told her to give Juliette this time alone – the old man with the half-moon glasses had said on his way out that this was often a very big moment for adoptees, the first concrete step on their journey back to their beginnings. It was terribly frustrating though. Renée felt almost desperate to find out, although she knew it wasn't her business, not really.

Renée picked up a leaflet entitled 'How to register a death' and sat in one of the booths reading it mindlessly, fiddling with a long black strand of her hair, twirling it round and round her forefinger like she was a little girl still. She was glad for Juliette, that she'd started this at last, sure that Juliette would feel so much better about herself if she knew the truth of where she came from. She almost shivered with excitement – once Juliette had her mother's name she'd be able to go about trying to trace her. Renée hoped it was a distinctive one, so it would be easier for them – no, *for Juliette*, she reminded herself. Maybe

Juliette could even go and visit her one day; Renée would be more than happy to keep her company, offer moral support if she wanted it. Renée's finger was hurting now, and when she looked down she realised she'd twisted her hair so tightly she'd cut off the blood supply to it.

When Juliette eventually came out of the anteroom her beautiful face was as white as her best friend's finger. Renée smiled encouragingly and went to speak, but Juliette just shook her head and beckoned her to come, so Renée got up and followed her out, untangling her hair as she walked. They made their way into the open courtyard and the sky was blue and clear, and the building was luxuriating in its own beauty like a gorgeous girl in the bath, but neither of them appreciated it as they hurried one after the other. Once they were out in the shivery air of the Strand and it was clear that Juliette still wasn't going to slow down, or say anything, Renée ran to catch up.

'Well?' she asked, almost panting.

'Well what?'

'What did you find out?'

'I don't want to talk about it.'

'Oh,' said Renée. She didn't know what to say. 'Was it upsetting?'

'Yes,' said Juliette, and there was steel in her voice that Renée had never heard before. 'You could say that.'

'In what way?' asked Renée, struggling to keep up as they passed the Savoy, where a group of wealthy-looking people swarmed out into the road, expecting the traffic to slow down for them.

Juliette didn't know why she was so upset, not really. Nothing had actually changed, had it? She struggled for an answer that would satisfy her friend.

'Because what is the point in chasing after someone who didn't want me in the first place? There is no point. It's pointless.'

'But you don't know that,' said Renée, breathless still, and not just from having to walk fast. 'You don't know that she didn't want you. Maybe she had to give you away.'

'I don't think so,' Juliette said, and her voice was sad suddenly. 'And whichever way you look at it, she didn't want me *enough*. I should just be grateful for having such lovely adoptive parents, and leave it at that.' She thought then of Giles and Cynthia, of what good people they were, how hard they'd tried, how they'd sent her to a lovely school, bought her a pony, of how much they'd always loved her, as if she were their own. And then she remembered how she'd always felt slightly inferior to her younger brother Barney, because he wore laughter around his eyes and never seemed to care where he came from. She wished she could have been more like him. She sighed. Life had been good regardless, hadn't it? She'd been happy with her lot; why was she stirring everything up now? (*Because Renée forced m*—, and before she'd even finished the thought she buried it, snapped it away somewhere dark and inaccessible in her brain.)

Renée said nothing more as they made their way down into the Tube at Charing Cross, and the atmosphere between the girls was tense, unfamiliar. They'd become so uncannily close, as if they'd known each other forever, but right now they were each in their own worlds. Juliette had set her mind to neutral, and was trying not to think at all. Renée was thinking of her own mother, across the Channel in a tiny apartment in Paris with her handsome French boyfriend. *She* knew how it felt not to be wanted too, she thought crossly. But maybe in Juliette's case there would be a happy ending; they just had to find it. They just had to find *her*.

60

Stephen sat behind his desk, sleeves rolled up deter-minedly, running his afternoon editorial meeting in the manner of a despot ruling a tin-pot country somewhere far away. His office was a complete mess – papers every-where, old editions of the newspaper dumped on the floor like in a hoarder's home – but his secretary and the cleaners never dared touch anything, it could get them the sack.

'OK, what have you got?' Stephen said. His deputy editor ran through the list of stories, an uninspiring lot including an A-list couple visiting Harrods with their kids and having a row in the food hall, a man being trapped for fifteen hours after his ceiling collapsed under the weight of his porn collection, the threat of another economic meltdown in Europe, a primary-school teacher who'd doctored her class's SATs results, a ten-vehicle pile-up on the M4 in which a baby had been killed, yet another rumble in the phone-hacking scandal.

'None of this is really front-page news,' said Stephen, ignoring the last story. 'Isn't there anything better?'

'Uh, sorry, Stephen, that's all we've got,' said Barry Smiley, his long-time assistant. 'What about going with the baby story, we've got a picture – of him *before* obviously,' he added hastily, knowing even Stephen wouldn't put a picture of a mangled baby on the front cover of a national newspaper.

'I don't know, pile-ups aren't that interesting these days unless there's at least twenty cars involved,' Stephen said. 'I think if *that's* all you've got maybe we should have a bit of fun with the porn-mag story, it is silly season after all.'

Stephen's favourite reporter, Maddie, poked her head round the office door. Barry scowled at her; she was a right brown-noser, always trying to muscle in on everything. He was convinced she was after his job, and it kept him awake at night.

'Sorry to interrupt, Stephen,' she said breathlessly. 'Hold the front page – I've always wanted to say that! – but a body has just been fished out of The Serpentine.'

'What, in Hyde Park?' asked Stephen, a little prick of adrenaline shooting through his neck.

'Yes, The Serpentine river! It's a woman, she's not been formally identified yet, but they think they've got the bloke too. Apparently he only went and dialled 999.'

'Well done, Maddie! Thank God *someone* is doing some work around here.' He looked witheringly at Barry, and Barry went puce with anger above his pink-striped shirt (which as it happened was beautifully ironed and cufflinked, unlike his boss's) at being upstaged like this. It was a bloody disgrace how Stephen humiliated him in front of this little upstart, after all he'd done for him over the years. He needed a drink.

'Oh well, I'll leave you to it then,' Barry said huffily. He stood up, but they didn't seem to have heard him. He walked slowly across the room, en route to his secret drawer, and then hesitated at the door. He tried to think of a punchline.

'And, in the interests of factual accuracy,' he said, always his forte, 'I think you'll find that The Serpentine is a lake, not a river,' but Stephen was still too wrapped up with Maddie to have heard him.

61

Camden

It became clear to Renée, once they were back at her aunt's house, that Juliette really wasn't going to talk about anything she'd discovered, or otherwise, at Somerset House – not now or, it seemed, later. It was strange how she'd clammed up like that – what could she possibly have found out that was so traumatic? A thought came to Renée then – what if her mother actually had turned out to be famous, joking aside? Or what if Juliette had known her mother; maybe she'd found out it was her neighbour or grandmother or something. Perhaps she'd discovered who her father was too, it wasn't always the case that it was 'father unknown', and there was something shocking about him. Renée was almost desperate to know.

'How was your day today, girls?' asked Linda as she stood at the stove stirring something comforting-smelling, a blue-striped butcher's apron tied neatly over her regulation jeans and white T-shirt. The aroma of paprika mooched through the air.

'It was fine,' said Renée.

'What did you get up to?'

'Oh, you know, a bit of shopping around Covent Garden, not much really.'

'I think you're forgetting something,' said Juliette then, and she sounded uncharacteristically harsh, pent-up. 'We went to Somerset House, didn't we, Renée?' She turned to Linda, whose face was flushed, from cooking presumably. 'I don't know if you know, Linda, but I'm adopted. Renée, for some reason, is obsessed with where I came from, so she forced me to go to Somerset House and –'

'I didn't *force* you,' Renée cut in, horrified. 'I thought you were happy to go.'

'Well, you were wrong,' said Juliette, but her anger had faded now. She knew she was being unfair – she'd only realised that she didn't want to do it once she'd done it, after all.

Renée looked close to tears, and Linda reacted quickly. 'Right, who'd like a nice cup of tea?' she asked.

'I'm *not* obsessed with where you came from,' said Renée, ignoring her aunt. 'I was just trying to help – I thought you said you'd feel better once you'd found out.'

Juliette knew Renée was right, she had consented, in fact had even been keen just a few hours earlier, but it seemed when it came down to it she wasn't ready to go there, not yet. It was strange how before all this adoption business Renée had seemed so in tune with her, had appeared to understand her more than anyone else in the world. But thinking about it, who else would get her?

She had no blood relatives after all; there were no genetic connections to help anyone read her deepest feelings. She felt embarrassed now at her outburst, especially in front of Renée's undeserving aunt.

'Don't worry, Renée, I'm sorry I got so emotional, I don't mean to take it out on you. I just don't think I'm ready to do this, after all.' She turned to Linda. 'I'm so sorry, Linda, I'm not usually such a nightmare, I promise.'

'No, no, that's fine,' said Linda. 'You don't have to apologise to me. Look, it's none of my business, but it's a big deal what you've done. Don't be too hard on yourself.'

'Sorry, Renée,' said Juliette again, as Renée just sat there, hiding under her orange fringe.

'That's OK,' muttered Renée, and the ever-obliging Linda served them tea and home-made fruit cake, and as snowflakes started to fall gently on the street outside and disappear into tiny shiny pools upon reaching the pavement, the crisis passed, for now.

62

Stephen was feeling even more pleased with himself than usual. OK, 'The body in the lake' was not the most original of headlines, but it was a cracking story, and he was hoping to get enough extra material for at least a double-page spread inside – plus he'd almost certainly be able to eke it out for the rest of the week too. He'd got Maddie straight onto the bloke they'd picked up; she was off now seeing what she could dig up on him.

Maybe today was going to turn out well after all. It had certainly started badly. He and Juliette seemed to be getting on more appallingly than ever, she was so bloody uptight these days, always shouting at the kids, presiding over a pigsty of a house. How on earth could they have so much domestic help and the place still look like that? He felt sorry for the children sometimes, especially Noah, and he was worried about his middle child, he seemed to have become so withdrawn lately. Stephen didn't know what had happened to Juliette, she certainly hadn't turned out to be much of a wife and mother, despite her early promise. He'd been so taken in by her beauty, her utter middle-classness, when they'd met at Bristol, and he'd been immediately smitten, had worshipped her like a precious painting, but she'd changed so much over the years, had become so bitter, and it was like she hated him as much as she did her mother now. Even worse, he was convinced she was having an affair these days, and the thought made him want to retch; he hated that she still had such a hold on him. He was annoyed that Terry still hadn't got back to him with an update from her supposed picnic the other night; he bet he'd lost her, the useless twat.

His phone rang, and it was her. She didn't usually ring him at work. His heart leaped, despite himself.

'Yes,' he said, which he knew didn't help marital relations, but hostility was their modus operandi these days.

'I'm at the police station,' she said carefully.

'Why?' he said. Christ, was she all right? Had something happened to the kids?

'Siobhan's dead.'

'*What?* How?'

'She drowned, in The Serpentine.'

Stephen felt his breath fall down, away from his chest, as though gravity had just got stronger. He felt a tightness in his throat.

'Weren't you with her the other night?' he said. 'In Hyde Park?' He wondered if Terry knew anything about any of this – he bet he did, the sneaky little cunt, no wonder he hadn't been returning his calls.

'Yes,' said Juliette. 'But the rest of us had left, it must

have happened after.' The lie came out surprisingly easily, and she was ashamed of herself.

'She was drunk,' she added, as if an afterthought, and gave a little sob.

'This is fucking awkward for me,' he said, thinking of the front page he'd been about to push the button on.

'Well, I think it's a bit more awkward for Siobhan, don't you?' his wife said softly, and put down the phone.

63

Bristol

Juliette stood alone in the phone box around the corner from her flat, a piece of paper propped up on the scratched black ledge in front of her. It was the torn-off back of an envelope that she'd received from her bank a couple of weeks earlier, and she had written the phone numbers on the patterned blue side of the paper, not the plain white side, for some reason she couldn't fathom now. The digits were hard to decipher, blue writing against a blue security pattern, the ink smudged and messy, almost as if she'd wanted not to be able to read it. There were only three numbers in W3, and two in W12. She'd copied out the fourteen others she'd found in the rest of London, just in case.

Juliette paused before she pressed the last digit of the first number. Should she really be doing this? What would Cynthia say if she knew? *She'd be devastated, that's what*, Juliette acknowledged, especially at her daughter doing it behind her back. Why hadn't she told her at least?

Juliette stood and watched her breath in the dankness

of the booth, little puffs of white going nowhere, just fading into nothingness. She took so long deciding whether or not to punch in the last '7' that eventually the phone must have thought she'd completed her dialling, and the wrong number tone screamed into the thin air like a warning. She clacked the receiver into the cradle, to stop it.

Why on earth was she doing this? It seemed insane suddenly. She thought of her own mother in Berkshire, kind and well-meaning, but ultimately unconnected to her. She thought of who her real mother might be.

What harm can it do, Juliette thought in the end. She wouldn't say who she was. She ran the forefinger of her left hand along the length of the number as she dialled it again. Her nail was thick with over-painting, but there were no actual chips in the bright-pink colour today, just a steep ridge of varnish that ran across the nail a quarter of the way down from the cuticle, where it had grown out from the last time she'd painted it.

The phone took forever to connect, but eventually those familiar thrum thrums started and Juliette's heart started to beat faster and louder, and she very nearly hung up but her breath had come up into her mouth so she closed it and it made her feel giddy and fluttery, and she was so distracted that she kept the call going until at last her heart settled down and she almost felt ready to speak, if anyone would ever answer. After twenty or so rings, just as she was about to give up, there was a clatter and a knock and a rustle and a few moments of silence, and then an impatient breathless voice finally said, 'Hello?'

Juliette panicked and went to put down the phone, but instead she froze and held the receiver away from her, in limbo, as if it were contaminated, which it was.

'Hello?' said the voice again, sounding far away, dis-embodied in the glass box. 'Who is it?'

'Um, is Elisabeth Potts there?' said Juliette, putting the receiver back to her ear at last. It reeked of stale saliva.

'No, there's no-one of that name here,' said the voice, irritated now. 'You've got the wrong number.'

'Sorry, bye,' said Juliette, and as she hung up her ears burned red with shame.

64

Berkshire

A few days later, Juliette sat opposite her mother in the sitting room of the house she'd grown up in – Cynthia said it would be better in there, although Juliette hadn't been quite sure what her mother had meant by 'better'. Barney was at school and her father was at work and the house felt only half-inhabited, as if ghosts instead of real people lived there. Juliette felt oppressed by the formality of the room today, of sitting across from her mother, perched on the edge of the sofa with a cup and saucer on her lap while Cynthia looked thin and sad in Giles' armchair. Why couldn't they sit in the kitchen where the sun streamed in and forced a modicum of jollity into the atmosphere, where the Aga gave the room some warmth, some substance? Juliette felt her heart beating fast in her mouth, and despite the wild erratic thuds it was a vacant, empty feeling somehow, above her tongue, and it wouldn't go away, even when she sipped her tea.

'What is it, Juliette, dear?' asked her mother eventually, once it was clear Juliette wasn't going to start the conversation. 'Why have you come home like this? Is there something wrong?' She paused. 'Is it Stephen?' she asked, although she knew it wasn't.

Juliette looked at her right hand, in its black lace fingerless glove, holding the delicate handle of the teacup clumsily, like a chimpanzee in one of those tea ads. Why couldn't she just have had a mug? She looked at her mother's hands, which although small were large-palmed and raw with washing, it must be all the cooking she did; she really ought to use hand cream. She looked past her mother to the window-ledge, full of knick-knacks and photos: of Juliette and Barney on the beach at Salcombe; of Juliette with Popcorn (the latter proudly wearing a blue and white rosette, his head at a jaunty angle, as if he knew he had won); of Giles and Cynthia on their wedding day, the looks in their eyes innocent, from a different era (the only photo of their wedding she'd ever seen, now she came to think of it); of Giles as a boy with his brother and their parents, and this picture was from another even earlier time, another universe – the dour dark clothes, the two boys' ears jutting out of their brutal haircuts, their parents looking old despite surely being still in their thirties, the grimly startled expressions, fear of the camera she supposed. She wondered why that picture had been framed at all, it wasn't a good one.

'Juliette,' said her mother again. 'What are you thinking about, dear?'

The question yanked Juliette out of the distant past, back to more recent events, to the furniture-polish smell of Somerset House, the inky curl of the letters, the thickness of the paper, the words. The phone box.

'You know,' said Juliette finally, but she didn't say it accusingly, just in a *let's get on with it* kind of resigned tone.

'You wanted to know where you're from,' said Cynthia. 'It wasn't for your course, was it, darling?'

Juliette shook her head slowly as tiny tears formed just above her eyelashes, and they sparkled like drizzle in sunshine.

'What have you done about it, Juliette?' said Cynthia. 'Have you done anything?'

Juliette put down her tea on the mahogany coffee table and the gentle clink of the fine bone china, of the cup and saucer chattering with each other sounded loud, explosive to them both.

Juliette stared out of the window, past the eclectic assortment of photos, towards the house across the street, and she saw that the neighbours had a brand-new car – it was red and shiny with a 'C' number plate, although she would never normally have noticed, she had little interest in cars.

Juliette sat silently still. She didn't know how to broach it, even though she'd come home specially, on a Friday – after her abortive phone search she'd felt like she'd explode with the not-knowing. Cynthia waited resignedly, looking at Juliette's black-lace hair band and tights and gloves and thinking it all looked a bit over-the-top, how the lace didn't go with the pink flowery skirt and Aran knit jumper and heavy boots, but she didn't say anything of course, she didn't want to hurt her daughter's feelings.

'Elisabeth Potts,' Juliette said in the end. 'Who is Elisabeth Potts?'

Cynthia tried not to react, but her back stiffened.

'Where did you get that name, Juliette?'

'You know, Mum,' Juliette said. 'It's on my birth certificate.'

Cynthia looked forlorn then, as if it were game over, although of course really it had only just started. This was the end of the family she'd tried so hard to create. She'd always been aware Juliette would want to know one day, but she felt like she'd failed her daughter somehow. Poor Juliette, she was too young still – she, Cynthia, should have managed it better. It was never meant to be like this.

'Maybe we ought to wait until your father gets home,' said Cynthia. 'We should all talk about it together, as a family.'

'NO,' said Juliette. She looked shocked at herself. 'I'm sorry, Mum, but I can't wait any longer.' And Cynthia saw that she couldn't, that she was bursting with hope and fear.

'It's just I know the name,' said Juliette. 'I know that I know it, but I can't think how, or where from.'

Elisabeth Potts. A name to remember? Juliette sat across the room from her mother, auburn hair glowing, her mind searching forensically over her past life, searching out the time, the place, she had first heard those two words. Elisabeth Potts.

65

Belgravia

Terry Kingston sat sullenly in the fluorescently bright interview room feeling thoroughly resentful. He'd been interviewed for over two hours now, and was fed up with saying the same thing over and over again. He'd known they thought he was dodgy anyway, but at the mention of his client's name, they had reacted first with disbelief and then with outright hostility, and it seemed to have made it all worse, not better. (The duty solicitor had shifted in his seat and wondered what the hell was going on here, this case he'd been randomly allocated suddenly looked like it might get even more interesting – it wasn't just dead girls in lakes and dodgy blokes in bushes, now there was a major newspaper editor involved too. This was bloody dynamite!)

'So what you're telling me is that you are a *private investigator* and that Stephen Forsyth is your client? *The* Stephen Forsyth, the newspaper editor?' The police-woman was openly sneering now.

'Yes, that's right,' said Terry, and he felt relieved, now it was out.

'And just what were you doing on *his* behalf?'

'I was keeping tabs on his wife. He . . . he thought she was having an affair.'

'And how do you know Mr Forsyth?'

Terry sighed. 'I'm his half-brother.'

The male police officer looked incredulous.

'You?'

'Yes, that's right.' *A loser like me*, Terry said in his head, but of course he didn't say it out loud.

The policeman seemed lost for words at this revelation, so the woman took over again. She was black with one of those faces that was plain until she smiled, and then was transformed by her beautiful white teeth, like the sun coming out. She wasn't smiling now though.

'And so you were in the park *spying* on Mrs Forsyth, and then what happened?'

Terry sighed again.

'I wasn't spying on her, I was being paid to keep her under surveillance.'

'Then what happened, Mr Kingston?'

'I told you, I was bored because it was clear to me that this was just a tedious women's night out, with them all going on about school admissions policies and salmon recipes and the like, but I couldn't leave in case Mrs Forsyth was going on to a rendezvous later in the evening, which was possible, I suppose. So I was just sat minding my own business . . .'

'Hardly,' said PC Williams, her gleaming teeth firmly

under wraps now, and he realised, quite perceptively considering the pressure he was under, that his misogynistic bent wasn't helping him here.

Terry tried again. 'I was waiting for Mrs Forsyth to leave, not really listening to the conversation, and once they'd moved from the Diana fountain I couldn't really hear the detail of what they were saying anyway – by then I think they'd all been drinking and everyone started arguing (he chose not to bring up some of the words he'd overheard, particularly the ones like *rape* and *murder*) and there was lots of screaming and shouting, and then one of them just seemed to totally lose it for some reason and ran off hysterically. The others were all packing up anyway, so they started to leave without her – they were really fed up with her, I suppose, and it was getting late anyway . . . and . . . and then . . . and then there was a splash.'

'Who heard the splash?'

'We all did.'

'How do you know they did?'

'Because one of them said, "What was that splash?"' He tried not to sound sarcastic, he knew it would do him no good. 'And then they all started discussing it, and they were nearer to me now, although they still couldn't see me, so I heard it all . . . And one of them said she was sick of her anyway, and . . . and . . . and that she could drown for all she cared.'

'Who said that?'

'I don't know, they all sounded the same.' (*Horsey, posh, drunk*, he meant.)

'And then what happened?'

'They started saying they thought it was a bird, but it obviously wasn't, it was much too loud to be a bird – but the weird thing was that after the splash there was no other sound. No splashing, no struggle, nothing. And then one of them said that if her friend really had gone and drowned herself she'd just say she'd already left and hadn't heard it, and that she was going home, she'd had enough of all the melodrama. And once *she* decided to go, they all went, she was obviously the ringleader . . . and I was about to follow, to keep up with my target . . . and then . . . and then I thought I couldn't just leave . . . just in case she *had* fallen in . . . so I ran and looked but I couldn't see anything . . . but the splash was so loud . . . I couldn't be sure . . . and I couldn't just leave her . . . and so that's when I called the police.'

PC Williams had been doing this job long enough to know when someone was lying. Up until five minutes ago she'd been convinced this shifty little creep had had something to do with it, the way he couldn't look them in the eye, his evasiveness around their questions. But she'd spotted his resemblance to Stephen Forsyth as soon as his name had been mentioned, knew the part about them being brothers at least might be true – and now the man seemed to have found his voice, become eloquent despite his hesitation, and she just knew that Terry Kingston, pathetic loser, small-time dick, was telling the truth at last.

66

Early one hot July morning, a week to the day after the picnic, Natasha had got a grip on the situation at last and was jogging effortlessly across Barnes Common, trying to get hold of Juliette (she was not only super-fit but the queen of multi-tasking). She didn't want to have to speak to her, although she thought she ought to at least try, and was glad in a way Juliette wouldn't come to the phone – her cleaner had answered and said she was 'indisposed', so perhaps she was having a breakdown. When Natasha couldn't get hold of Camilla either, on a whim she tried Renée's mobile.

Renée sounded thoroughly miserable, which undoubtedly wasn't helped by having to talk to Natasha.

'Are you all right, Renée?'

'Well, what do you think? This is bloody awful. Poor, poor Siobhan, I still can't believe it.' She hesitated. 'I feel terrible about lying to the police as well.'

'Shush,' said Natasha, although in actual fact there was

no-one to hear either of them. Renée was cooped up alone in her tiny flat, which was the epitome of flea-market kitsch, in the less salubrious part of Battersea, the part where the gangs still roamed and the petrol stations had grilles between the staff and the customers. Natasha was at this precise moment running through a particularly remote part of Barnes Common, swamped by trees with oversized leaves and great herds of cow parsley, that even the dog-walkers rarely reached. 'That's why I'm ringing. Have the police called you?'

'No,' said Renée, wary now. 'Why should they have? I've given my statement.'

'Well, they called me,' said Natasha. 'And they've said that the bloke who called 999 originally, the one they arrested, they've said he heard us all talking, and he's told them we heard the splash.'

'WHAT?' screamed Renée, and then she started swearing, saying fuck fuck fuck over and over like a mantra, before moving onto panting, virtually hyperventilating, down the phone – and then there was a tremendous crash in Natasha's ear.

'Renée? Renée? Are you there?'

'Yes, sorry,' said Renée finally, after much clattering. She seemed slightly calmer now. 'I dropped my phone. Oh my God, what are we going to do? We'll be arrested. This is horrendous.'

'No we won't,' said Natasha. 'I've looked it up on Google – I went to an Internet cafe, they'll never be able to trace the search back to me. We haven't committed a crime as such. As long as we say we heard a splash but that we thought it was just a bird, we'll be OK. And even if he did hear us say something about her drowning it was obviously a joke.'

'But we've already said the opposite,' said Renée, moving over to the window, staring down at the choking grey of the main road below, crying now. 'We've given our statements, we told the police we didn't hear anything. We'll get done for perjury.'

'I've looked that up too,' said Natasha, and she sounded almost pleased with herself. 'We haven't perjured ourselves, you can only do that in court. We can just change our police statement, people do it all the time apparently.'

'Really? But . . . but that makes us look terrible . . . and surely . . . even if we don't get done for that . . . surely it must be a crime to leave someone to drown? Isn't it negligence or something?'

Renée's obviously spent a lot of time agonising over this, Natasha thought. She hoiked her Lycra shorts out of her bottom as she jumped across a ditch. She should've been proactive and looked into it, like I have.

'No, we haven't committed any crime,' she continued, still not remotely short of breath despite her pace. 'We weren't responsible for her in the eyes of the law for a start – that's only the case if she were a dependant, a child or something, not a grown woman. We simply say we didn't go back when we heard the splash *because we thought it wasn't her*. I'm pretty certain the absolute worst that can happen is that we can have a civil action against us, not a criminal one. That's called tort law, I've read up on it. But we can talk to lawyers about that if we need to, once everything's in the open.'

Renée was too busy thinking about Camilla and her bloody raspberry torte, how the picnic had been all her idea, how if they'd never met up in the first place then Siobhan wouldn't be dead, to really take in any more of what Natasha was saying. She'd had quite enough shocks lately. She couldn't believe Natasha could be so matter-of-fact about her friend's death, almost like she was discussing her team's monthly sales performance or what to get for dinner. She knew Natasha hadn't really got on with Siobhan in recent years, even before that final devastating night – they'd become the exact opposite of each other by the end, Siobhan the ditzy single girl and Natasha the uber-Superwoman – but even so, it was a bit callous. Natasha seemed to have lost any kind of heart these days, Renée thought, was more driven and ambitious than ever. She imagined her now, head-to-toe in designer running gear, about the only thing she ever wore when she wasn't in one of her hideous suits, face tight from Botox, sprinting home to set up a spreadsheet about probable outcomes. She was ghastly, really she was, how had she changed so much, how had they ever been friends?

67

Belgravia

Sergeant Hunter looked at the beautiful pale woman sat across the table from him. Her lawyer looked out of place in the scruffy interview room – in his pinstriped suit and yellow silk handkerchief he would have been more at home in a gentleman's club; he had that air about him, as if this was all beneath him. Sergeant Hunter didn't think he needed to ask any more questions; she was the fourth woman he'd interviewed in the last two days and she was just repeating the same boring account of the evening – they'd obviously all got together and colluded to make sure they got their stories straight, despite the monumental acrimony they'd had towards each other by the time they'd left Hyde Park, according to Terry Kingston.

Now there was an odd bloke, Sergeant Hunter thought. He'd seemed like such a creep at first, but it turned out he'd been the only one who'd tried to save the dead woman, after her so-called friends had all just upped and left her to her fate. And it appeared he'd only lied at first to try to protect his half-brother – it seemed now they were finally getting to the bottom of exactly what had happened it was Terry Kingston who had more morals than the rest of them put together.

Sergeant Hunter wasn't interested in the interview with this woman. They'd had the pathologist's report back and nothing she was saying added to it. No, it seemed he'd have to let her go. He asked her a few more questions, just for the hell of it. Let her sweat a bit, he'd thought. Even if it did turn out she was criminally in the clear, which seemed likely, seeing as the funeral had already been approved to go ahead (what had become of the British criminal-justice system!), morally she and her friends were guilty as hell in his book. Typical selfish middle-class values, he told himself, somewhat bigotedly – give me my Sandra and the lads at the snooker club any day over these stuck-up cows.

Sergeant Hunter took a final glance through his notes to check he'd covered everything. He looked up, saw her frightened frigid face next to her lawyer's fleshy smug one, sighed and said, 'OK, madam, that's all, you're free to go.'

68

Royal Leamington Spa, The Midlands

Juliette drove Sissy to the funeral in her Range Rover.
The others took the train – Natasha and Juliette were no
longer talking if they could help it, now Juliette's affair
with Natasha's husband was out in the open, and it seemed
Juliette would never speak to Renée again either, after all
the things she'd said about Stephen at the picnic, not to
mention the further vile accusations she'd made in Juliette's garden. Anyway, it was more practical that way – it
would have been unbearable in the car with everyone. It
was a nightmare, but despite everything they had to go:
they were some of Siobhan's oldest friends, and they'd
been together on the very night she'd died. They couldn't
not go.

As Juliette parked up in the narrow car-lined lane, she
couldn't believe what a huge event the funeral was. The
media were there and an outside screen had been erected
for all the mourners who wouldn't fit inside the church.
Juliette was horrified by the photographers – who immediately recognised her and began taking photos – but

more than that she was shocked by how many people had turned up, for Siobhan. She'd had no idea Siobhan had so many friends. 'It must be because it's all over the news,' she overheard Natasha whisper, as Natasha sat down behind her in the church, and Juliette thought there was no need for cattiness at a time like this, but of course she didn't say anything.

The service had an unbearable poignancy that inked through the air and magnified everyone's sadness. Siobhan's father, an elegant old-fashioned-looking man, stood tall through his grief as he addressed the congregation, dark suit immaculate, tie militarily straight, hand-made shoes polished, as he talked of his love for his funny, eccentric, warm-hearted daughter, who although at times could be a little outspoken perhaps, undiplomatic even, had empathy and generosity that more than made up for it. He spoke of his and his wife's pride at how well Siobhan had done over the years, how she had grown into such a capable young woman who'd achieved so much in her career (it appeared she'd just been made a director at her publishing company; how come she'd never told them that?), how much her boyfriend Matt had adored her, although she often didn't seem to realise it. Derek had choked a little at this point, and stopped, seemingly unable to go on, and after a few seconds the vicar had taken his arm and guided him gently back to his seat, where Margaret had grabbed his hand and held it tightly, as though letting go would cause something to break.

*

284

Matt's speech was even more devastating, if anything. Natasha thought it odd that only Camilla and Sissy had ever met him before, as it seemed he'd been going out with Siobhan for ages, and he was much better-looking than she'd expected – how had Siobhan pulled such a dish? Matt spoke of Siobhan's lust for life, her success in her career, her courage, her risk-taking, her integrity. He talked of her love of acting that she'd discovered in just the last year or so, when she'd joined a group and even been in a play in a small theatre in Chiswick. Natasha and the others were stunned – *how come she'd never told them?* It was like the service was about a different person to the one they'd known.

But it was when Matt spoke about how Siobhan could never do too much to help someone and was such a wonderful friend, that Natasha felt uncomfortable, and the others succumbed to remorseful tears. Although the service, as these things are wont to, teetered into over-indulgence at times, the odd thing was it felt real, heartfelt, not just false flattery in death. Natasha found herself recalling the time when Nigel had cancer, of Siobhan helping Sissy through the pregnancy, the birth, although Sissy had been so delirious with grief she'd barely noticed. She remembered Nigel's death ten years later, of Siobhan being there for Sissy, and then *every* weekend for months afterwards, of how Sissy's kids had adored Siobhan. When the music signalling the end of the service started up ('Wishing I Was Lucky', by Wet Wet Wet) the irony felt unbearable, and Natasha wondered who'd picked it. Siobhan had adored that song, had played it over and over

285

again in the flat in Bristol, and although Natasha had pretended it had driven her mad, she'd secretly loved it too.

As Natasha sat there, her thoughts in turmoil, she finally acknowledged that she'd misjudged Siobhan, not appreciated the person she'd become, and probably always had been. She'd written her off in recent years as nothing more than a calamitous irritant. Natasha felt faint. She had failed her friend in life and *had left her in death*. She was despicable. They were all despicable. As she looked desperately around the church, searching for something, someone to comfort her, she could see the shame on all their faces, every last one – even the one who had no need to feel ashamed, the one who'd already left and truly hadn't heard the splash.

69

St Pancras, Central London

Three and a half weeks after the funeral, Siobhan Benson's parents travelled from their home in Royal Leamington Spa to the coroner's court for the inquest. They were still in shock. Margaret hadn't slept for longer than a couple of hours at a time, not since the police had knocked on their door on that terrible Sunday afternoon nearly two months earlier, and the exhaustion had changed the shape of her face: it looked skull-like now, as if the flesh around her eyes had been prematurely gouged out by maggots. Derek stood tall and stiff, with a muted, sad air about him, and as they walked from their Audi past the waiting photographers he put an arm around his wife's shoulder, but the contact didn't comfort either of them. There was no comfort to be had.

The coroner felt for the Bensons (the most difficult inquests were always when it was somebody's child involved) and he ushered them away from the throng into a private room and offered them coffee, as there was still half an hour to kill. No-one spoke. Largely to break the silence, the coroner went over what was about to happen, although the Bensons were already vaguely aware of it. He gently reiterated that they'd only be trying to establish the cause of death today, not who, if anyone, was responsible. He showed them the list of people he'd be calling as witnesses. Margaret Benson looked at the names, recognising many of them, and felt sad that her daughter had even been out with these women. Siobhan had been so hurt over the years at their various put-downs and slights, Margaret had tried on several occasions to suggest that maybe she shouldn't see them so often, maybe even leave some of those relationships in the past – it was no good keep getting upset, dear, she'd said. But Siobhan hadn't wanted to – they were her friends, she'd insisted, and besides, they all had so much shared history, accumulated like books over the years, and you never got rid of those, did you? Margaret knew that her daughter only really saw Camilla and Sissy by the end, she'd never failed to give Sissy support with those poor children. That was the thing about Siobhan, her mother thought, her throat constricting, she'd always wanted to help people. And now, following one of the most innocent activities you could hope to partake in – a picnic in the park with some old college friends – her only child was dead.

The inquest was underway but Margaret could barely follow it. She understood a few things. She understood that her beloved daughter, Siobhan Alice Benson, had died, aged forty-four, at approximately 22:35 on Thursday 7th July 2011 at The Serpentine Lake, Hyde Park, London.

She understood that she had died through drowning – they were quite unfussy in the way they said that, there seemed to be no fancy medical term for that way of dying. But from this point onwards Margaret struggled to keep up with what was going on. Apparently, the pathologist said, there were marks on the side of the deceased's head consistent with a heavy object, perhaps a poly-amide something or other, but not necessarily so. (*What did he say? How did she get the marks? Did someone hit her with the polya-whatever-it-was-called?*) He said Siobhan might have been unconscious when she hit the water. (*Is that why she didn't scream?*) A post-mortem analysis estimated that she had 164mg of alcohol per 100ml of blood at the time of her death. (*Did that make her drunk? Is that why she drowned?*)

Margaret's head felt thick, as if she had a heavy cold, and the words were finding it hard to punch through to her brain. She was struggling to remember the meaning of quite basic expressions, let alone the technical ones. Eventually the pathologist finished and sat down, looking chipper, self-satisfied. He was small and geeky, and Margaret was dismally reminded of an excited little boy with a bucket of worms, one of those ghoulish types who'd been born to poke over dead rotting flesh, into unex-plored cavities, her precious daughter's body nothing but a macabre journey of discovery for him.

Through her bewilderment Margaret still started – even though she'd been expecting her – as the first of the witnesses took the stand: the shock of flaming hair, pulled back as if in penitence, the exquisite pale face. She listened more intently now, as Juliette explained her relationship with 'the deceased', described how the evening had somewhat disintegrated, with 'the deceased' running off into the night after what Juliette described as a 'bit of an argument'. Margaret heard Juliette admit (quietly, her voice choking) that they'd all been drinking, were all rather drunk in fact, and that no-one had known where Siobhan had gone, they'd just assumed she'd gone home. And so, she said, when they'd heard a splash it hadn't even occurred to them that it might be Siobhan, they'd thought it was just a bird or something – after all, there was no struggling or splashing afterwards – and so they'd left without going to check (Juliette looked ashamed at this point, like she might cry). Margaret watched the coroner nod and ask Juliette to take her seat, and apart from the deep screaming red of Juliette's hair the scene felt blank, colourless, unreal to her.

The next bit Margaret couldn't understand. She knew why everyone was gasping and covering their mouths with horror, it was clear Terry had said something dreadful (' "She can bloody drown for all I care," I heard one of them say, Your Honour,') but she struggled to understand the implications. Did Siobhan's so-called friends know that the splash was her all along? *Did they deliberately leave her to drown?* No. Surely not. Margaret slumped suddenly in her chair and, as Derek stood up shouting for a doctor, the coroner hurriedly adjourned the inquest.

Fortunately, it turned out Margaret Benson had only fainted, and a shot of brandy that appeared from somewhere amidst the mayhem appeared to sort her out. Afterwards Derek explained to his wife what she'd failed to comprehend: that Terry had told the inquest the details of the conversation he'd overheard, which was that the women had agreed at the time to say they hadn't heard the splash if it turned out Siobhan really had drowned – and how he, Terry, couldn't be sure exactly which individuals had been involved in the conversation, it had been too dark to see. Derek told his wife how Terry had said he'd seen one of the women stride off into the night half a minute before the others, so she possibly really hadn't heard anything, had left with a clear conscience at least. Amidst the chaos it seemed that no-one knew which woman it was though, and because of the disruption none of the rest of them gave evidence that day.

70

Canary Wharf

On the afternoon of the inquest, Stephen Forsyth was sent home from work. It was all too awkward. Following the euphoria of his newspaper breaking the original story of the body in the lake (online, at least, they even beat *Sky News* to it), over the following weeks other less convenient facts had kept revealing themselves, like rampaging acne. Facts like the dead woman being a friend of the editor's wife. Like there having been a group of other women present at the time, *including his wife*. Like the fact they'd all been arguing just before the woman died, as witnessed by a small-time private detective who had quite remarkably turned out to be Stephen's very own half-brother.

As the limo (probably the last one he'd get out of this fucking job) crossed Tower Bridge Stephen didn't bother with the view, he was too busy seething. Those early revelations had been awkward enough, but Stephen had managed to ride out that storm; he had a thick skin, it hadn't been too bad. It had only been a matter of time after that though – he'd known it would almost certainly all come out at the inquest, even though he'd offered Terry so much money to change his story, just a little. It wouldn't have changed the outcome, he'd argued, but Terry wouldn't budge, the sanctimonious wanker – he just kept saying he'd already made a statement, he couldn't alter his story now. Stephen had tried his hardest to bully him into it, although deep down he'd known it was madness, but he'd been desperate; and besides, he'd got away with worse before. So now, because of his weaselly half-brother's sudden penchant for integrity, the rest of the unsavoury facts that would ruin Stephen's hitherto soaring career were out.

Stephen had known he couldn't hope to have survived putting his own wife under surveillance while all the phone-hacking shit was going on, but it was Juliette's leaving her friend for dead, she and her friends apparently saying they didn't care if she drowned, that had caused the most sensational headlines, had finally finished him off. As the car crawled past the dismal sights of the New Kent Road down towards the Elephant and Castle, he let out a groan of humiliated rage, which the chauffeur politely ignored, he'd been doing this job long enough to know when to keep his mouth shut. Stephen was finished, and it was all Juliette's fault, the fucking bitch.

Back in Canary Wharf, Stephen's assistant Barry Smiley was jumping for joy, totally cock-a-bloody-hoop. He'd been as gobsmacked as everyone else when the story had started leaking out, in tantalising dribs and drabs at first, and then building relentlessly to the brilliantly shocking revelations of the inquest. He'd been amazed when everything had turned out to be true too: usually in these situations all manner of fantastical stories get bandied about before the less lurid facts are slowly extracted out of the morass of half-truths – but in this case the more wild the rumour the more accurate it had turned out to be. All it had taken was one emergency meeting less than two hours after the curtailing of the inquest for the publisher to decide to grant Stephen what they were euphemistically calling a 'compassionate leave of absence', and put Barry temporarily in charge.

But no-one was feeling very compassionate. Barry knew Stephen had been sidelined just so they could crack on with reporting the story, and although he ought to have felt sorry for his long-time boss, for the way his world had come tumbling down, Humpty Dumpty-like, he'd still been smarting from Stephen favouring that upstart reporter Maddie ahead of him, belittling him like that in front of her when she'd come bounding in like a bloody spaniel with her precious sodding lake story. So when Barry had been asked by the publisher to take over the reins, just for a few days initially while they worked out what to do, he had taken tremendous joy in sanctioning every ghastly detail to be printed. He had zero loyalty to his boss now – and why the hell should he after all he'd done for Stephen over the years, and for what? Barry had also delighted in transferring Maddie from the news desk to cover *Big Brother*, which no one watched any more, and he'd relished having Stephen's office cleaned out – he, Barry, couldn't possibly work in all that mess. It was retribution time. It was bloody brilliant.

71

Sardinia

The bedroom was still so brutally hot Nigel needed to do something, and quickly. He felt frantic, useless, frantically useless. He stared helplessly at the phone his daughter had fetched for him. He didn't know the Italian number for emergency services, and there was no one to ask. Maybe Sissy didn't need an ambulance anyway, he thought – he shouldn't panic, he just needed to cool her down. What else could he do? An idea came to him and, although it wasn't a particularly good one, action felt better than inaction. He raced to the walk-in store cupboard where Stephen and Juliette kept everything that there was no other place for: deckchairs and beach toys, a tool kit, a broken barbecue, spare faded cushions for the outdoor furniture, fishing gear, a battered straw picnic basket. *Yes.* Tucked on a high shelf right at the back was the silver electric fan, still in its box, that he'd remembered seeing. He clambered over the folded-up deckchairs and with his fingertips edged it off the shelf, catching it mid-air as his body bent half backwards into the sun-loungers.

Nigel ran back to the bedroom where his wife was lying with her eyes closed, breathing raggedly, her face obviously badly burned, and he took the fan out of its box and searched ineffectually for a socket, looking everywhere, seeing nothing. The ones for the bedside table lamps were hidden behind the bed, inaccessible. There must be another one somewhere, surely. He scanned along the skirting boards, and then for maybe the fourth time along the length of the frieze of the tastefully naked couple pastel-painted across the back wall, the one against which the bed was butted up – and finally, there in the corner, amongst the tangled twining grapevines, he found the socket. It was quite a way from the bed, but the cord should be just about long enough to reach her.

Nigel plugged in the fan but it refused to work. He checked its settings, made sure it was definitely switched on. He jiggled the plug around. As he wiggled the cord increasingly manically (he still wasn't sure it would do much good, but he didn't know what else to do, proving useless in a crisis) the fan leaped into life, and his heart jumped – thank God – and then the whirring stopped, fading out limply, as if it couldn't be bothered, as the electricity cut again. He cursed it. Maybe he should run next door, try to find someone else who could call a doctor, perhaps send Nell; she was sensible. He couldn't think straight – his mind had always been so clear in the face of his own impending death, but at the thought of anything happening to Sissy, he was derailed, a mess. Yes, he'd get Nell to go for help. He'd ask her in a minute, once he'd got this sodding fan going.

Nigel jiggled the plug in its socket yet again, and it seemed to move more freely than it should, as though there was merely space behind it, rather than wall. The fan jittered in and out of life, teasing him. The TV ads were deafening from the lounge, and there were some groans he didn't like the sound of, this was Italy after all, you never knew what they might put on, even in the middle of the day.

'Turn that TV off now!' he yelled, but the children ignored him. He shoved in the cord harder and waggled it angrily, furiously, and at long, long last the fan started up its shiny revolutions, rhythmically in synch with the moans from the living room, and at the very same time a blue crack of electricity flew through the air from the socket, and then it flew through Nigel, and the fan stopped again.

72

Wandsworth

Early on a Wednesday morning in September, not long
past midnight, Stephen Forsyth sat in the office in the
eaves of his two-million-pound house – perfectly located
close to the common and just five minutes' walk from his
favourite (Michelin-starred, no less) restaurant on Belle-
vue Road – with his own newspaper's site open on the
twenty-seven-inch iMac that graced his vintage Danish
desk. His wife lay passed out on the bed in the luxurious
guest room below. Although Stephen was ridiculously
drunk, he could still just about focus on the text. The
next day's stories had been published two minutes earlier.
It was the fourth one, on this, the day after the inquest,
which attracted his attention. 'Mother who abandoned
her son for love' was the headline. 'Loner Kingston', ran
the copy, enthusiastically endorsed by Barry a couple
of hours earlier, 'developed a deeply entrenched dis-
trust, verging on hatred, of women after his own mother
Eileen walked out on him, according to an unnamed
source. Terry Kingston, who quite sensationally is the

secret half-brother of this paper's editor, Stephen Forsyth, who is currently suspended (Barry must have had that bit put in, Stephen fumed), was the prime suspect in the initial inquiry into the death of Siobhan Benson, 44. Kingston's mother left the family home when her son was just two years old to move in with her former next-door neighbour, a mere half a mile away, and she soon bore a new child, Stephen. According to our source, Terry Kingston never forgave her.' Stephen finished reading, put his head in his hands and sobbed snottily, like a toddler.

Ten or so hours later, Juliette and Stephen sat sullenly opposite each other across the solid oak table, which he noticed was badly scratched in one place (had one of the kids been scribbling again, did she ever fucking supervise them?) in their large German-manufactured kitchen. Its white high-gloss finish was sparkling, the surfaces unusually clear of the normal detritus associated with a household made up of a (before now) largely absent father, sluttish mother and three unruly children. The housekeeper had been so titillatingly embarrassed by the revelations of the *Daily Mail* when she'd arrived that morning it had given her a rare flare of energy, and she had taken to the kitchen as if to a human catastrophe clear-up – an earthquake perhaps, or maybe a hurricane. She had donned her pale-blue housecoat and pink Marigolds and whipped through the room, emptying the dishwasher, piling all the clean stuff onto the island (making the place look temporarily worse), putting away the cutlery with dangerous efficiency: large knives deftly dispensed to the magnetic rack on the wall, knife-thrower-like; forks and table knives and spoons and teaspoons tossed into the appropriate sections of the cutlery drawer expertly, like quoits at the fair; ladles and serving spoons zealfully attached to hooks like hanging victims.

Mrs Redfern had then turned her attention to all the crap on the draining board: dinner plates stacked up, still full of leftovers; two wine glasses, one smeared with gash-red lipstick; three (three!) empty wine bottles; an assortment of dirty bone-china mugs from Heals and Harrods and various unheard-of stately homes; half-full tumblers of orange juice and water; flattened individual smoothie cartons oozing gunk; a lone squashed pear with a single bite out of it. *It's an absolute bloomin' disgrace this house*, she'd thought, as she picked bills and colour supplements out of slimy puddles on the counter-tops, shook sticky unidentifiable drips and burned crumbs off them onto the work surface, scraped the resulting mess off the counter into her rubber-gloved hand to be dispatched into the bin, dunked the dishcloth in hot soapy water and cleaned the Corian (*whatever that is*, she harrumphed, *all that money and you're not allowed to use Flash on it, I ask you*) surfaces so they shone. She'd then vacuumed and mopped the floor like a maniac before whirling upstairs, uncharacteristic energy not yet spent, to attend to the children's rooms – on her way stomping noisily past the firmly shut door to the master bedroom in the hope that someone might come out; sneaking a hopeful peek into the spare room, where she tantalisingly saw a pair of beautiful bare feet hanging over the end of the bed; listening fruitlessly at the bottom of the stairs up to the office in the eaves.

Stephen and Juliette were not appreciative of Mrs Redfern's earlier efforts as they sat at the table nursing monumental hangovers – in fact they didn't even notice that the kitchen was tidy for a change. Juliette probably wouldn't have done anyway, even on a good day, and Stephen was too wrapped up in the horror of his apparently imploding life. It was disastrous. The press was still getting tremendous mileage out of the body in the lake story, especially Stephen Forsyth's involvement, there were just so many angles. And now on top of all the damage that had already been done to Stephen's reputation, this week the *Sun* had taken delight in the unveiling of Juliette's affair (as it turned out it *was* bloody true, the whore – and not just with anyone, but with that fucking snake Alistair Smart!). Stephen felt sick to his stomach. That wasn't even the half of it, it got way worse than that. Last night with his wife, in their drunken, violent shouting match (Juliette had gone for him first, he hadn't meant to catch her eye, he'd just been defending himself, for fuck's sake), she'd told him that Siobhan had claimed *he'd* been to blame for Nigel's death in Sardinia, and that when she'd blurted it out Renée had gone nuts and started calling him a murderer. Stephen was terrified – he knew he wasn't guilty of *murdering* Nigel, but he must admit he'd always felt slightly responsible, and if it got out he definitely could be accused of fraud, or perverting the course of justice or something – or maybe even manslaughter, he didn't know the Italian law on that.

How the fuck would Siobhan have known about the socket though? He thought he'd dealt with all that. Sissy must have known somehow, and must have told her. He tried to clear his head, ignore his wife as she sat half-dead across the table from him. OK, he'd known he'd done up the apartment on the cheap, even been aware that the electrics were faulty, but he hadn't meant to *kill* anyone, and it's not like he had wired the sodding plugs himself. And he *had* felt terrible about Nigel, killed off by electricity, not cancer, in the end, and after everything he'd been through. But really, Stephen told himself yet again, as if saying it often enough would make it true, Nigel had been lucky to be alive anyway, he'd been read the last rites ten years beforehand, no-one ever thought he was going to pull through. The cancer would probably have come back anyway, it usually did, and Nigel had had ten good bonus years. And at least the kids' screams at discovering Nigel had alerted the neighbours, so they'd managed to get Sissy to hospital in time; they hadn't been left as orphans, thank Christ. They could so easily have lost their mother, might well have done save for the accident, if all Nigel had been doing for her severe heatstroke was plugging in a fucking fan. Surely it was better for them to have had their father die rather than their mother?

As Stephen sat with his head in his hands, he remembered how much he'd panicked when he'd first got the call about Nigel's death, had known he had to do something – you never knew with the Italian authorities, it definitely could have got nasty. So he'd contacted Terry's brother-in-law, Gianfranco, as soon as he could, just in case the police did end up getting involved, and Gianfranco had sorted it all out, had had the socket repaired by someone who knew what they were doing – Stephen's offer had been far too attractive for him not to.

Stephen had always thought that would be the end of it, but it turned out Sissy had somehow known what he'd done all along. And now, thanks to Siobhan, apparently so did the rest of Juliette's friends. He was fucked, especially as someone had already leaked it – even if the press hadn't actually implicated him yet there'd still been a story about someone dying in his holiday apartment. What if some dogged reporter decided to check it out further? He couldn't go down for murder though, he told himself, he definitely wasn't a murderer . . . it had been an *accident*. He hadn't wanted Nigel to die, he'd quite liked the bloke. How dare anyone call him a murderer?

As Juliette slumped further into her chair, Stephen thought of all her fucking bombshells last night, all the revelations, the other rumours circling – and he didn't know what the hell he was going to do about any of them, now they were surfacing, rotten and stinking like Siobhan's bloated corpse. He was finished, surely.

Stephen let out a howl, and it sounded villainous, comedic, although in truth it was desperate. (Juliette barely looked up, it was like she'd been drugged or something.) He'd been humiliated, abandoned, well and truly shafted. His life was being picked over as if by vultures on a stinking rubbish dump, and although he tried not to acknowledge it, Stephen realised it was what they call comeuppance, retribution. He thought about Nigel,

Juliette, Renée, and he felt defeated, ready to succumb, penitent even. He deserved what was coming to him.

As Stephen continued to look across the table at his ghost-like wife, whom he had adored once as an example of what he could become, he thought of the hateful, damning things they had screamed at each other last night, and he wondered whether the children or, worse, the neighbours had heard, resulting in yet more ways for damaging stories to get out. And as he stared at the puffiness around his wife's left eye, Stephen wondered where a rope or some kind of lead was, so he could go out to the garage now, before he had to face anyone.

73

Berkshire

'Hello, Giles, it's me, Cynthia . . . Yes, yes, I'm fine. I'm so sorry to ask, but are you able to come home? . . . Yes, I know it's the middle of the day, it's just Juliette's here . . . Yes, yes she is, she got the train, I picked her up from the station . . . Now, yes please . . . She wants to know about her mother . . . Yes, I do mean her . . . Yes, yes, she has . . . All right. (*Long pause.*) Hello, yes, I'm still here . . . You can? Oh, thank you! See you soon, dear. Bye-bye.'

Juliette looked at her mother, at the lines around her eyes that were beginning to attest to her approaching middle-age, and she felt sad for Cynthia, could see how hard it was for her too, but it couldn't be helped. She had to discover the truth at last – it was as if once she'd started this, had found out the name, made the fruitless phone calls, the real story had to come unfurling out, whatever it might prove to be. She'd waited her entire life, but it seemed she couldn't wait any longer. She needed to know *now*.

Cynthia seemed unsure what to do with herself while

305

they waited for Giles, so she made her excuses and went upstairs to put away the clean laundry, blowing her nose as she went, and when she'd finished she came down to the kitchen to make more tea, and her eyes were red. Juliette had moved from the living room and was already sitting at the kitchen table – its blue and white gingham oilcloth and bowl of jaunty yellow tulips made her feel better somehow. Juliette smiled nervously at Cynthia, too on edge to notice her mother's pain. Yes, she thought, it was much nicer in here, with the dog asleep on his bed in the corner, this was where she wanted to hear her story. She took off her lace gloves and looked at her hands, at the wide palms, the chipped polish, the long snaking lifeline. She studied her fingerprints, unique to her, made by someone. She waited.

74

Barnes

Natasha sat at her dining table looking out onto the garden, a huge glass of wine and today's newspapers in front of her, a cigarette to her lips: it seemed that once she'd started smoking again after Siobhan's death she'd been unable to stop, especially since the inquest. As she flicked through the pages, she decided that she really did have to divorce Alistair now, there was no alternative course of action after all this – the past few weeks had been intolerable, really they had. Her whole carefully constructed world had come tumbling down, her sham marriage revealed, the hardness in her heart right there for all to see, in three glorious double-page spreads of a gutter tabloid. All their secrets had been paraded like trophies: the affairs, the feuds, the abandonment of their friend, the role of Stephen's unsavoury half-brother, even something about Nigel's death – how on earth had they dug that one up? The one thing that hadn't leaked out, thank God, was that she and the others had changed their story – that they'd lied to the police at first, and only admitted later what they'd heard, what they'd said, when called back in for further questioning after Terry Kingston's statement had directly contradicted theirs. Not that it had helped at the inquest, of course – it had still been clear they'd deserted their friend, they'd still come across as callous bitches (*She can bloody drown for all I care*), just not lying ones. Their lives would be forever blighted by it.

Natasha wondered for the millionth time what had actually happened that night, how Siobhan had really died. She supposed no-one would ever know for sure. They'd never charged Stephen's brother with anything, and they hadn't managed to turn up any other potential murderer – but neither had they ever been one hundred per cent certain what had caused the dent in her head. And of course no-one knew what Siobhan had been thinking at the time, and it was too late to ask her. Maybe she did it deliberately, Natasha thought, surely that was the best answer of all, if she'd had to end up dead, that she'd intended it. She'd seemed so miserable that night anyway – with her job, her boyfriend – and then she must have regretted some of the things she'd said, they'd been so horrendous; and besides she'd been completely paralytic, couldn't possibly have been being rational. Yes, maybe that was it.

Natasha stood up. She was in her office attire: trademark suit, crisp blouse, high heels. Her dangly earrings looked incongruous, ridiculous, her pathetic attempt at cheering herself up, moving on, getting over Siobhan's death – after all, she'd been fond of Siobhan once, wouldn't wish what had happened to her on anyone. Natasha had been planning on going back into work this morning, but now it came to it she found she still couldn't face it. No, she'd have to continue to lie low until all the stories had died down – but now Stephen had been suspended that didn't seem very likely any time soon. His own newspaper's coverage seemed to be even more vicious than the others' – he could never go back there after what they'd written about him and his family, and she wondered briefly what would happen to him, not that she gave a shit of course, not after what he'd done.

So, thought Natasha, shaking off her maudlin mood, snapping into proactivity – if she wasn't going back to work today she needed to do something productive, the kids wouldn't be home for hours. She left the warmth of the dining room, with its plate-glass windows giving onto the huge slimy-looking pond Alistair had insisted on having dug in their garden, rammed full of monster carp that she vehemently hated but which he refused to get rid of.

Yes, that's it. She'd go and sort things out with her husband, start the ball rolling, now was as good a time as any, now she'd made up her mind at last. As she climbed the stairs, she noticed the bare patches on the carpet, a single long loose thread. Maybe she could request some samples, the carpet needed replacing and she never usually had time to sort things like that out, not unless she had a project on. She might as well make an effort to get the house looking nice, she'd be staying in it with the children, obviously. Perhaps she could also order some towels from The White Company while she was at it, they could do with some new ones.

When Natasha reached the closed door to her husband's office, she felt suddenly unsure of what she was doing. It was unlike her to hesitate once she'd made a decision, but she still wasn't feeling quite right – which was hardly surprising, she tried to remind herself. As she stood there hesitating, her fingers on the door handle, she briefly remembered how much she'd loved Alistair once, been mad for him, couldn't get enough of every single part of him. She'd believed in him then. In between climbing her own career ladder and shagging his brains out, she'd channelled her endless energy into helping him professionally, launching his book career with her normal invincibility, never taking no for an answer; she'd been so sure of his talent. He'd have been nothing without her.

So where had it all gone wrong? Natasha acknowledged now that Alistair had started to get fed up with her years ago, perhaps even before the wedding itself (maybe looking back she had been a bit dogmatic about it all), and she knew he'd definitely found it difficult once the babies had come. She'd gone back to work after two months each time, and it had been so hard juggling her job, securing her promotions, running the house, organising the children, she'd ended up exhausted. No wonder she'd gone off the whole sex thing, it was normal, it was just that no-one ever admitted it. She sighed as she remembered Alistair's hurt at her rejections, felt a rare stab of sympathy for him. Maybe she shouldn't have put so much effort and energy into her own self-improvement, become so obsessed with keeping up with everyone else; perhaps she should have concentrated more on her marriage . . . but she'd needed every ounce of resolve and drive to have made it to university in the first place, to escape the dismal future that surely would have been hers if she'd stayed in Glasgow, and it seemed her ambition just didn't have an off switch. Poor Alistair, she'd been a lousy wife, Natasha saw that now.

And then she remembered that her husband had screwed one of her oldest friends – and not just Juliette, but that little strumpet author too. Possibly even worse, he'd passed off Lucinda Horne's books as his own, was a loafer, a *fraud*. Any remaining nostalgia for her marriage vanished in that moment, was gone for ever.

Natasha shifted her weight onto her left side, easing the pain in her bunions, and wondered how to do it. Knock? Barge in? She listened, but it was quiet. She turned the handle. It was time to confront him.

It was only when the door failed to open that she realised it was locked. *She didn't know he had a lock on it.* He's probably wanking in there, she thought with disgust, and it was the most perceptive insight she'd had about her husband in years.

Natasha didn't bother knocking, or waiting to see if Alistair had heard her and would come out anyway. She turned around and stomped back downstairs to the dining room, where she took a seat at the table facing the fish, opened her laptop, lit up yet another cigarette, and demanded the divorce by email instead.

75

Berkshire

Juliette looked younger than her nearly nineteen years as she sat opposite her mother in the kitchen of her childhood home. Cynthia couldn't help but notice how beautiful her daughter was. She was glad Juliette had taken off the fingerless gloves she'd had on earlier, Cynthia wasn't too sure about the whole Madonna look. She wouldn't have said anything though, Juliette always seemed too fragile to take any kind of criticism, no matter how well-meaning, and especially not today.

After what seemed like forever they heard the sound of wheels on the gravel, the car door slamming, the key in the lock. They waited, unable to look at each other, as they heard shuffling and rustling in the hallway. *Finally* Juliette's father came into the kitchen, looking older, anxious. A cold wind swept in with him, and Juliette shivered.

'Hello, Daddy,' said Juliette. 'Thank you for coming home, I'm so sorry to be such a drama queen.' She paused, not sure what else to say.

Cynthia pushed a mug of tea (cups and saucers were reserved for the front room) across the table at Giles, and it was brown and swampy, stewed.

'You start, Juliette, dear,' said her father, taking a sip and trying not to grimace, his voice low and steady.

Still Juliette said nothing. Where did she begin?

'It's all right,' he said. 'You can tell us, love.' His kindness made her eyes prick.

'Elisabeth Potts,' she said finally. It was all she could think of to say. She took a breath. 'She was my real mother.' Juliette saw Cynthia flinch. 'Oh, sorry, I mean my birth mother.' She looked at Cynthia. 'You know her, don't you, Mummy?'

'Oh no,' thought Cynthia. '*Oh no.*' Although she'd always known a lot more about her daughter's adoption than she'd ever let on, what could she ever have said? How do you tell a little child the truth of how they came into the world, why they are not wanted, when you don't even know yourself? As she sat there, unsure where to begin, her mind wandered back through the past nineteen years. She remembered how for years Juliette had been obsessed with who her real mummy was, why she had left her, where she lived, what colour her hair was, whether at her real mummy's house there was a swing in the back garden, like at her best friend Sara Day's house. Cynthia had found it all terribly upsetting. The adoption people had said not to tell her she was even adopted until she was older, that tended to be the advice in those days, but Cynthia was quite progressive like that, knew that wasn't good for her daughter, and had always tried to tell her at least a version of the truth right from the very beginning. Sometimes she'd regretted her candour. She remembered hating having to have discussions with Juliette about how her real mummy had loved her but wasn't able to keep her, and no, she really didn't know why, but what she did know was that there must have been a very good reason (what harm could one little lie do?). And Cynthia would always go on to tell her daughter that they were all very lucky to have each other, and how much Juliette was wanted by her new parents, how much she was loved, but Juliette had gone on and on about her 'real mummy' until sometimes Cynthia had wanted to scream. In the end the eight-year-old Juliette had caught Cynthia at a bad moment, as she'd just been let down by one of the mothers who normally made cakes for the school's summer fair, and for once Cynthia had snapped.

'Look, Juliette, I've told you all I can about your mummy. *I'm your mummy now.* I really don't want to hear anything more about it.' And she had stormed out of the kitchen and banged the door behind her, which was most unlike her, and although she had apologised profusely, little Juliette had never mentioned her real mummy again, and even when Cynthia had tried to bring up the subject herself, Juliette never wanted to talk about it any more. In fact, it wasn't just that she didn't speak of it, it had seemed to Cynthia that she'd closed it down somewhere deep in her mind, and she'd stopped wondering, stopped caring, stopped thinking about where she had come from originally. From that point on she was just Juliette Greene, from Swallowfield, Hampshire, with a mummy and daddy who might not be her real parents but who she knew adored her, and a beloved pony, Popcorn. Who needs two mummies anyway?

Cynthia looked at Giles. He nodded, almost imperceptibly. She gulped. Her mouth felt dry. The words sounded like they were coming from someone else, someone far away, in another room perhaps.

'Elisabeth's my sister,' said Cynthia.

76

Wandsworth

The weird thing after the grotesque showdown with her husband (who decided, once he'd sobered up, not to hang himself after all) was that all Juliette wanted was her mum, her real mum. She knew better than to call her though, she'd learned her lesson over the years, and she didn't think she could handle Elisabeth Potts' dismissive platitudes, Juliette preferred silence to those. Stephen had been surprisingly compliant since the night she'd confronted him – he was obviously shit scared she'd leak something. She must admit she was tempted, she was so horrified by what he'd done, someone needed to make sure he got his comeuppance – or perhaps she ought to go to the *police* instead of the papers. Why should he keep getting away with everything? She knew she wouldn't do it though, she couldn't do that to the children, they were unsettled enough as it was, particularly Noah. If her friend wasn't going to press charges then she wouldn't stir it up, it wasn't her business, not really. She was only married to Stephen, she hadn't actually been involved, thank goodness.

Juliette lay in the enormous bed with the luxurious mattress that she'd shared with Stephen for so many years and shuddered. She would never share it with him again, not after this. Their marriage was *over*. She turned her head into her pillow and let out a sob. Poor Cynthia wouldn't do. She wanted her mother.

The phone rang and rang downstairs. Juliette ignored it as ever, her head still buried in the pillow – Mrs Redfern could get it, she seemed desperate to know what was going on. Eventually the phone stopped and Juliette welcomed back the silence, like an old friend. Then the door opened, just a little, enough for half a curly grey head to make an appearance.

'Juliette, are you awake?' she said. 'It's one of your friends, I think. She says it's important.'

Juliette groaned and took her head from under the covers. Her hair was wild in the half-light. Mrs Redfern tiptoed across the luxurious deep-piled carpet and handed her the phone. She slumped it against her shoulder, barely holding it, and it was slippery against the silk of her nightdress.

'Juliette?'

'Yes,' she said.

'It's me, Camilla. I was just calling to see how you are. You never return my calls.'

'Oh.'

'How are you doing?'

'Not bad,' said Juliette. She started to cry, silently.

'Why are you blanking me, Juliette? What have I done in all this, except maybe be a little bossy over what to make for the picnic? I can't help it, it's my upbringing.' She attempted a laugh.

'I'm not blanking you, Camilla,' said Juliette. She hesitated. She didn't want to be rude, Camilla of all people didn't deserve it. She decided in the end to be honest for once, it might do her good.

'It's just that I can't forgive myself for Siobhan's death, for leaving her like that. You don't have to live with the guilt – I know it sounds odd but you're lucky in a way, you'd gone, you didn't hear her.' She didn't mention Stephen, she couldn't face referring to what he'd allegedly done, although Camilla knew that too of course, everyone had bloody heard the night of the picnic. Juliette wept and had to stop talking for a while as Camilla waited, quietly. 'I just can't see any of you now, it's all too painful. I'm so sorry,' she said, and went to put down the phone.

'Stop, don't go,' said Camilla. 'You were drunk, you didn't know what you were doing, and anyway you didn't really think it was her, of course you didn't! You're not to blame, really you're not. Look, I'm at Mummy's in Holland Park, shall I pop over? Your cleaner said you're still in bed, and it's the afternoon, Juliette. You need your friends at times like these, I should know. Remember how you looked after me when Daddy died?'

Juliette remembered that time, twenty-five years ago,

how they'd all rallied round Camilla after her father's dreadful sex scandal, how they'd taken her off to Siobhan's uncle's cottage and looked after her, only for her father to hang himself the day after they'd got back, deep in the woods on his country estate. Camilla had still managed to stick out university though, and Juliette knew it was because they'd all pulled together, put a cocoon of love and support around their friend, as people who all live together at college tend to do at the time. They'd stuck together through everything back then, even though they'd all been so different – Camilla had been so totally posh in her stripy shirts with the collars turned up, and Juliette and Siobhan were Madonna wannabes, while Renée was punky, and Natasha always looked like she was going for a run, a vision in Lycra even then, and Sissy had looked like someone's little brother. But they'd all got through things *together* in Bristol. They'd been real friends back then.

'OK,' she said, in the end. What harm could it do? All the harm had been done.

'I'll get a cab, I'll be there in half an hour. So get off your skinny arse and put the kettle on!' And the way she said the word *off* rhymed with *wharf*.

'OK,' said Juliette. 'Thanks, Camilla. See you soon, bye.'

'Ciao, ciao,' said Camilla.

77

Berkshire

Juliette sat quietly opposite the tulips, which seemed to have drooped, lurched downwards under the weight of the revelation, disbelief trickling down her face, as Cynthia recalled exactly how Juliette had recognised her birth mother's name. She could remember every detail of that morning, what, ten or eleven years ago now, when they'd spent Christmas at Cynthia's mother's house, down in the New Forest. Juliette had been such an inquisitive little girl and her nana had loved her so, doted on her, more than poor Barney (as everyone knew but no-one dared acknowledge), and they had shared such a wonderful bond. Juliette had been an absolute poppet, so eager, so helpful – setting the table for Christmas, making glittery name tags for everyone, putting up the Christmas cards her nana had saved for the children to do on lengths of silver ribbon (not that Barney had bothered, he'd just ripped a couple up and been told off), alternating the sizes and shapes, making them look perfect. It would have been the 27th or 28th of December, the first day of post after Christmas. Juliette had been sitting patiently at the kitchen table, her bowl of Weetabix neatly eaten, waiting for Barney to finish so they could both get down, when the letterbox had clattered and her nana had asked her to run and pick up the post before her badly behaved dachshund Dexter got to it, he loved chewing it up. There had been only three items – a plain envelope with a cloudy window addressed to Mrs P. L. Simmons that looked boring to Juliette, a bill perhaps; a thin insubstantial-feeling card for Mrs Penelope Simmons; and another small square card addressed to someone unknown, and then in a different-coloured ink, as though written at a later time, a c/o alongside Penelope's address. As she sat in her cosy warm kitchen with not a teacup out of place, Cynthia went over that morning in vivid technicoloured detail – how she'd noticed as she buttered her toast that her fuchsia nail varnish had chipped, she must take it off; how she'd nagged Barney to finish his cereal (Golden Nuggets they were, she had scolded her mother for buying such junk, and Penelope had said, 'Oh it won't hurt them just this once'); how she'd watched Juliette come back into the kitchen and read out each envelope in turn, showing off what a fantastic reader she'd become; remembering Juliette's nana saying, 'Yes, you can open them, dear,' hearing Juliette reading, quite innocently in her little girl's voice, 'Elisabeth Potts – like pots and pans! – c/o (pronounced 'cee oh') 3 Willow Grove, Lyndhurst, Ha—' And then she, Cynthia, jumping up from the table and snatching the card off her daughter and saying, more sternly than she ever had, 'That one's not for you,' leaving poor

Juliette looking tearful, violated, and Cynthia knowing she had handled it badly, attracted way more attention than she needed to have, but it had been the shock of course.

Cynthia felt strangely calm, now the secret was out at last, and she wondered whether they should have just told Juliette years before, and to hell with Elisabeth's rights, sod what her sister had wanted – after all, she'd been so unfathomably selfish about everything. But it was too late to worry about any of that now, Cynthia had done her best, it was what it was. She looked across at her trembling daughter (or should she think of her as her *niece* now, what on earth was the etiquette?) who she loved more than anything, and as the colour slowly returned to Juliette's face, Cynthia sat patiently and waited for her to speak.

78

Wandsworth

The two women sat together on the bench at the bottom
of the gently fading garden, where the roses were brown
now and only held their shape until the wind blew them
into little fluttery petal bombs, flamboyant reminders of
the seasons passing. The air had a sharpness to it, as if
warning them that there wasn't much of summer left, but
the sun felt warm enough on their faces, and at least sitting
side by side Juliette didn't have to look her friend in the
eye. They chatted for a while about James and the kids,
and it was clear to Juliette that Camilla's married life was
so simple, based on real love and mutual respect, accept-
ing each other's differences, giving to each other rather
than transacting like a business arrangement – and she
realised how most of her friends' marriages weren't like
that at all. Camilla moved on to her favourite subject
now, filling time, telling Juliette about a super recipe
she'd found for making instant ice cream ('It's so easy,
Juliette, you should try it'), and Juliette told Camilla how
the kids were doing in school (not great), how little Jack

in particular had been unsettled since his father had moved out, how Flo seemed to be struggling with all the after-school activities and extra tuition and pressure she was under to get into secondary school, and how Noah just ran wild, immune to discipline, so Juliette simply didn't know what to do with him. Finally the conversation had faded out to nothing and they had both just sat there for a while, in silence.

It was Camilla who spoke first.

'So what are you going to do, Juliette?'

'About what?'

'You know.'

'I don't know.'

'About getting better.'

'I guess I just have to try to carry on, look after the kids, try to be a better mother, what else can I do?'

'You need to get your head straight, that's what. You owe it to the children, especially now you and Stephen have split up.'

Juliette sighed. 'I've tried all that. I've read every therapy book under the sun over the years. I've even tried writing it down – that's why I first went to Alistair, I never meant . . .' She looked sheepish, and Camilla knew it was Natasha she regretted betraying, not Stephen now. 'Nothing's worked,' Juliette continued. 'I'm officially a nutcase. I yelled at Noah again this morning, just for slopping his drink. I just seem to have so much rage in me . . . He hates me, and I can't say I blame him.'

Juliette's eyes started to fill, and although Camilla had told her that of course he didn't hate her, Juliette had hunched into herself and shaken her head and said, 'Yes, he does, he does,' and she'd confessed to what a hopeless mother she was, and how desperately she loved her children and didn't want to be fucking up their little lives but just didn't seem to know how not to, and she started crying really hard then, and Camilla hugged her until the weeping had stopped and then suggested, ever so gently, that maybe Juliette could get some help with her anger issues, and Juliette nodded, acknowledging it at last.

'You do know why you're so angry, don't you?' said Camilla. 'It's not just about the kids – or Stephen – or even Alistair.' Juliette coloured again. 'It's not even about what happened to poor Siobhan, although of course that's dreadful. It's all that business with your mother.'

'No it's not,' replied Juliette.

'Yes it is, Juliette. I told Renée at the time not to rush you. We were all so worried about it, once you told us what you were doing. I mean, one minute you didn't seem remotely interested in your birth mother, and the next you and Renée were dashing off to find her. It's a huge deal doing something like that, especially before you're ready. You just never had time to come to terms with it.'

'No, it wasn't even that.' Juliette hesitated. She'd never told any of them the real story: what she'd found out twenty-five years ago, who Elisabeth Potts really was. It was humiliating somehow, the rejection (by a young married couple, not a desperate teenager) even worse than she'd imagined. She'd felt ashamed that no-one, not Cynthia, not her grandmother, had told her the truth. She found over time she didn't blame them though, she'd known how hard they'd tried to get it right. No, she only blamed Elisabeth. The revelation of what Elisabeth had done, explained to her by her devastated adoptive parents in their sunny kitchen so long ago, had felt too painful, too overwhelming to take in, and so it had seemed easier to leave it all alone at first. It had been another few months before she'd tracked down and confronted Elisabeth, met her for the first time, and as Juliette thought back to that day, not long before the end of her first year at Bristol, she realised that it hadn't helped at all. In fact it had made it all worse.

Her old friend looked at her in the watery sunshine.

'Tell me what happened, Juliette, you need to talk about it.'

And so, for the first time ever, maybe because she'd hit rock bottom and had no-one else to turn to, Juliette did.

79

Berkshire

Juliette sat fiddling with her lace gloves, which she'd put back on, looking at Cynthia like she was mad. The yellow tulips between them were sickly in the sunlight. She finally spoke.

'What d'you mean, your sister? That . . . that makes you my . . . my *aunt*.' She thought of Cynthia's small square hands, the same shape as hers. How had she never noticed? '. . . That makes Nana my *real grandmother*, for goodness sake. What on earth do you mean?'

Cynthia picked at one of the tiny pearly buttons on her cardigan. 'Well, the thing is, darling, Elisabeth didn't feel ready to have a child. She was still so young, hadn't finished college . . .'

'And who was Alan Potts then? He's on my birth certificate too. It says he was my father. Was that her *husband*?'

Cynthia looked helplessly at Giles, and Giles looked distraught for a moment, and then he spoke.

'Yes, Juliette, he was. They'd got married a few months earlier.'

'But then why didn't they want me? Why didn't they keep me?' She was shrieking now. 'What was wrong with ME?'

'Oh, Juliette, nothing was wrong with you. You were so beautiful.' Cynthia started to cry, horrified that she was causing her daughter such anguish after having tried so hard to protect her for so many years. She continued, her voice wavering.

'Elisabeth just felt too young to have a baby, darling. They didn't have a house or anything, they were living with Nana . . .'

'She was twenty-two,' said Juliette. 'That wasn't that young in those days.' Her face was fixed, grim within the halo of hair. No-one spoke.

Pots and pans: Nana's house. That was where she'd heard the name. Of course. Elisabeth Potts was Nana's daughter too.

'So what happened to her? Where did she go?'

'Well, when she said she wouldn't keep the baby, none of us believed it at first. And then she seemed so deadly serious that your father and I discussed it and . . . and we offered to take you ourselves. You see, we . . . we had struggled to have our own child, and Nana was so furious with Elisabeth, so desperate not to lose you . . . it seemed to make sense on so many levels.' Cynthia cleared her throat. 'So we applied, and . . . and I'm afraid Elisabeth was so angry that she didn't want to speak to us any more, and so she didn't. We knew the baby, you I mean, had been born in Acton but we didn't know where Elisabeth went after the adoption. So we lost contact.'

Juliette struggled to keep up with what Cynthia was saying. 'Why didn't you tell me?' she said finally, and her voice had an edge to it that Cynthia hadn't heard before.

'Oh, Juliette, we wanted to, but if you have your baby adopted you have the right to anonymity until the child turns eighteen. It's only then that you would have been allowed to trace her.'

'So why didn't you tell me when I turned eighteen?'

'We were planning to. But we weren't sure how you would take it . . . and you never asked, never seemed interested, so we assumed you weren't ready.' Cynthia paused, recalling the time she had snapped at her eight-year-old daughter, 'I'm your real mummy now,' and it seemed she still hadn't forgiven herself. 'And then you were going off to university, and we didn't want to unsettle you, it's such a big step, and then the time just never felt right after that. We did our best to get it right, but sometimes we didn't. I'm so sorry, darling.'

Juliette ignored the apology. She knew she was furious, she wasn't quite sure who with yet.

'And what about Nana? Did she ever see her?'

'I'm not sure. I think sometimes, up in London. We didn't really talk about it.'

'So Nana would know where she is now?'

Cynthia looked into the bottom of her mug, where the dregs lay.

'Yes, I suppose she would, Juliette. I suppose she would.'

80

Wandsworth

The sun had gone behind a cloud, one of those flighty ones that keeps changing shape, and the temperature dropped sharply. Both women shivered.

'Bloody hell,' said Camilla. 'Why would she want to give her own baby away, if she was happily married?'

'Oh, it gets worse,' said Juliette. 'D'you know what she did then? Got pregnant almost immediately. And then she *kept* that baby, another girl. Now why would she do that? Abandon me and then keep the next one? It's evil.'

'Is she still with your father?'

'No, they split up years ago. Apparently it was all her who wanted to get rid of me, he couldn't understand it either. I think he resented it in the end. That's what my grandmother told me anyway.'

'So, she had a new husband, you were born in wedlock, she had another child straight after . . . There must have been something really devastating, it doesn't make sense otherwise.'

'Maybe it was my ghastly hair,' said Juliette, and as they tried to laugh they looked at each other and it came to them both at the exact same time, and Juliette couldn't believe she hadn't ever thought of it before.

81

Elisabeth

Cynthia was always the more serious daughter in the Simmons household, a typical firstborn really. Elisabeth was the pretty, fun one, seven years younger, with long wavy hair and laughter streaking through her soul. The sisters had adored each other, despite their different temperaments, the difficult age gap – Penelope had done well on that count, ensuring she handed out her love evenly between her daughters, minimising resentments. They'd even shared a room until Cynthia left home to get married to a nice young engineer called Giles. Elisabeth had been bridesmaid of course, and she had been pretty as a picture, everyone kept saying, but Elisabeth had shushed them, not wanting to upstage the bride.

Elisabeth had missed her sister after Cynthia left home, but she was happy enough – she did well at school, went on to nursing college, had loads of friends, plenty of boyfriends, and then when she was twenty she'd met a lovely boy at a dance, and she'd known he was the one, from the minute he'd asked her to Rock Around The Clock, and she'd been relieved that she'd saved herself, for him.

Marrying Alan turned out to be the happiest day of her life, although the wedding night had been something of a let-down – she'd been scared stiff and it had been awkward and painful and altogether embarrassing. They'd sat up afterwards, smoking in bed, unable to sleep, both wondering what the fuss was about. But the next day they'd driven to Dorset and had stayed in a beautiful little cottage just a short walk up the cliffs from the beach and they'd practised like crazy until they'd really got the hang of it; several times a day for a whole week seemed to sort it. The weather was balmy and the sea was clear and lovely and warm for swimming. Life couldn't get better for Elisabeth. It could only get worse, and it did.

82

Cleveland

Renée was on the kitchen floor, Volume Two of *Tyler's Educational Handbooks* open next to her face, its pages bent at the biology section, the radio blaring the usual dismal news in an inappropriately cheerful tone. The man was heavier than he looked and she couldn't move, was fully pinned down, stripes forming on the undersides of her thighs from the edges of the tiles beneath her.

'Get off me, you bastard,' Renée screamed as she struggled against him, but that seemed to provoke him, arouse him further, and he brought one hand down from her neck to maul roughly at her top, and then he tried to pull at her shorts, but they were denim and belted and he couldn't get them off.

Even through her panic Renée knew this was serious, she could see the madness in his eyes. She'd read something somewhere and it came to her then, so she stopped struggling and went limp as the man pawed at her, and at first he didn't know what to do, he had nothing to fight against – and then she started moaning, as if she were even *enjoying* herself, and that seemed to really confuse him, put him right off his stride. He loosened his hold on her throat, just a little, while he undid his belt, tried to get his trousers off, and she managed to move enough to get her hand down there and he let her although he didn't much like it, it was all rather odd, he preferred it when they were scared shitless, and soon her hand was free enough for her to take hold of him, and she caressed him, as if he were precious, and he released his grip still further – and then when her hand had just enough free-dom she started to twist, hard, until he was screaming in agony, and she twisted further and harder, with both hands now, and once he was in too much pain to be able to stop her she got to her feet and kicked him between the legs, repeatedly, like she was kicking a door in, and then she grabbed her book bag and fled from the house.

83

Wood Green, North London

Juliette was shocked when her mother opened the door. She looked so old these days, but, Juliette reasoned, she was in her mid-sixties now, what did she expect? Elisabeth had that pinched look to her face, of someone who has suffered, and the lines around her mouth were like a hangdog's, largely thanks to the packet a day habit she still hadn't conquered.

'Oh,' said Elisabeth. 'Goodness. I wasn't expecting you. Why didn't you ring? Now's not convenient.'

'It never is, is it, Elisabeth?' said Juliette, but she sounded less hurt, less bitter than usual. Today she just felt sadness to the moon and back for her mother. The hatred had gone elsewhere.

'When can I come back?'

'Well . . . Oh, you might as well come in now you're here, but you can't stay long, I have to go out. What d'you want to drink?'

'Nothing, thanks,' said Juliette. She moved inside the cramped cluttered hallway, and she could smell damp faintly, wet washing perhaps. Elisabeth ushered her through to the kitchen, which was small and dark, and one of the cupboard doors was hanging at slightly the wrong angle, like it might fall off, and the work surfaces were scratched and stained. There was a gleam of grease covering the once-white walls, and paint was peeling in one corner. The washing-up had been done – a single bowl and plate and mug – and the ancient-looking dishcloth was hung over the tap to dry. My God, this place is depressing, thought Juliette.

Juliette sat at the tiny table, which was still wet from wiping. A copy of the *Daily Mirror* was lying folded next to an unhappy-looking spider plant, open at the crossword. It was half done.

'What d'you want, Juliette?' said Elisabeth. She stood with her back to the sink, arms folded. Her jumper was navy, acrylic, worn-out. 'Do we have to go through it all over again?'

Juliette didn't know what to say. She had literally got in her car, dropped Camilla back home in Chelsea and driven straight over to Wood Green, ignoring Camilla's protestations. She hadn't been thinking.

She looked at her mother, at the grief etched into her skin like knife wounds, and she started crying.

'Oh, for God's sake,' said Elisabeth.

'I know why you gave me away,' said Juliette, snivelling.

'What do you mean? Of course you do, I've told you enough times over the years.'

'No, I know the real reason.'

'What do you mean?'

'You know,' said Juliette.

84

Dorset

On the last day of their honeymoon, the one with no clouds and sky blue as china, Elisabeth was on the beach devouring an Agatha Christie, her second of the holiday. She was smooth peanut-brown, the darkest her pale skin would turn in the sun, and she wore a red polka-dot swimsuit with a white frilled skirt that kept flapping up in the breeze, revealing the perfect curve of her behind. Alan stood towelling himself after his swim, and as he looked down at his young wife lying on her stomach, legs kicking, back arching so that she could read, dark hair loose in the sunshine, he thought again what a total smasher she was, and he felt the desire build in him yet again, was there no end to his ardour?

'Shall we go in a minute, pet?' he said. He paused. 'We might have time for a quick lie down before dinner.'

Elisabeth looked up over her shoulder. 'You randy bugger,' she laughed. 'I need to finish my book, I'm just about to find out whodunnit.'

'I'm all clean now, love,' he said. 'I don't want to get all sandy again. Shall I go ahead then, take everything up, get the kettle on for a brew?'

'Yes, fine, I'll only be ten minutes. D'you mind?'

'Of course I don't.' He leaned down and put one hand into the sand as he kissed her, tried to put his tongue in her mouth.

'Stop that,' she giggled. 'There are children about.'

He looked at her green eyes, her flowing hair, her breasts squashed together by her position, and he wanted to reach out and touch her right there, hold her, make love to her, bury himself into her. My God, he had to stand up, before it was obvious.

'All right,' he said. He moved reluctantly away from her and packed everything up, the picnic, the Thermos, the beach ball, the frisbee, and when it was safe he folded up his towel, put on his shorts and shirt, and left her sundress and sandals neatly beside her.

'I'll see you soon, my darling.'

Elisabeth looked up quickly from her book, she'd just found out the murderer was Vera, she needed to know how it ended.

'Bye, love,' she said, and blew him a kiss full of promise.

When Elisabeth finished her book just twelve minutes later, there were only two family parties left on the beach. The children were still running squealing in and out of the sea, and as it was such a perfect evening none of the adults seemed inclined to move, although it was gone six o'clock. As Elisabeth put on her dress she noticed one particular little girl, laughing and naked, and she felt a tiny pull of joy that perhaps she might have one of those herself soon; she wouldn't be surprised if they had a honeymoon baby after the week they'd had. She smiled to herself. Yes, she'd be quite happy with that.

The walk up the cliffs to the cottage was steep, and although it wasn't far it puffed Elisabeth out; she smoked too much even in those days. She stopped for a second, panting, looking back the way she'd come, and she could see the people, small now, still settled in their deck-chairs, and a dog cavorting across the sand after a ball, and the green of the sea, reaching out for ever, to the end of the world. She shook her head back and shut her eyes and put her face to the sun, and it still felt warm, like it was blessing her. And that was when she felt a hand over her mouth, and something cold and hard against her throat, and that was when she got pulled off the path and into the bushes, down into the thorny bushes that scratched and hurt her, but not as much as he did.

85

Cleveland

While her friends were still out at the bar getting drunk, and Stephen was downstairs waiting to continue where they'd left off, Renée was standing under the shower, watching the grit from her body run red into the tray. The fierce streams of water penetrated through the alcohol and sobered her up very slightly, made her heart a little steadier and her legs a little stronger.

Renée felt ashamed of her behaviour now, and not only because of Juliette. Although she knew rationally it wasn't her fault, she couldn't stop thinking about the man in his kitchen, couldn't stop blaming herself: 'So all I need you to do (*giggle*) is sign here.' (Provocative lean forward – had she been fucking mad, she'd known he was a weirdo; she must have been on auto-pilot, irrefutable proof of the book company's fail-safe training methods.) She'd been unbelievably lucky to have got away, she might even have been *murdered* if she hadn't managed to fight free of him – what man does that in his own home unless he's going to kill you, dump your body, destroy the evidence?

And now here she was, less than two weeks later, drunk, making out, rolling around in the dirt like a sow on heat. And with *Stephen* of all people.

Renée realised as she stood there, water pouring over her like from a bucket, that she wasn't falling for Stephen after all, absolutely not. What had she been thinking? She must simply have been lonely and drunk and depressed – unnerved by bookselling, freaked out by the double dose of trauma on that terrible day a fortnight earlier, what with almost drowning too. It couldn't have helped her state of mind, and this line of thought comforted her in a way. It really wouldn't do to sleep with Stephen, he was her best friend's boyfriend after all. She had her standards. OK, it was embarrassing, but they hadn't done anything much more than snog, thank goodness, and she knew that Juliette would eventually forgive her if she left it at that – she and Stephen *were* officially on a break, after all. Thank God Stephen had tripped over in the driveway, pulling her down with him like a lassoed calf. Getting all that orange grit over her bare legs and arms had brought her to her senses, had bloody hurt for a start. Who knows what would have happened if they'd ended up in the house still all over each other? They wouldn't have fallen into bed though, seeing as there weren't any beds to fall into, maybe they'd have jumped into *floor* together.

Renée stopped herself. She knew it wasn't funny. She couldn't bear to lose Juliette's friendship for a start, she was far more important to Renée than Stephen ever would be, but it was more than that. She was vaguely aware that her attitude to men had been somehow changed since the attack – she needed to be careful, she thought, she mustn't get unhinged by what had happened, as though she were an open door to push against these days. But then again, *what was the point of saying no when no-one listened?*

As she pulled back the shower curtain she was swaying again. It was almost as if the streams of water had created a force field around her, keeping her upright, and now she was standing just in air she found she was still horribly drunk.

I need to go to bed, she thought. No, not bed, *floor*, and she giggled again. *Get a grip, Renée*. She pulled her towel around herself and unlocked the bathroom door to find Stephen standing outside on the landing, big and bulky, in only a towel too, as if he were waiting for the shower. He took one look at Renée, barely covered, and grabbed at her and started kissing her again, and although in her head she didn't want to any more she found herself snogging him back, there was something about the alcohol and the steamy heat and his solid-looking body that made the desire build in her all over again, and he propelled her along the corridor and into the room he shared with Jason, one of the other (mainly under-tree-dwelling) booksellers – but Jason wasn't there, he was still getting hammered at the bar. Stephen pushed the door shut behind him and started kissing her even more passionately, and she didn't much like it now; his breathing was heavy and ragged, and anyway her towel was coming down, they should stop, and although she tried to push him away he bent her backwards until she thought she was going to hit the floor, but he managed to get down on one knee and catch her somehow, and before she knew what was happening he was heavy on top of her and she could feel the roughness of the carpet beneath her, and he carried on kissing her like he was trying to eat her, his tongue rigid and choking, and then she realised he was pushing himself into her and although she screamed at him to stop his face was vacant and his eyes were cold, and he started moving backwards and forwards, hard, fast, and each time he thrust into her he hurt her deep inside herself and she beat her fists against his chest and screamed at him to stop, get off her, but he didn't seem to want to hear, he was in his own world, looking down at her as if he owned her, and it was only once he'd finished that he seemed to realise she was even there, and he sank down next to her and muttered something although she couldn't work out what, and then he turned over and went to sleep.

86

Wood Green

Elisabeth never broke down, just spoke slowly, mechanically, for the first time ever, of the events on the last day of her honeymoon, and as she spoke she felt like it had happened to a different girl, in a parallel life. She never faltered, even as she described to her daughter how she hadn't screamed, because of the knife, how much it had hurt, how she had run back to the cottage and locked herself in the bathroom, shouting through the door that she'd just fallen over, that she was fine; how she had scrubbed at herself, had screwed her torn costume into a ball and disposed of it later in the dustbin; how she'd finally come out, smiled, dressed, cooked dinner, but said sorry, she was too tired for anything else tonight, after all. She'd been too tired for anything for weeks, apparently. Elisabeth told her daughter how much she desperately hadn't wanted to be pregnant, had wanted to be sure she wasn't, before she resumed anything like that with her poor bewildered husband. But then when her period hadn't come she'd been terrified, and she'd told Alan she didn't want to have a baby, and she'd even tried to abort it (abort *me*, Juliette thought), but it hadn't worked, and so she'd suggested they have it adopted, and her husband had gone mad and said no. But he gave in, in the end, Elisabeth had been so insistent, and even though they arranged the adoption she thought secretly she still might keep it — what were the chances of it being the rapist's rather than her husband's after the honeymoon they'd had? But when the baby had been born and she'd seen that unmistakable curly red hair, even at birth, that had been it. It had destroyed her marriage, she told Juliette. She left unsaid what it had done to her.

Juliette tried to process what Elisabeth had told her. She and Camilla had guessed right: her father was a rapist. She, Juliette, was a *product of rape*, a mistake, the end result of a vile act, an unnatural aberration. As Elisabeth looked bleakly, helplessly at her daughter, Juliette felt like she was brittle, might even break.

Juliette thought of her own husband then, with whom she had shared a bed for so many years, raping her best friend long ago in America. She'd known for two months now, since the night of the picnic, when Renée had screamed it out through the trees and across the water, that it was *Stephen* who had raped her, not the stranger she'd always claimed — although he'd tried to as well — before collapsing in hysteria. Juliette had been trying to deal with the fact that her husband was a rapist, and now it turned out her father was one too.

Juliette sat for long empty minutes in the kitchen of

346

her mother's grim little council flat. To her astonishment she found that, in a place beyond the horror, she started to feel oddly exhilarated, free even – of guilt that she hadn't ever really loved Stephen, at least not how you should love your husband; of rampant hatred for her mother, whose actions she could finally understand – and although she knew it was the shock (the pain of who her father was, what he had done, the way she'd come into the world not yet able to sink in), she felt in this moment a connectedness at last, an understanding. She felt desperately sorry for Elisabeth then, and for Renée too. She spoke gently.

'So that's why you were so against poor Mum having me.'

Elisabeth flinched at the word *Mum* and it surprised Juliette. Usually she didn't react to things.

'Maybe it sounds selfish,' Elisabeth said. 'But I didn't want any reminders in my life. How could I look at you, and not think of how you were conceived? I tried to get Cynthia to understand, but I couldn't bring myself to tell even her the truth – I felt so ashamed, and besides I couldn't bear poor Alan to know – and when she wouldn't listen, insisted on carrying on with the adoption, I just cut myself off from her and the rest of the family. I'm not proud of it, but it's all I could think to do.'

'But why did you have another child so soon afterwards?'

Elisabeth hesitated.

'I don't know, that's what people did I suppose. And it

must have been to do with my body as well. It had carried you and then it had nothing. My milk drying up was excruciating.'

Elisabeth looked far away, as if deciding what to say next, if anything – and then she continued, but almost like she was talking to a ghost, a phantom daughter, a gorgeous girl from another life, not the one sat opposite her now in her miserable kitchen in North London. She had never said the words out loud before, it was as if they bewitched her.

'Once you were gone I found that I craved you, Mandy, and I so wanted to believe you were Alan's, but when I saw you I knew you weren't, I just knew it. So I had another child, another daughter, to . . . to take your place I suppose.'

Juliette said nothing, just stared at her mother. *Amanda Lily*.

'You just called me Mandy,' she said.

Elisabeth seemed young again, girlish for an instant, and then it was gone. She looked straight at her daughter.

'You'll always be Mandy to me, Juliette.'

And that's when Juliette cried, and instead of scolding her for a change, so did Elisabeth.

87

Cleveland

Late on a putridly hot night in a furniture-less house in Midwest America, Renée found herself back in the grimy shower, barely ten minutes since she'd last been there. Her party mood had vanished, to be replaced by feelings of helplessness and revulsion. She sobbed drunkenly as she scrubbed and scrubbed at herself, as if willing the fluid out of her, repulsed yet again at what had happened, trying to work out just what it was that *had* happened, *why* it had happened. As the water grew half-heartedly tepid and then fully cold, she was finally able to put a label to it. Rape. That was the word. *She had been raped*.

Renée was shaking as she turned off the shower, unable to stand the onslaught, and she leaned her back against the cold cracked tiles and slumped down to a squat, head between her legs, long dark hair sodden and straggling in the tainted water that hadn't yet gone down the plughole. She cried and cried until she couldn't seem to stop, the snivels coming in strangled little pants, her heart beating frantically like it was about to stop. It was only when she heard the front door go and realised the others were home, and in drunken high spirits at that, that she pulled herself together. She ran naked from the bathroom up to the room she shared with Sissy, and hauled herself into her sleeping bag although she was still soaking wet. She lay quietly shivering on the horrid green carpet, and although there was no mattress to comfort her and her bones stuck into her at funny angles she didn't mind the pain, perhaps she deserved it. She rolled over in the now-sopping bag, onto her side, away from the door, trying to pretend she was asleep in case Sissy came in – although if anyone were to look closely they would see that her body was trembling through the nylon, like a giant brown caterpillar shaking on a leaf in the breeze.

Stephen awoke suddenly and there was a body snoring next to him, and he couldn't work out whose it was. He lay there, uneasy, feeling like he'd been run over, his head especially, but yes, his body too. His knees were sore, the flesh tender, and as he sent his hands down to check on them he could feel the still-sticky wounds, on his right knee more than the left. What were they? How had he got them?

And then he realised – *carpet burns*. He didn't need to wonder at where they'd come from. As soon as he worked out what they were, his memory of the evening flicked back in, as if a channel in his brain had been switched on by remote control. He felt sick, aware of exactly what had happened now, although he refused to put a name to it. *What the fuck had he done?* What would Juliette say? What would Renée say? What would the *police* say?

Stephen's body spasmed and his eyes started to prick, threatening tears of self-interest, so he knew it must be serious. He tried not to think them but the thoughts came anyway. *Why hadn't he stopped, when it was clear that she wanted him to, when he'd heard her screaming the house down for him to get off her?*

Stephen had always been aware of how much he liked to get his own way, right from when he'd been a little boy, but he knew what had happened last night had taken his inherent sense of entitlement a step too far. She'd seemed so keen though, and then had changed her mind at the very last minute, the fucking prick tease. What did she think men were like? Didn't she know that beyond a certain point there was no turning back? Stephen felt a little better when he took this line of thought – phew, it was her fault, not his – but deep somewhere inside himself, where his heart still resided in those days, he knew it wasn't true.

Stephen lay sprawled on the floor, trying to think straight, attempting to work out what to do, how to make sure Juliette never found out – and through the thickness of his headache he realised his first task was to stop Renée telling anyone. Who would she tell though? After all, it didn't look good on her either – out of her mind on cheap booze, barely dressed, one provocatively short towel loosely fastened. Maybe she wouldn't say anything, it was too damaging for her as well, on so many counts.

He wondered whether he should acknowledge to Renée what he'd done, admit it was rape – and before he had time to even get to the end of that thought the voice in his head swooped in and said, 'Noooo . . .' and so he never admitted it again, which was a shame, as a *genuine* apology then, a proper confession, if only to himself, *might* have saved him from his ultimate path of never feeling obliged to tell the truth, of going for what he wanted at any expense, of no moral code being too sacred.

Maybe *this* was the moment that made him.

Stephen knew on that stifling morning in Ohio that there was only one option open to him to get him out of trouble, in the short-term at least: he had to cry, grovel to Renée, pretend he'd completely misread the situation, *had thought she wanted it too*, tell her the last thing he'd wanted to do was hurt her, take advantage of her, etcetera, etcetera – and he needed to do it fast. It might just work, if he played it right. He lay next to Jason, who was snoring and farting in gaping boxers on top of his grubby-looking sleeping bag. He couldn't possibly do it here. Sissy would be in Renée's room, he couldn't risk a confrontation in front of her either, she was such a goody-two-shoes, and far too close to Juliette to risk knowing anything. He would just have to camp out outside their bedroom door, wait for one or other of them to come out, so he could get Renée alone. Yes, that's what he'd do – the girls' room was at the top of the house so no-one else would see him, and Sissy would just think he was being lovesick if she came out first. As he lumbered to his feet, a crack went through his skull. He bunched his sleeping bag in front of him, the nylon sticking to his weeping knees, and staggered towards the stairs.

*

After Sissy got up, assuming her friend was still asleep, Renée continued to lie on the thinly carpeted floor of their bedroom, contemplating exactly how she felt about what had happened last night. She found that her feelings kept evolving as the morning sunshine invaded. At first they'd been pretty clear-cut, unequivocal, but it all seemed more complicated now. She kept trying to label her feelings, choose words to explain them, as though that might make it better somehow. She chose carefully: *helplessness, disbelief*, as Stephen pushed her to the floor; *fear, revulsion,* as he forced himself into her; *anger, fury*, as she beat her fists into his chest when he refused to stop; *repugnance, disgust*, as his face contorted when he ejaculated inside her; *shame, revulsion*, as she staggered away from him and into the shower; *guilt, shame*, but not at him, at herself this time, that maybe she'd encouraged him, had even been asking for it; *shame, responsibility*, as she realised it must be her fault, she must give off some kind of signal. It was all she deserved. She was a slag.

Renée knew emphatically that if she couldn't respect herself, how could she expect men to respect her – no wonder her father never had, no wonder men came onto her like they did. She hunched into her sleeping bag although the room was too hot for it, ignoring the knocking at the door, as she tried to decide what the overriding emotion was, the single word, above all the others, that she could use to explain her feelings, and she lay there and lay there until in the end – that was it – she decided unequivocally what the word was, and the word was *shame*.

88

Val Gardena, Italy

The view from the apartment was straight down the valley, and all that could be seen was roof-tops and pine trees against flat blue sky, and pink mountains like blancmange, and green, green grass – and over to the left was a tiny little church with a cute pointy spire, whose raucous bells belied its toy-town appearance, and that Siobhan thought would be a wonderfully romantic place to one day get married.

Around mid-morning on the third glorious day of her holiday, Siobhan half-staggered out onto the balcony, oblivious to the view for once. All she was wearing was a towel, with a second one wrapped turban-like around her long honey hair. She looked incredulous, like she couldn't believe what she was hearing.

'What do you mean, he's dead? He can't be, he *survived*.'

The person on the other end of the phone continued gabbling, and although they weren't making much sense Siobhan finally understood. She rewrapped the towel around her body – accidentally giving the German hikers across the way a tantalising glimpse of her long, lean body – and tucked it in tightly, whilst just about holding onto the phone between her left shoulder and ear.

'Where did you say she is, Cam? . . . Is she still in the hospital? . . . What, in Sardinia? . . . Are her parents there yet? . . . *What?* Well, who is with her? . . . What about his parents? Who's looking after the kids? . . . My God, that is ridiculous.'

When Siobhan finally hung up, she walked carefully back into the apartment, before her legs gave way as she collapsed onto the sofa.

'What's going on?' said Phil.

'It's Sissy,' said Siobhan. 'Her husband's died.'

'What, the one with cancer?'

'No,' said Siobhan. 'Well, yes, but he's not died of that . . . He's been electrocuted.'

'*What?*'

'I have to go to her,' sobbed Siobhan. 'She's there on her own. Camilla says her parents are on some religious retreat in India.'

'Don't be stupid,' said Phil. 'We're on holiday.'

'Holiday?' said Siobhan. 'How can I be on holiday at a time like this? What am I meant to do? Go on a nice hike for the day? Do a spot of sunbathing?'

'Well, there's nothing else to be done,' said Phil. 'There's no point ruining our holiday.'

'Oh, my *God*,' said Siobhan. 'You mean it, don't you? You really do mean it.'

'What are you talking about?' said Phil.

'I'm sorry, Phil, I'm nearer to Sardinia than anyone, I

355

could get there quickest. She needs me. I have to go and help her.'

'Siobhan!' said Phil. 'It's not your responsibility. Why d'you always have to think it's up to you to sort things out? Plus it would take you just as long from here as it would from London. Why can't you just let her family deal with it?'

'Because she's got two little kids who've just lost their father and who need looking after, that's why.' She stared at her boyfriend as the realisation hit her. Had she really spent the last three years waiting for this selfish wanker to propose? 'I'm sorry, Phil,' she repeated. 'I'm going downstairs to see if they can help me get a flight. I take it you won't be offering to come with me.' She got up from the sofa, went into the bedroom, pulled on a clean pair of knickers and threw on an old sundress. She shoved her feet into her new plimsolls, breaking their backs. She turned as she left the room, her hair stringy and wet over her shoulders, looking younger than her forty-two years, perhaps because of the train tracks on her teeth which she'd finally had fitted. 'And I'm sorry, Phil, but I think we need to talk about "us" when I get back.'

'There is no "us" if you leave,' said Phil.

Siobhan stopped still and looked back at her boy-friend, her grief sharpened into agony now. All her hopes and dreams for their relationship, for this holiday, flitted past her like starlings on the breeze. She took an age to respond.

'Well, I'm sorry, but I guess there's no us then,' she said. And then she packed her stuff in five minutes flat before making a dramatic exit that would have been perfect, if she hadn't had to go back ten minutes later, as she'd forgotten her passport, and if her heart hadn't been broken yet again.

Siobhan managed to get a flight from Venice to Olbia that afternoon, and she stayed with Sissy for three whole days, which is how long it took Sissy's parents to turn up. She took on two traumatised children, a widow in hospital with heatstroke and hysteria, and a newly single status. But Siobhan coped better than anyone would have expected. She played endless games of Uno with the kids in the hospital canteen, regaled them with terrible jokes, and then stroked their hair and cuddled them wordlessly when their inevitable tears came; and she sat for hours holding Sissy's hand; and she tried her hardest to help Nigel's distraught, bewildered parents, dealing with all the hospital bureaucracy as best she could in her pidgin Italian – and it seemed that in this crisis she came into her own, her usual scattiness replaced with determined utility. And then once Sissy was home, Siobhan visited her every weekend, helping her decorate the scruffy old house she and Nigel had just bought, taking the children on trips to the park to give Sissy a break, doing her best to make things easier for her friend. Even when Sissy finally confessed to Siobhan the truth of how Nigel had died – but begged her not to say a word, saying she couldn't deal with the fallout – Siobhan had understood. But although she'd complied with Sissy's wishes she'd secretly prayed that Stephen would eventually get his comeuppance, some day, somehow. And she'd secretly dreamed that she, Siobhan, would one day find a man who loved her as much as Nigel had loved Sissy.

Part Three

Part Three

89

Speke, Liverpool

In a smart end of terrace house not far from the Hale
Road – the only one of the row with tidily blooming
petunias in plastic hanging baskets – a small neat woman
was preparing to cut up newspapers. Her husband was at
the races and she was taking advantage of some time to
herself, about to make a scrapbook about her youngest
son, Stephen.

Eileen Forsyth liked making scrapbooks. She had a
cupboard full of them, stuffed with Stephen's achieve-
ments. She'd always been so proud of him: of how well
he'd done at school, how he'd made it to university,
moved to London, got a job at a local newspaper, over
time risen through the ranks to become one of the heavy-
weights of the media world, even sometimes *on telly* no
less. It had been his destiny, she'd felt, she'd always known
he was special. She'd spoiled Stephen rotten of course,
and she thought that must have helped, turned him into
the man he was. And although she never acknowledged
it, inside she knew that this deluge of love for him was

because she'd left her other, somewhat less appealing son with his father, like a consolation prize, while she'd buggered off to start a new family. Showering Stephen with enough love for two had seemed the obvious thing to do in the circumstances. It had helped her cope with the guilt.

Today, though, Eileen found herself uncharacteristically hesitant in her crafty pursuits. She'd been armed and ready, scissors poised, glue stick unsheathed, surveying the headlines of the papers spread out in front of her, deciding which one to attack first. But despite it being an incredible story it seemed no-one was coming out in a very good light. Of course Eileen had been shocked when it turned out the body in the lake story had involved not one but both her sons. She'd been appalled when the early headlines surfaced: that Terry was under suspicion for murdering the poor woman, that he'd been trailing Juliette, like some kind of pervert, and she'd been glad then that she'd washed her hands of him, convinced she'd been right all along, he was obviously a loser. But as she sat alone at her glass-topped dining table with the lace tablecloth underneath, dressed in smart polyester trousers and a matching cream blouse, a new picture of the saga started to emerge. It opened her eyes to her sons, made her see each of them in a different light, and she hesitated.

Eileen sat quietly pondering the two men, as dispassionately now as if they were fictional. Stephen was ruthless, she'd always known that – even as a small boy he would go to abnormal lengths to get what he wanted (*like her*, came the thought, and she buried it). She didn't know

Terry any more, of course, not even what he looked like until she'd seen the pictures in the papers (and she'd recognised him like a shot, he looked so much like Stephen), but from the little she'd heard over the years he hadn't made much of a success of himself, his most notable achievement seeming to be having relocated from the lea of one Ford factory to another.

But it was when Eileen read the coverage of the inquest and realised it was *Terry* who had tried to save the woman, the only person who had from what she could tell, that she felt proud of her eldest son somehow. In fact she was perversely more proud of that than anything Stephen had ever done, it being a selfless act rather than a selfish one, and she'd begrudgingly admired it, known that neither she nor Stephen had that kind of thing in them. She'd even thought for a moment of ringing Terry – but she hadn't spoken to him in nearly forty years, what in heavens' name would she say?

So after long minutes of vacillation, self-contained, practical-minded Mrs Forsyth (formerly Kingston) finally did the only thing she could think of under the circumstances. She did use her scissors and glue stick to make a scrapbook that day – not one about Stephen after all, but about Terry this time. She kept it, the only evidence of love for her eldest son, hidden away in a cupboard, for it one day to be found by house clearers, and thrown away.

90

Lucinda Horne couldn't believe how many people had turned up to her latest book launch, the third in the *Bottersley Dog School* series. It seemed extraordinary that everyone had come to see *her*, not Alistair Smart, that they didn't totally hate her after all. It had been excruciating when Alistair's wife had gone to the press about her and Alistair's 'little arrangement', as he'd liked to call it, and it had all come out as front-page news – yet another weird offshoot to the long-running saga about the woman who drowned in The Serpentine.

The bizarre thing about the whole business was that Lucinda had felt most betrayed when it turned out that Alistair had been sleeping with Stephen Forsyth's wife at the same time as he'd been seeing her. That was when she'd realised how naive she'd been about it all, but when you're a writer getting nowhere in your bid to be published, who knows what lengths you'd go to – and besides Alistair Smart had been such a hero to her for more than half her life she probably would have done *anything* for him. What an idiot she'd been! Maybe she should have taken her parents' advice and got her head out of her books, out of either reading them or writing them, every now and again to see what real life was like. She damned well knew now though, and so far, after a somewhat bumpy start, she found she rather enjoyed it. She was so lucky the public had forgiven her, had seen *her* as the victim in the scandal, and she'd taken her publicist's advice to tone down her appearance and now kept her wondrous breasts firmly under wraps. ('You don't want the children's fathers lusting after you, dear,' her publicist had said. 'Not after that Alistair Smart business.')

Poor Alistair though, she felt so sorry for him – career washed up, thrown out of the family home, his own children embarrassed by him at school, having to endure the other kids constantly woofing at them. His wife had been an utter bitch from what Lucinda had gathered, the last time she'd rung him, he'd sounded desolate, even though he'd just found out his publisher had decided not to sue him for breach of contract after all. And when Lucinda had read last week on the Internet that he'd checked into the Priory for sex addiction she'd felt awful. She could understand now that he might be an addict – he really had been quite obsessed with sex, rather glassy-eyed about it all in fact – but she'd thought that was quite normal behaviour at the time; after all, she'd had nothing much to compare it to.

Lucinda sighed. She did hope he'd get better. Despite his failings he was still Alistair Smart to her, her inspiration. She'd be nothing without him.

The mother of the little girl in front of her coughed self-consciously.

'Oh, sorry, it was Amelia, wasn't it?' The woman and her daughter nodded, excited smiles fixed on their faces under matching brown bobs.

'To dear Amelia,' she wrote, 'enjoy Wowser and the gang's latest adventure, love Lucinda.'

Her publicist scowled. 'You'll have to go faster than that,' she whispered. 'Look at the queue.'

'Oh, sorry,' said Lucinda. She sat back, shook her silky blonde hair out of her face, and turned to the little boy waiting expectantly in front of her.

'Hello!' she said, smiling guilelessly. 'And what's your name, young man?'

91

Renée's Aunt Linda lay drowsily in the velvet-swagged four-poster bed, mulling over what an unbelievably fantastic day she and Sam had just had. The grounds of the old abbey sloped down to the Thames, and they'd had the service right there on the grass in the autumn sunshine, a last-minute weather-related change of heart. The venue had been super, completely devoid of that conference feel so many of those places had, where people sat through countless boring team-building events, drinking gallons of bottled water and sucking Fox's mints all day. Linda had loved Sam's dress, it was so flouncy and feminine, not at all Linda's style of course, but even though Sam had thought she was way too old for it, they'd both thought what the hell, we can get married at last, why not? Linda had looked good too, in a pale-blue trouser suit, and she knew the pictures would be stunning – with the water glinting behind them, the swans wafting along, the newly-wed (OK, newly civil-partnershipped, but it was close enough) smiles ones of jubilation, of their moment having arrived at last.

The day would have been absolutely perfect, in fact, apart from one ugly incident, and Linda tried not to let it upset her – it didn't really matter, not in the grand scheme of things. It was unfortunate though that Renée had got so incredibly drunk at the reception, and had had such a horrific go at her mother, which pretty much everyone had heard. Linda's big sister Simone had come all the way from Paris for the wedding, and although obviously she hadn't deserved that kind of treatment, secretly Linda had found herself sympathising with her niece a little. She just wished it hadn't had to happen at her and Sam's wedding – but it was the first time Renée had seen her mother in years, and it obviously still hurt. Sam hadn't been at all happy about it, fuming to Linda that Renée and Simone should sort out their issues in private instead of ruining their day, but she'd known not to interfere. Linda had smoothed everything over in her usual implacable way, she hadn't worked in A&E for over thirty years for nothing, and Renée had calmed down eventually, thank goodness.

Poor Renée, thought Linda, she'd never been quite the same since her friend had drowned last summer, although Linda had always known it went much further back than that – certainly to her mother, maybe to her father, definitely to when she'd come back from America all those years ago. She'd just drifted in and out of jobs and relationships, grown apart from her former best friend, never properly settled down to anything after university. She seemed to have so little self-respect now for some reason, but whatever it was that had messed her up, she was beginning to show it on her face, her looks had become quite ravaged these days. Linda wondered sadly what would become of Renée, maybe she should suggest she go for counselling or to AA or something. When she and Sam got back from Barcelona she'd take Renée for dinner, try to work out how to help her. Perhaps she could even suggest Renée got back in touch with Juliette, help facilitate some kind of reunion between them. Linda still remembered Renée and Juliette turning up on her doorstep in Camden all those years ago, so fresh-faced and eager, so obviously firmly best friends, despite the ensuing friction over their trip to Somerset House. It was such a shame they'd fallen out, and when Renée had finally sobbed to Linda about it the last time they'd got together, albeit after a bottle and a half of red wine, Linda had thought she'd been almost as upset about that as about her friend drowning.

Yes, Linda decided, she would talk to Renée, after the honeymoon. It was the least she could do for her niece, she was terribly fond of her, and everyone needed a mother figure. After all, Simone had never been there for Renée.

As Linda lay deep in thought in the voluptuous bed she heard Sam give a little snore, and she turned on to her side to put her arms around her new wife, and she shivered inside, both with worry about Renée and with happiness about Sam – and then she buried her face into Sam's ample shoulder, and drifted off to sleep.

92

Tower Bridge, Central London

The sun was weak and wintery as Stephen stood on the ledge of his tiny apartment overlooking the river. It wasn't a balcony as such, but it was just big enough to stand on, get some fresh air. He quite liked living here, although he missed the kids, obviously: the view was amazing and his cleaner kept the apartment spotless, which was a relief after the sluttishness of Wandsworth.

Stephen was feeling peculiarly optimistic this morning. It had been nearly five months since Siobhan had died, four since Juliette had thrown him out, despite her concerns about the effect it would have on the children, and although he'd lost his job, at least he'd had a whacking big pay-off. Things had finally calmed down on the PR front too now, thank fuck. Once the media had latched onto the story of how the women had *abandoned* their friend, left her for dead (a prime example of the amorality of our times, according to the *Daily Mail*) the focus had shifted to them. So although his wife's antics had indirectly got him the sack they'd perversely also let him off the hook in the end. The interest in his own loser of a brother, his dysfunctional family, his penchant for spying on his wife, had disappeared after a while. Chip paper, he thought with a sly smile. And, almost unbelievably, the rape story had never surfaced, even though there were at least five people who knew now – apart from him – from what he could tell. Juliette had confronted him, the night he'd hit her, and although he'd denied it she'd seen it in his eyes – and anyway she'd said that Renée had confessed at last, at the picnic, admitted she'd lied about the other man in Cleveland raping her. Renée had probably made that whole episode up, he thought, the fucking drama queen. According to Juliette, the only other person Renée had ever told before the night of the picnic was Siobhan, years ago, and she was dead and buried, which was probably just as well. So he was almost certainly safe now: Renée wouldn't want to go through the ordeal of a trial, especially not with her sexual history, no-one would believe her; and even Juliette wouldn't do that to the father of her own kids, no matter how much she might hate him herself. The others wouldn't do anything either, they'd follow Renée's or Juliette's lead. Yes, he was off the hook, he was sure of it – and, he reminded himself for the millionth time, it hadn't been *actual* rape, not really, more of a drunken misunderstanding. He'd honestly thought she wanted it too, it wasn't his fault she'd changed her mind too late.

Nothing more had been said about Nigel's death in Sardinia either, although Stephen was much more nervous about that story leaking. He'd been shocked when

Juliette had told him how Sissy had known what he'd done all along, how it came out at the picnic that Sissy had heard through her delirium Nigel cursing the socket, saying there was something wrong with it; how she'd not trusted using it herself to plug in her hairdryer. But when the emergency services had turned up, she'd been carted off to hospital and put on a drip while another ambulance had taken Nigel's body away, and the police hadn't even been called. So when the report into Nigel's death had concluded that it was accidental, with no reference to the faulty socket, Sissy must have known then that there'd been a cover-up, but had been too scared or distraught to do anything except accept the verdict.

Stephen still felt terrible about Nigel dying like that, he hadn't intended it to happen, no way. It really had been just an unfortunate accident – he'd been trying to do the guy a favour, for Christ's sake – but he'd panicked, hadn't known what else to do apart from hush it up. Nigel was dead anyway, no investigation would have changed the outcome. It would have wrecked his, Stephen's, life too – and what was the point of that?

Stephen looked down absently at a police boat on the river, cute as a bath toy, cutting through the water. So that's why Sissy had hated him over these past years, they'd always got on all right before that, especially since they'd gone to America together – in fact he'd thought she'd liked him, before.

What got to Stephen the most though, he realised in this rare moment of reflection, was not what Sissy or Renée thought of him these days (he couldn't give a toss about that), but the fact that Juliette despised him now, after what had been said at that fucking picnic. There had been no going back after that. They were finished.

Stephen sighed as his eyes glistened in the early sunlight – it was too bright out here – and he dabbed at them with his sleeve. Life goes on, he thought, there was no use moping, and even though he missed her sometimes (which annoyed the hell out of him) he knew he was better off without her – she may be beautiful but she was a lousy housewife, useless mother, unfaithful bitch. He looked at his watch. He'd better think about getting ready in a minute; his meeting to discuss a possible new tabloid launch was at eleven. The hacking scandal had done him a favour in the end – he'd managed somehow to avoid being implicated, and people were dropping like flies these days, which meant there were a couple of very juicy openings in the offing.

Stephen cheered up at this thought. It was a beautiful December day, he might even walk to Soho House, it was an interesting route and the exercise would do him good, make him nice and hungry for his lunch with Maddie later.

93

Lambeth, South London

Terry came out of Elephant and Castle Tube station and looked around bewilderedly – at the semi-subway he found himself in, the despondent-looking stallholders displaying handbags and scarves and sunglasses that all looked the same, the seemingly identical roads as he emerged onto the roundabout. He'd only ever come out at Lambeth North before and he was disorientated, but he definitely didn't want to be late. He knew he shouldn't stress, it wasn't as though he was on a date or anything, it was just a casual visit to a museum, to indulge a shared interest in military history, that was all. He was pleased though that he'd had his hair cut, he didn't look so insipid with it shorter, and he liked his new Levi's and bomber jacket, they almost made him look trendy.

It was strange, he'd always found women so hard to talk to before. Maybe that's why he'd married Maria all those years ago, she'd been quiet and sweet and barely spoke English – plus she'd mothered him at first, before she'd got fed up with him. But with this woman it was different. They'd got chatting after the inquest had been adjourned when Siobhan's poor mother had passed out – he'd found her crying outside when he'd popped out to call the vet to check on Humphrey, who'd had gastroenteritis and was still under observation. He'd asked her if she was OK – and because she was so overwrought and he seemed kind, she'd told him in a timid little voice he'd recognised from Hyde Park that she couldn't believe what she'd done, leaving Siobhan to die like that.

'No, I heard you,' he'd said. 'You wanted to go back and check on her, it was the others who persuaded you it was nothing. You cared, I could tell you did. You have nothing to feel guilty about.'

And then Terry had taken her back inside and they'd sat together amidst the panic, and somehow or other he'd made her feel better. They'd got on to talking about anything and everything: Frank Sinatra, the Franco-Prussian War (she told him she'd done History at Bristol, was passionate about it, especially military history, which was odd for a woman, he'd thought), Terry's rats, Sissy's cat: how getting Coco had been a godsend in helping the children cope after their father's death. And that had led to Terry telling her about his poor sick spaniel, and she had seemed so concerned about Humphrey it was endearing, really it was, not like Maria who'd seemed to almost hope he'd die – although she probably didn't care either way now that she'd buggered off with one of the tenors from the Barking and Dagenham Choir. Being splashed across the papers putting out the rubbish in her dressing gown, after her husband had been implicated in *murder*, had given her the perfect excuse.

As Terry walked towards the museum he saw the familiar green dome and the white columns and the two huge guns, and there she was, already there, although he was five minutes early himself, standing between the cannons, in jeans and a puffa jacket and Converse trainers, her hair messily longish, like a teenage boy's – his first ever female friend.

'Hello,' he said, and hesitated, unsure how to greet her. He held out his hand, was that the protocol?

'Hello, Terry,' said Sissy, and she shook it, politely.

'Shall we go in? It's freezing out here.' She nodded shyly, and they walked together, side by side, towards the entrance.

94

Wandsworth

The Roman soldiers were lined up smartly, twirling prettily in the faint breeze, the ghost-breath. Light rain was falling half-heartedly past the windows, almost as if it couldn't be bothered. It was quarter past four.

Noah Forsyth's teacher sat back in her chair, relieved, as his parents left the room. That hadn't gone as badly as it might have done, and it was good that they'd discussed it. It was hard being a teacher sometimes – you ended up being responsible for far more than a child's education, and you had to be careful not to overstep the line to wanting to become their mother too. But she'd thought about it carefully, discussed with the head beforehand what she was going to say – and anyway she owed it to Noah, he was such a sweet little boy, underneath.

It was odd how Mrs Forsyth seemed to have softened these days, Miss Pridmore thought. She knew it had been hard for her to come into school when she and her husband were still being splashed all over the news all the time, and it must have been particularly awful for her to have been virtually accused of being a murderer like that. Still, she thought, there was no way *she* would have left a friend in that situation, no matter how drunk she was – sometimes it seemed the more money people had, the fewer morals they possessed, even if they did just about manage to operate within the confines of the law.

But somehow today Mrs Forsyth had seemed less uptight, less angry than normal, and Noah certainly seemed happier of late too. It was funny how kids sometimes seemed to fare better after the parents had split up – Miss Pridmore had seen enough children throughout her career to know that staying together wasn't always the answer. Mrs Forsyth had seemed genuinely interested in what she'd had to say too, as though she was trying desperately hard to support her son. Even the husband had turned up for a change, and although the atmosphere between Mr and Mrs Forsyth had been terribly strained, it was a step forward – he never used to come when he and his wife were still together.

Miss Pridmore made a note in her diary to book the session for Noah with the school counsellor, and then she shuffled her papers, adjusted her glasses, took a deep breath, and went over to the classroom door where she welcomed in the parents of Rupert Rees-Smith, who, she would be obliged to inform them, was having trouble with his maths.

95

Gusty rain was hammering at the windows, water streaming downwards as if in a race to the bottom, the sky still dark even though it was morning. It was a lousy day for commuting and Camilla's husband was soaking. He took off his Burberry trenchcoat, shook the rain from it, hung it on the coat stand, switched on his computer, sat down at his desk, and picked up the *FT*.

James was glad that Camilla seemed to be feeling a bit better at last, despite the apocalyptic weather this morning. She had taken Siobhan's death last year so hard, almost as hard as her father's from what he could gather, and although she didn't have to live with the guilt that the others would bear for the rest of their lives, she still seemed to blame herself. James did his best to tell her that just because she'd organised the picnic, that didn't mean it was in any way her fault Siobhan had died, she hadn't even been involved in any of the arguments. But Camilla kept saying that she'd known how paralytic Siobhan was and yet had left without her anyway, even if she *had* been drunk herself, and that made her as culpable as anyone. And of course she was also devastated that the group had finally broken down, although James was convinced it was for the best, it had been far too long coming in his opinion. Thank God Camilla had the boys to think about – she was helping Christian with his university choices at the moment, and although she'd blanched when he first said he wanted to go to Bristol, she knew that that was what his heart was set on, it had one of the best reputations for Mathematics, and she would never want to stand in either of her sons' way. And anyway, James thought as he downloaded his emails (thirty-seven *overnight*, what had happened to people talking to each other?), it might do her good to go back there one day, and remember the good times she'd had with the others, realise that their friendships *had* been real once, before the inevitable ups and downs and outright tragedies of life had got in the way.

Part Four

Part Four

96

Hyde Park

The park was still and moonlit. Clouds seemed to be gathering, as if sensing the danger. A bat flew over silently, but she didn't see it, not even in the reflection on the water. The women's voices were far enough away to be nothing more than low-level bitching now, not in-her-face vitriol, and it was a relief to her.

She knelt at the lake's edge with her head between her knees, oblivious to her surroundings, to the blackness of the water. She was breathing hard, panting almost, trying not to sob. She just couldn't take any more of those women tonight, their feuds, their hatred — Natasha screaming at Juliette that she was shagging her husband, and Juliette not even denying it, and Natasha trying to go for her, pull her hair like they were five-year-olds; Renée sitting there sobbing about having been raped, and although she felt desperately sad for her friend, *really*, just blurting out twenty-five years too late that it was Stephen who'd done it, not the stranger in Cleveland after all, while they were all totally paralytic, was not the way to go about it. Siobhan had told Renée so many times to go to the police, go to counselling, get help, get closure, but Renée wouldn't. She preferred to drink herself senseless and shag other people's husbands, as though she didn't deserve any better.

As Siobhan slumped at the lakeside, she knew her behaviour had been far from perfect too tonight. She'd been in a terrible mood by the time she'd got there, she'd had such a lousy day, and they'd all been mean to her, as usual – and then she hadn't helped matters by inflaming everyone over Stephen. She must have been mad to insinuate that Stephen had had something to do with Nigel's death, she'd kept it secret for so long – and although she'd tried to cover it up, pretend she hadn't said anything, she knew it had been her words that had kicked everything else off. Running off screaming had been ridiculously melodramatic too, but she couldn't bear to hear any more – she'd simply had to get away once they'd all got going, screaming at each other like they were harridans in some dreadful soap opera.

Was it really all her fault? It had been years coming, Siobhan realised, and they'd all drunk far too much, even Sissy; and Renée had just gone straight in there, given the sniff of an opportunity. She obviously hated Stephen, *despised* him, and Siobhan couldn't blame her, not at all. Even Siobhan had to admit Stephen seemed despicable these days, a serpentine man, but really, Renée calling him a murderer, a rapist, in front of everyone, spitting out the words like they were poisoned meat, was too awful. Siobhan actually felt a tiny bit sorry for Stephen, although she knew that she shouldn't. But he was the one who had to live with Nigel's death, with what he'd done to Renée, even if he hadn't directly planned either. He still had to sleep at night, knowing someone had died, that he was a crook, a rapist.

What was odd though, Siobhan had always thought, was how Renée had seemed all right with Stephen when she'd first got back from America, acted almost normal with him still, although it was clear their affair had been very short-lived, in fact pretty much a one-night stand. At the time Siobhan had just assumed that Renée had cooled it with Stephen because she hadn't wanted to upset Juliette, ruin their friendship over a man.

But, months later, Renée had eventually confessed to Siobhan that it was *Stephen* who'd raped her, and she'd broken down as she'd described how much he'd grovelled to her afterwards, told her he'd thought she wanted it too, and apparently Renée had fallen for it, accepted it – at first. She hadn't spoken of it again for years, and now it seemed to Siobhan that the impact must have grown over time; as if the further away Renée had moved from what had happened, the more it had affected her – and the more intense her hatred for Stephen had become.

Siobhan gave a great heaving sigh. Renée's outburst had been bad enough, but then on top of all the drama Natasha had got stuck in too – once she'd finished attacking Juliette she'd had a go at her, Siobhan, almost seeming to enjoy ganging up on her, like a playground bully, when what she should have been doing was tearing a strip off her adulterous husband. Only Camilla had risen above it all, nothing seemed to enrage her, apart from inappropriate picnic contributions perhaps. No, Camilla and Sissy were the only two Siobhan was going to see from now on – she'd steer clear of the others, even poor Juliette, who would never be happy while she stayed with Stephen, and especially not now. She never should have gone out with him in the first place, Siobhan thought, through the Prosecco, she was always too good for him. She'd tried to tell her, but what can you do, people never listen to the truths that don't suit them, and Juliette had always seemed too vulnerable to be on her own for long.

The clouds moved silently across the moon, and the night became velvety dark. As Siobhan knelt quietly, trying to breathe slowly, ignore the still irate voices from beyond the bushes, she calmed down a little, began to regain some control. And then she thought she heard something near her, and she raised her head and looked up. She felt nervous suddenly, and a feeling of doom drenched through her, as though she were drowning in fear.

Words and images tumbled through her head in the darkness, and they were scarier than any movie she'd ever seen. Her heart thudded and seemed to stop. Someone was there, she was sure of it, someone in the bushes. It wasn't one of her friends, definitely not, she could tell it was a man. *Who was it?* As her brain flipped in on itself in panic, the clouds passed by and the moon reappeared, as if on cue, to light up her nightmare.

Stephen!

What was he doing here? She was consumed with terror, with what she'd said about him, the secrets she'd unleashed. She knew he was ruthless. Maybe he wanted to silence her. Perhaps he was a murderer after all. Perhaps he was going to murder *her*.

As their eyes made contact she thought she'd pass out with dread and horror and drunkenness. She opened her mouth to scream, but before she had time to, her would-be murderer looked more shocked than her suddenly, and instead of running over and stabbing or strangling her, he turned on his heel and legged it, stifling a sneeze as he went – and as he disappeared along the path she realised it wasn't Stephen after all, he was too slight for a start, her nerves had obviously got the better of her. But then who was he? Why had he been spying on her? Siobhan's head restarted its spinning, sending her thoughts haywire, and she dropped back down onto the hardness of the concrete, trying to quell the nausea.

Her phone rang. She sat up and grappled in the depths of her bag, and got to it just before it went to voicemail. Her fears vanished when she saw who it was. She felt giddily drunk, euphoric, relief flooding through her.

'Hello,' she said, but even through her joy her voice was slurred and faintly hostile, she couldn't help herself.

'Hi, Shiv,' said Matt. He paused. 'Are you all right? Are you at your picnic? How's it going?'

'Terrible,' said Siobhan, and she started to cry, despite feeling better, or maybe because of it. The man in the bushes seemed to have definitely gone, thank goodness, she must have imagined he was after her. Maybe she'd even imagined *him*, she was drunk after all.

'Listen, I'm sorry I haven't called before. It's just that

the reception here's rubbish, and I've been a bit distracted lately, you'll understand why soon.'

She panicked again, convinced suddenly that he was about to dump her. 'Matt, I'm sorry,' she said. 'I've had an awful evening. Is it OK if we talk about this another time?'

'Of course, it's just that, well . . . look, where are you?'

'By the side of the bloody Serpentine,' she said. 'We all had a terrible row and I ran off like a total drama queen, but you should have heard it, the things that were said, it was poisonous. Then I thought there was someone in the bushes, but maybe I was wrong, I don't know, and I'm covered in wine and chocolate and I look like a tramp, a pissed daft tramp.' She began to cry a little harder.

'Someone there? What d'you mean? Are you OK?'

Siobhan listened. Everywhere there was stillness; even the women were quiet now. She tried not to alarm him.

'Oh, I must have imagined it, I'm fine.'

'Are you sure, Siobhan? I don't like the sound of it. How are you getting home?'

'I don't know, try to flag down a taxi I guess.'

'I wish I could come and get you, make sure you're OK, I wish I wasn't in the bloody Kimberleys.'

'It doesn't matter, there's no-one here now, I'm sure of it. I'll be fine. I'll see you after the weekend.'

'Come round on Sunday, my flight gets in early morning. Come round then.'

'You'll be knackered.'

'I'll be OK. I can't wait to see you. Oh, *please* don't cry again. I . . . look, this isn't quite how I envisioned it, but I

hate to hear you so upset . . . so when I get back . . . I . . .
Oh, fuck it . . . (*Deep breath.*) Siobhan, when I get back
I've got something to ask you.'

Siobhan felt a hot sweet feeling course down her neck,
through her back, like you get when you say hello to a
stranger and they respond to you, smile at you unexpect-
edly. She stopped crying, stopped breathing.

'I've already spoken to your father, don't worry, I've
done it all properly. Listen, I've got to go in a minute, the
truck's waiting for me.'

'OK,' she said. '. . . Matt?'

'Yes?'

'I'm a nutter.'

'That's OK, I like it.'

'Ma – att?'

'Ye – es?'

'I really, really love you.'

'I really, really love you too, Siobhan, I really, really
do. I always have. See you soon. Look after yourself, OK?'

'I will, don't worry, I'll be fine,' she said. 'The others
are still here, they'd hear me if anything happened, I'm
good at screaming. I love you, Matt. Bye.'

Siobhan shoved her phone into her bag and sat there
for a while, stunned, savouring Matt's words, delighted
chills still coursing through her spine. Finally she pushed
up on her hands and hauled her legs around, resting
drunkenly for a moment on her left arm and left thigh, as
if she were posing for an old-fashioned swimwear shot.
She smiled her killer smile, teeth perfectly straight these
days, hugged the knowledge to herself like a newborn

baby. She felt totally fine about getting home now – the park felt brighter, safer, in fact the whole world felt lovelier, she loved everything about it. There were definitely no more strange men lurking in the bushes, and there was bound to be a cab up on the bridge, she'd be home in no time. She even felt more optimistic about her friends now – she'd be sure to ring everyone in the morning to make up, even Natasha. After all it was her own lapse in discretion that had kicked everything off – thinking about it, maybe it was all her fault, the least she could do was apologise to everyone. And they *were* all friends still, always had been, always would be, they'd been through so much together. Her mind waltzed a little, full of love and Prosecco. She'd invite them to the wedding of course – in fact, maybe they could even be bridesmaids! She'd love that. Yes, she'd sort everything out tomorrow. It would all be all right tomorrow.

Siobhan's head spun as she fully stood up, and she tottered on her ridiculous heels, and she tripped clumsily on the trailing strap of her handbag, and as she fell she gashed her head on the rowlock of the little boat, the one that they'd left there with a hole in it, and as everything went black a splash – was it a bird or a woman – sounded into the soft summer night.

Acknowledgements

So many people have read this book along the way, but editorially I'd especially like to thank the brilliant Maxine Hitchcock at Penguin, my husband, my aunt Val Young, and my friends Claire Lusher and Tracy Morrell, all of whom had some fairly strong things to say that I at some point or another acted upon. To my long-suffering agent and saviour, Jon Elek, and to everyone else at United Agents. To Francesca Russell, Francesca Pearce, Kimberley Atkins, Sarah Arratoon, Sophie Elletson, Louise Moore, Lydia Good and all the other people at Penguin who worked so hard to bring this book out. To my friends Jackie Parker and Lisa Parsons for undertaking the essential job of vetting the manuscript, and my other friends from university who have shown such understanding and good humour about this novel, and who have supported me for so many years in so many ways. To all the people who championed the book when it was launched as *A Serpentine Affair*, particularly the amazing band of book bloggers, who show so much love and enthusiasm for books, and such generosity of spirit in helping promote them. To my husband and son and the rest of my close friends and family, especially my dad who still hasn't read any of my books (although he has seen *Gone Girl*). And finally to everyone who has enjoyed my books, and who has even written something nice about them, thank you so much.

Reading Group Questions

1. Do you think it's possible to stay friends with the people you knew when you were young, or is it inevitable that you grow apart?

2. Which of the women in the novel did you empathise with the most? Who did you feel least sympathy for?

3. Betrayal is a key theme in the novel – in what different ways did the women betray each other? In your opinion, whose actions were worse? Do you think any of the relationships could, or should, have been reconciled?

4. Were the women wrong to not return to the park when they heard the splash? Were they culpable by their lack of action?

5. Even though they weren't at the reunion, how much are the men in the novel to blame for what happened that night?

6. Are any of the women victims of their own circumstances? Do you think any of them should have taken more responsibility for their own behaviour?

7. 'If you'd done no wrong and you told the truth what harm could possibly come to you?' To what extent do

you agree with this statement? Should some secrets be kept no matter what?

8. There are two rapes in the novel – why did neither woman go to the police? Do you think things would have been different if they had?

9. How is motherhood depicted in the novel? How do the relationships the women have with their parents affect them over the years?

10. Did the final scene change your feelings about anything else in the novel?